What Goes Around
Comes Around

What Goes Around Comes Around

DARRIEN LEE

SBI

STREBOR BOOKS

NEW YORK LONDON TORONTO SYDNEY

Published by

SBI

Strebor Books
P.O. Box 6505
Largo, MD 20792
http://www.streborbooks.com

© 2004 by Darrien Lee
Originally published in trade paperback in 2004.

Cover Illustration: André Harris

ISBN   0-7432-9599-4
LCCN 2003112285

First Strebor Books mass market paperback edition March 2006

10 9 8 7 6 5 4 3 2 1

Manufactured in the United States of America

For information regarding special discounts for bulk purchases,
please contact Simon & Schuster Special Sales at 1-800-456-6798
or business@simonandschuster.com

DEDICATION

This novel is dedicated to the men and women
of the United States of America's armed forces
as they strive to protect our freedom.

ACKNOWLEDGMENTS

First and foremost, I would like to thank God for the gift of creativity that is bestowed upon me. To my church family at Wayman Chapel A.M.E. Church, in Columbia, Tennessee, your guidance, love and prayers are everlasting.

My motivation to be successful can be found in the eyes of my beautiful daughters, Alyvia and Marisa. I do this for you and your father, Wayne, and I know you're proud of my accomplishments. My eternal love is expressed with every hug and kiss.

There are so many special friends who have encouraged me to stay focused and on the right path. Words cannot express the gratitude I have for friends: Buanita Ray, Robin Kennedy Ridley, Sharon Williams Nowlin, LaTonia Davenport, Monica Bradford Baker, Brenda Campbell Thomas, and Tracy Dandridge. We share some interesting stories from our past and present and are confident that our secrets are safe.

I love you guys!

To The Mocha Review Bookclub members, your drive and dedication are priceless and I thank you for being in my corner.

The new friends I have obtained over the pass few years are many but I would like to give a special shout-out to Charaine, China, Samantha, Tresia and Bianca. I smile every time I get an encouraging email from you. Keep 'em coming!

André Harris, your talent leaves me spellbound every time your paintbrush hits the canvas. The book cover is breathtaking and once again, you saw my vision and produced a masterpiece. Thank you so much!

V. Anthony Rivers, you are like a brother to me and with that comes certain expectations. You always know what to say to lift my spirits when I'm down, push me when I am stubborn and support me in my endeavors. You're a great listener, adviser and have never let me down. You Go, Boy!

Phylishia, Emily and Edward Jr., you've known me all my life and I know as your sister, I've made you proud. Thanks for everything! The same love and affection goes out to my wonderful sisters-in-law, Juanita and Sheledia; and brothers-in-law, Lee, Troy and Pat. I would also like to thank all my other family members in New Orleans, Lousiana for supporting me. Send me some gumbo!

To my nieces, Marquita, Ashley, Jessica, Paige; and nephews, Tylan and Edward III, I have mad love for you! My heart is overflowing with affection for my mother, Ines; and mother-in-law, Sylvia, who offer support and love, which is required for me to be successful. Thanks to special cousins Venus Boston, Vanessa Harris Maston, Nichelle Braden, and Rolanda Perkins.

The Strebor Family and Zane have been extraordinary in providing me a platform to showcase my work. Words cannot express the admiration I have for each and every one of you.

CHAPTER ONE

The weatherman had forecast at least another five inches of snow. Winston Carter, III, better known as "Skeeter" by his friends, was trying to get used to Northeastern snowfalls, but it had been difficult. These winters were far worse than what he experienced growing up in the South. As he stood to close his briefcase, his cellular phone rang.

"Hello?"

"Hey, Skeeter."

He smiled. "Hello, Venice. Before you say another word, I'm putting my coat on right now."

"I'm just checking because I know you. You've cancelled the last two dinner dates, and I will drop-kick your butt if you try and cancel on us tonight."

Venice was the wife of his best friend, Craig Bennett. Their relationship hadn't always been this close, but over the years, they were able to settle their differences and become close friends. On this night, Winston was to join his friends for dinner. He had been tied up at his law firm with heavy caseloads for several weeks, which accounted for the cancelled dinner invitations. Winston buttoned his coat and said, "I'm on my way, woman. What did you cook anyway?"

Venice smiled. "Don't you worry about it. You just get over here. Oh! I need a favor."

He cringed. "Oh Lawd, you don't need me to pick up any personal items, do you?"

"You're so stupid, Skeeter." She laughed. "Listen, Arnelle put her car in the shop this morning, and it's not ready yet. I was supposed to go back to the clinic and give her a ride home. I'm tied up here with dinner. Can you swing by and give her a lift home…please?"

Skeeter frowned. "Dang, Venice! You know we don't get along. Why don't I come and help with dinner and then you or Craig can go pick her up?"

Arnelle was Venice's partner at her sports medical clinic. Winston was used to women falling at his feet, which left him confused why Arnelle seemed to despise him. Ever since they'd met, she'd acted uninterested with anything he had to say or do in her presence.

Venice pulled the succulent roast out of the oven. "Skeeter, it's on your way over here so stop acting childish. Arnelle does like you."

Frowning, he answered, "Sure, I can tell by the way she rolls her eyes every time I try to talk to her."

Sighing, Venice pleaded, "Do it for me, okay?"

He locked up his office and walked toward the elevators. Thinking about what he was about to encounter, he changed the subject by asking, "How are the kids?"

"I have one on each hip, and Brandon's clinging to my leg."

Winston let out a baritone laugh. "That's a visual. Wait…are you serious?"

"I'm just kidding. The twins are napping, and Brandon's helping Craig set the table."

"You owe me big time for putting me in the same space as that woman."

"Okay, okay," Venice said, giggling. "I love you and thanks a lot! Make sure you drive safely, and we'll see you soon. Did you remember to bring a change of clothes, in case the weather gets worse?"

He punched the elevator button and answered, "Yes, Mother."

"Just for that, no dessert for you. See you soon, Skeeter."

"Pray for me."

He climbed into his truck and maneuvered through the snowy streets. He tensed up, knowing his peace and quiet would soon be interrupted.

∞

Arnelle hung up the telephone and started gnawing on her nails. She couldn't believe Venice was going to make her ride with him. While they had some unfinished business to discuss, Winston had avoided the subject totally, so she'd done everything she could to stay out of his way. Maybe the distance between them was the best thing for now; until they could sit down and discuss what had happened between them rationally. She stood with her hands on her hips, remembering Venice's words: *Arnelle, it's going to take a cab two hours or more to arrive. You can do this, just this once.*

She vowed to pay her partner back one way or another. Glancing at her watch, she realized Winston would arrive shortly. He was still very handsome, and was always able to shake her foundation whenever he was around her. She had never been very experienced when dealing with men, but the ones she had been in contact with proved to be nothing but heartache. Her desire was to right the wrong she had done to him and try to put her life back together. It only took moments to turn out all the lights and lock up the office. She would wait for him in the lobby.

∞

Winston turned into the circular driveway in front of the Bennett Complex. He took one last deep breath as he brought his huge truck to a halt. The snow was coming down even harder now and before he could be a gentleman and open the door for Arnelle, she climbed in on the passenger side and buckled her seatbelt.

"Dang, woman. Where's the fire?"

She turned to look at him with the most beautiful eyes he had ever seen.

"Look, I appreciate you giving me a ride home. But, if you don't mind, I'm tired and just want to get home, okay?"

He stared at her. "Why do you always have to be so mean, Arnelle?"

"You know why. You've been giving me the cold shoulder ever since we ran into each other again. Look, I'm sorry about what went down between us, okay?"

"I don't know what you're talking about, and what do you mean...*again?* You must have me mixed up with someone else."

"I don't have you mixed up with anyone else! How could you forget about me...us?"

He stared at her for a moment and tried his best to remember her, but he couldn't and he didn't understand why. He knew he had dated a lot of women, but Arnelle wasn't the type he'd forget.

"You must have me confused with someone else, Arnelle? We've never met."

Turning away, she wiped away a lone tear. "No, I don't have you mixed up. The reason I know for sure is because we have a..."

His cell phone rang, interrupting her. Arnelle sighed as Winston answered the phone.

"Hello?"

He stared at her as he listened to the caller. He was trying to figure out what the hell Arnelle was talking about.

"Yeah, I'm still here, but I'm kind of busy right now. I'll have to get back with you later. A'ight?" Hanging up the phone, Winston said, "Sorry about that. Now, what were you saying?"

Arnelle looked at him...really stared. This wasn't making any sense. She wasn't getting anywhere with him so she decided to leave things as they were. It was obvious he had moved on with his life and she couldn't blame him; after what she'd put him through.

"I'm sorry, Winston. If I could take everything back, I would. I just hope you'll find it in your heart to forgive me. You don't have to worry about me bothering you ever again. There, I've said it. Now please, just take me home."

Arnelle leaned back on the headrest and closed her eyes. She didn't want to talk about it anymore. She inhaled Winston's masculine scent, and it was wonderful. She didn't know what the fragrance was, but it suited him perfectly. He sat and stared in total confusion. He had no idea where their weird conversation was coming from. Puzzled, he responded, "I'm sorry, but you're mistaken, Arnelle."

With tears in her eyes, she replied, "Forget about it."

"Fine with me," he muttered before pulling out onto the street. The roads were full of motorists trying to get home in the heavy snow. Occasionally, he would glance over to see if Arnelle's eyes were still closed, and they were. He tried to figure out what she had meant by her statements. Why was she apologizing to him? He remembered asking Craig and Venice if they knew why she seemed to despise him so much. She was the only woman he hadn't been able to charm, and that puzzled him. In fact, what he had for her was a strong attraction, and it was getting harder for him to hide it.

When they reached the suburbs, they encountered treacherous driving conditions. These streets had not been traveled as much and even his four-wheel drive vehicle was having some difficulty. Winston turned into Arnelle's neighborhood and was met with roadblocks and a state trooper.

"What's this?" he asked.

Arnelle sat up and opened her eyes. The state trooper walked over to Winston's side and he rolled down the window.

"What's going on, officer?" Winston asked.

"Do you live in this neighborhood?"

Arnelle leaned toward Winston and answered, "I do, officer. What's the problem?"

"There've been several accidents in this neighborhood, so we had to close this area. It's just too risky to chance any more accidents."

Arnelle's eyes widened. "But I have to get home," she said, her voice high-pitched.

"Where do you live, Ma'am?"

"Dakota and Pine."

The officer shielded his eyes from the blizzard-like snowfall.

"Ma'am, Dakota and Pine is one of the worst areas, and it's too far to walk from here. I suggest you stay with friends or family for the night and maybe we'll open it back up tomorrow."

"Are you crazy?"

Skeeter could feel Arnelle's warm breath on the side of his neck as well as smell her flowery scent. The officer's irritation showed.

"Ma'am, I'm sorry, but you can't go past this point. Good evening."

He walked back to his vehicle and climbed inside.

She stared at Winston. "Why didn't you help me?"

"Hey," Winston said, throwing his hands up, "this wasn't my battle. Besides, what did you expect me to say?"

Her emotions had gotten the best of her.

"What kind of lawyer are you, anyway?"

Winston looked at Arnelle like she had lost her ever-loving mind. This woman was driving him crazy. She was the total opposite of the kind of women he dealt with, so why did he want to get to know her better? It was obvious there was some type of issue she had with him. He just didn't know what it was. He closed his eyes, trying to be as patient as possible.

"Arnelle, I'm not going to argue with you. I'm tired and hungry, and I have somewhere I have to be. Now, where do you want me to take you?"

Angrily, she said, "Drop me off at the first hotel you come to."

"Hotel? Woman, please."

"Just drive, Winston!"

"You can't tell me what to do, Arnelle!"

Disgusted, he pulled off and within minutes, he was in Craig and Venice's driveway. Before he could get out of the truck, Arnelle stormed through their front door.

"Venice!"

Arnelle went straight into the kitchen and found Venice and Craig locked, as usual, in a passionate embrace.

In unison, they asked, "What's wrong?

Arnelle folded her arms. "Don't you ever put me in the same space with him again! He is the most stubborn man I've ever known!"

Craig laughed. "What did you do to him?"

"Don't start with me," Arnelle replied, her finger pointed at Craig. "My neighborhood has been closed because of this snow, and I can't get home. I left your friend outside."

Craig continued to laugh as he walked out of the kitchen in search of Winston.

Arnelle paced back and forth across the kitchen, ranting and raving about Winston. Venice let her vent for a while, and then said, "Calm down, Arnelle. He's only a man. Damn! Why don't you like him? If you ask me, I think you like him more than you're pretending. You always get like this when he's around. What's going on with you two?"

"Nothing."

"You might as well go on and give him some loving and maybe that will take the tension out of the both of you."

Arnelle put her finger in the cake batter. "I can't believe you went there. Winston's pissing me off. We have some issues to work through, but he's avoiding it."

Venice smacked Arnelle's hand. "Well, whatever it is, you guys need to hurry up and straighten it out. We're all friends, and I want us to be able to get along, okay? He's a nice guy, Arnelle. I admit, we didn't hit it off at all in the beginning, but he's really a sweetheart."

Arnelle rolled her eyes. "Whatever. Look, since I'm stranded here, do you still have my gym bag I left at the clinic? It has a change of clothes in it."

"It's in the hall closet and if you want to take a shower, make sure you use the one downstairs. I'd hate for you and Winston to accidentally run into each other in the upstairs shower. He'll probably stay over tonight, so try to be nice to him."

Laughing, Arnelle said, "I'll do my best, and payback is hell, Venice."

"I'm so scared. Get out of here and go relax. Brandon is going to be so excited that you're here."

"I can't wait to see him, either."

∞

Craig ran into Winston as he walked through the front door. He folded his arms and asked, "What's up, Bro?"

Walking past him and up the stairs, Winston solemnly said, "Not right now, Craig. I'm going to take a shower and try to calm down. A'ight?"

"Take your time. You know where everything is."

Before Winston could get to the top of the stairs, he mumbled, "That woman is crazy."

"I take it you're talking about the witch doctor?" Craig asked.

Winston gripped the railing and nodded. "Yeah, man. She was yelling the whole way over here." Turning, he asked, "Hey, have you or Venice said anything to that woman about the things I told you?"

Frowning, Craig said, "I haven't, but I don't know about Venice. Why?"

"She said some weird things on the way over here; that's all."

"Oh, I see. Anything you want to talk about?"

"Not yet. I need to chill out first 'cause she's a trip!"

"She sure is beautiful when she's angry, huh?"

"Go to hell, Craig."

Winston could hear Craig laughing as he entered the guest room where he had spent many nights. He sat on the bed and placed his hands over his face, letting out a sigh. He hated to admit that Craig was right about Arnelle being beautiful when she was angry. To Winston, she was beautiful twenty-four/ seven. He tried to dismiss the fact that she was drawing him in against his will. He just wished he knew why she hated him so much. Moments later, he stood under the hot steamy water of his shower.

After stepping out, he wrapped a towel around his wet body and reentered the bedroom. He found Brandon using the bed as a trampoline.

"Hey, Uncle Skeeter!"

"What's up, Brandon? How long have you been in here?"

Brandon stopped jumping and sat on the bed next to Winston.

"Not long. I didn't know you were here, but I knew you were coming."

Brandon put his feet into Winston's large sneakers and walked around the room. Winston proceeded to rub his body with lotion as he watched Brandon use his shoes as toys. He eventually tripped over them and said, "I wonder if my feet are going to be big like yours and Pop's."

Winston stood and removed the towel, and seven-year-old Brandon said, "Ooh, I wonder if my penis is going to be big like yours, too!"

Winston froze. He never thought Brandon would pay attention to him dressing, let alone comment on his male form. Playing the comment down, Winston slipped into his boxers and said, "Don't rush things, my man. How is it that you're calling it a penis already?"

"Because Momma said that's what it was. My friend Jamal calls his a pee-pee."

"I see."

"Uncle Skeeter," Brandon began, smiling, "did you know girls have virginias?"

"It's vaginas and yes, I know," Winston stuttered. "Just remember what I said about rushing things, okay?"

"Okay, Uncle Skeeter. Did you know Miss Arnelle was here?"

He took a deep breath, sighed, and said, "Yes, she rode over here with me." Brandon stared at Winston for a moment and asked, "Don't you like her? I do. I love touching her hair. It's so long and pretty."

Winston was now fully dressed in some jeans and a pullover. He bent down to lace up his sneakers and said, "Well, Brandon, I've tried to be friends with Miss Arnelle, but I don't think she wants me as a friend."

"Why not?"

"I don't know, but let's not worry about her. I came over here to challenge you in a snowball fight, but you have to eat all your dinner. Have you been taking care of Clarissa and C.J.?"

Brandon sat back on the bed. "Yeah, Uncle Skeeter. I've been taking care of them, but I hate holding their stinky diapers."

"Don't forget," Winston said, as he rubbed his hand across Brandon's head, "somebody had to hold your stinky diapers when you were a baby."

"I know," Brandon said, as he jumped on the bed. "And I will eat all my dinner so we can go out and play."

"Good, now get down off the bed before your mom comes in here and goes ballistic on both of us." He took Brandon by the hand and left to join the others downstairs.

∞

When Winston and Brandon entered the dining room, Brandon ran over and gave Arnelle a hug. Craig was feeding the twins, and Venice was in the process of putting dinner on the table. Winton's eyes met Arnelle's briefly and it was then he realized she had changed into jeans also. The pink cashmere sweater accented her shapely figure. He figured that Venice must have loaned her some clothes because Arnelle didn't have a bag with her. He also couldn't take his eyes off the long, wavy hair spilling over her shoulders and down her back. He remembered Craig telling him that she had Navajo blood in her and her beauty reflected it. He stood motionless as he watched Brandon sit on her lap and run his hand through her thick mane. Even though she'd angered him only moments earlier, he felt his body starting to betray him. The last thing he wanted Arnelle to see was him getting aroused just from looking at her. He turned to walk out of the room, but Craig stopped him.

"Sit down, man. I could use some help here."

Venice and Arnelle looked at Winston as he sat down and took a bowl of baby food from Craig and fed Clarissa.

"Ok, Princess," Winston warned. "Don't give me any trouble tonight."

Clarissa smiled at him as he brought the spoon up to her mouth. He'd fed the twins before and was beginning to be a pro at it. He leaned in and gave Clarissa a wet kiss on the cheek, then over to little C.J., repeating the gesture. Clarissa sneezed, spraying his face with baby food. Everyone laughed, even Arnelle. Brandon put his hand over his mouth and laughed the loudest. Venice walked over and handed him a towel to wipe his face. Winston looked at Clarissa and said, "Sweetheart, you're going to pay for that."

She squealed with laughter as he kissed her again before rising to wash up.

"You might as well wait until she's done," Craig warned. "She'll probably do it again."

Winston sat back down. "You're right. Now, Princess, I'm warning you."

He pointed his finger at her in a playful way, and then tickled her before continuing to feed her.

∞

After feeding the twins, Craig and Winston took the twins upstairs, bathed them and put them to bed. When they walked back into the dining room and sat down, they realized Brandon had been keeping the two women entertained while they waited on them to return.

"Momma, I was talking to Uncle Skeeter, and we're going out to play in the snow after dinner."

Venice glared at Winston. "I don't know, Brandon. It's cold outside. Maybe you guys should wait until it stops snowing."

"Ahhh, Momma."

Minutes later, everyone joined hands as Craig blessed the food. It was mostly silent; except the occasional chitchat about the weather and work.

"I know something ya'll don't know," Brandon said in a sing-song voice.

"And what might that be, Lil' Man?" Venice asked as she picked up her fork.

"Uncle Skeeter has a big penis just like my daddy's, and I'm going to have one just like them when I grow up. Pops, I haven't seen yours yet, so I don't know if it's big or not."

Craig spat his tea out and started laughing as Venice screamed, "Brandon!"

Slumping down in his chair, Brandon whispered, "Well, he does, Momma."

Arnelle didn't even flinch. She just arched her eyebrows and stared at Winston as he showed his obvious embarrassment. She knew he dared not look her way. Venice stood and said, "Brandon, you don't say things like that; especially at the table. Now you apologize to Skeeter."

Brandon lowered his head. "I'm sorry I told everybody you had a big penis, Uncle Skeeter."

Clearing his throat, he answered, "Apology accepted, Brandon."

Craig was still laughing as he wiped up the tea he'd spat out. He looked up at Winston and burst out laughing again.

After dinner, Craig and Skeeter cleaned up the kitchen while Venice and Arnelle retired to the den to enjoy the fire the men had built. Brandon was sent upstairs for his bath since he had lost the battle to go out and play in the snow. Venice gave Arnelle a slice of cake and a cup of cappuccino before settling down on the sofa.

"Arnelle, I hope you'll be comfortable in the guest room."

She folded her legs under her and sighed. "I'm sure I will, but I'll need something to sleep in."

"Well, since Skeeter is here, do you want something sexy? I mean, since he has a big penis and all."

Arnelle threw a pillow at her and yelled, "Venice! Stop it!"

"I'm just teasing you." Venice laughed. "I'll go find something for you to wear. I'll be back."

When she left the room, Craig and Winston entered, talking about sports. Craig immediately went for the cake.

"Skeeter, you want some?"

Winston went over to the fireplace and threw another log on the fire. Arnelle was silent as she sipped her cappuccino. She had to admit, the man could wear a pair of jeans.

"Nah, man. I'm cool."

Craig turned to Arnelle and asked if she wanted another piece. She declined, unfolding her legs and placing them on the floor.

"No, thank you. I think I'll turn in."

Winston turned and stared down at her, not showing any particular type of emotion.

He asked, "So soon, Arnelle?"

She stood less than two feet from him. Winston couldn't believe how tall she was. She was the perfect height. Hell, he was beginning to feel she was the perfect everything. The only problem was she hated him. She placed her hands on her hips and explained, "I'm just tired. Is that a crime, Winston?"

He stood his ground, folded his arms, leaned in within inches of her ear and whispered, "No, it's not, Arnelle, and I hope you have sweet dreams."

She backed away. "Thank you. Goodnight."

He couldn't help but watch her curvaceous body exit the room. Once again, his body betrayed him. Craig sat in the oversized chair, eating his cake. "Man, you need to put that thang on a leash. The witch doctor's not going to fool around with you. You're too much of a playa for her, and she hates you, remember?"

Winston braced himself against the mantle as he willed his body back to normal in silence. Craig mumbled, "You're sad."

"Oh, like it doesn't happen to you every time Venice walks into the room."

Craig bit into the slice of cake, laughed and said, "It's all about control, partner."

"For some reason, control is the last thing I think about when looking at that woman. I don't know why I can't just forget about her. She's not even my type."

Craig sat up. "Do you want me to tell you what's up?"

Winston sat down, sighed and said, "Knock yourself out."

"You want her because you can't have her. She's not like all the others you've played around with. With them, it was all about you, and they did everything they had to do to please you. Arnelle is not like that. I will tell you this, though. If you decide to pursue her, it's going to take effort and, frankly, I don't think you're up for the job."

"Craig, I don't know what to think or do about Arnelle right now. Something is going on with her because she's been saying some weird things to me."

"Like what?"

"It's strange. She said we've met before, but I don't remember her. It's weird."

"Damn, Skeeter, have you fooled around with that many women that you don't remember her? If so, no wonder she's pissed off at you."

Standing, he said, "I don't know, Craig. There have been a lot of women, but I know for a fact that I would remember kicking it with her."

"Maybe she has you mixed up with someone else."

"That's what I told her, but she seemed sure."

"Well, what's done in the dark will eventually come out in the light," Craig said, smiling. "Give it time. Hopefully you'll remember and she'll be more specific."

Winston didn't respond. He just took a sip of coffee, sat back against the plush sofa and stared into the roaring fire.

CHAPTER TWO

ater that night, Winston found himself tossing and
turning in bed. He tried to sleep, but every time he
closed his eyes, there *she* was. He kept remembering
what Craig said about Arnelle. He still didn't know what to do
to remove her from his thoughts. Arnelle had now become
a distraction for him and, in his profession, that was a no-no.
Frustrated, he threw back the covers and headed for the
kitchen to raid the refrigerator.

When he walked into the kitchen wearing only shorts and
his robe, he stopped in his tracks. What he saw was an unexpected pleasure and the source of his sleeplessness. Arnelle sat
there, whispering softly to Craig Jr., feeding him his bottle.
Immediately, she became aware of his presence without even
turning around.

"What are you doing up so late, Winston?"

He folded his arms and leaned against the doorframe. "How
did you know I was here, Arnelle?"

With her back still to him, she answered, "You'd be surprised
at what I know, Winston."

Electricity shot through him with her comment. *Does she also
know how much I want her?*

Arnelle stood and faced him as she placed C.J. over her
shoulder to burp him. Her eyes pierced his thoughts and heart.
He tried his best not to lose his composure, but seeing her
standing there, with that silk robe brushing against her brown
skin did something to him. Coming further into the kitchen,

he towered over her. He could hear Arnelle take a breath as he reached up and ran his hand down the baby's small back in a soothing motion.

His closeness made her nervous. Stuttering, she said, "He's asleep."

Without breaking eye contact, he answered, "I know."

"Winston, I'm sorry about earlier. I know you're upset with me, so you might as well go ahead and get it out of your system because I can't take this much longer."

He frowned.

"Arnelle, I'm sorry that officer wouldn't let you go home, but that was no reason for you to go off on me."

"I'm not talking about that, Winston."

"Then what are you talking about?"

She stared at him and noticed he didn't look away. They stood there for what seemed like an eternity staring at each other. She looked deep into his eyes.

"Arnelle."

His voice snapped her back to reality.

"I'm sorry, Winston. Forget about it."

Yawning, he answered, "You sure do know how to confuse a brotha."

"I don't mean to. I just want things between us to be better than they were."

Silently, he reached over and pushed a strain of her hair out of her eyes. "Were?"

"Yes."

"Arnelle, I have to be honest…I don't remember you and I'm sorry. If that's why you're so upset with me, I understand. I hope you can forgive me. Where did we meet?"

Confusion settled in her stomach as she answered, "It's late, Winston. I don't feel like getting into that tonight."

"I understand. I will say that I have to be senile not to remember a woman as beautiful as you."

She blushed. Seeing Winston in fewer clothes than normal was not what she wanted or needed right then.

Extending his hand, he whispered, "Can we please try and start over? I'm exhausted from all the yelling we've been doing at each other. Truce?"

Shaking his hand, she answered, "Truce."

She had been unable to sleep since going to bed and had volunteered to put the baby monitor in her room in case the twins woke up. No matter what she did to try to sleep, her mind wandered to him. She had been without a meaningful relationship for almost three years and was starting to feel the strain both physically and emotionally. She prayed every night that she would be able to recover her lost love, but too much had happened.

Releasing his hand, she said, "I need to get C.J. back to bed."

Winston looked at her in awe and asked, "Where are the happy parents?"

"They took first shift, and I volunteered for the second."

He continued to stroke C.J.'s back lovingly, then said, "You handle the kids well; especially Brandon."

"So do you, and Brandon's my man."

Taking a step backward out of his space, Arnelle picked up the baby bottle and said, "Goodnight, Winston."

"Goodnight, Arnelle."

∞

When Winston woke up the next morning and entered the kitchen, he found out that Arnelle had called a cab and gone home. Craig had offered to drive her, but she'd insisted that he stay at the house with Venice and the kids.

Craig raised his coffee mug in salute and yelled, "Look what the cat dragged in!"

Winston slowly walked over to the counter and poured himself a hot cup of coffee. Craig sat smiling and asked, "What happened between you two last night that made Arnelle run out of here like a firefighter?"

"What are you talking about?"

Craig folded his arms across his chest. "I know you two were in the kitchen together late last night."

"You were spying on us?"

"This is my house, remember? Besides, I got up to check on the kids and realized she had C.J. I was coming downstairs to see if she wanted me to take him, and I heard you two talking. Don't worry, I didn't hear anything. Anyway, I just went back to bed. When I got up this morning, she was dressed and had already called a cab. She wouldn't let me drive her home. So, are ya'll cool?"

Winston sipped his coffee. "I don't know what we are and to tell the truth, you were right. I don't have it in me to deal with Arnelle. She's too complicated."

Craig stood and laughed. "I have a feeling you're not throwing in the towel yet."

"I don't know."

"I hear you, Bro."

∞

Arnelle sat in her office days later, twirling an ink pen with her fingers. She was feeling homesick for the first time since coming to Philly. She missed the warm Texas evenings; especially sitting out on her parents' porch and watching the sun set. She also missed her daughter, MaLeah; the source of all her determination to succeed. She was in the middle of her "terrible two" stage. Leaving her with her parents temporarily was difficult but necessary. She didn't want MaLeah with her until spring, since the winters were so severe in Philly. She was very reluctant about leaving her parents in Texas to watch over MaLeah since her father had announced his candidacy for mayor. She knew he had to concentrate on his campaign and keeping up with her two-year-old could be a distraction. The telephone rang.

"Bennett Sports Clinic. How may I help you?"

"Hello, Arnelle, remember me? I used to be your best friend."

Arnelle froze at the sound of the deep baritone voice.

"What do you want, Cyrus?"

He laughed. "You know exactly what I want."

Arnelle held her ground, though she could feel herself growing agitated. "I can't do it, Cyrus!"

With firmness in his voice, he answered, "You owe me, and you know it!"

"Why can't you just face this thing?"

"Come on, Arnelle. I'm sure your daddy wouldn't be too pleased with what I could tell him about you; especially since he's running for mayor. The media would love to get hold of this kind of information."

"Are you trying to blackmail me?"

"I'll do whatever it takes. You're supposed to be my friend. You owe me!"

"Go to hell, Cyrus! I'm sick of you calling here bullying me."

Arnelle slammed the phone down and practically ran from her office. When she turned the corner, she ran right into a tall, hard body. Strong, firm hands kept her from falling to the floor.

"Excuse me! I'm so sorry!"

Arnelle lowered her head and tried to hold in the tears but was unsuccessful. She looked up into Winston's eyes and broke down crying in his arms. Startled by her response, he embraced her.

"What's wrong, Arnelle? Did somebody hurt you?"

She shook her head as he led her back into her office and sat her on the sofa. He retrieved some bottled water from her small refrigerator and handed it to her.

He sat next to her and asked, "Arnelle, why are you crying? Where's Venice?"

She took a sip of water and wiped her tears away with her hand. "I'm fine, Winston."

Even though he knew she wasn't, he said, "If you insist."

"Thanks for being here for me though."

"You're welcome," he said softly.

"Venice went out to lunch with Craig." She wiped her nose with a tissue. "They should be back shortly."

She still wouldn't make eye contact with him. She just stared at the bottle she held in her hands. Winston was angry, knowing that someone had caused her pain.

"Who upset you, Arnelle?"

She finally looked at him. "You're getting a little personal, Winston. I'm allowed to cry sometimes."

Reaching over, he wiped a lone tear from her cheek. "I'm not trying to get in your business, Arnelle. I'm just concerned and wanted to make sure no one had hurt you. You are a friend of my best friend. I just wanted to make sure no one messed with you."

She stood and so did he. He was dressed in a dark gray suit; looking every bit the great attorney that he was. His neatly trimmed goatee outlined a pair of luscious lips and for a moment, she couldn't take her eyes off them. The slight contact she was having with him caused chills to run over her body.

Clearing her throat, she asked, "Was Venice expecting you?"

"Not really. I just dropped by to see if I could take Brandon to the ballgame Saturday."

"Brandon will love that."

"We've been before. It's really cool. We always have a good time."

"I'm sure you do." She folded her arms. "Thanks again for being concerned. I'll be fine...really."

He shoved his hands in his pockets. "Well, I guess I'd better go. I'll just leave Venice a note on her desk."

His eyes were doing a number on her, and she tried her best not to let it affect her.

Looking into his warm eyes, she asked, "Why are you doing this, Winston? Don't you feel anything for me?"

"I'm concerned about you, and it bothers me to see you cry."

He wasn't about to reveal what he was really feeling for her lately.

"No, besides that?"

"Is there something you're not telling me, Arnelle? We never had a chance to talk about where we met."

Panicking, Arnelle waved him off nervously. A part of her wondered if Winston's act was indeed an act, or if he wanted to see her sweat.

"I'm sure Venice will call you as soon as she gets back. I'll walk you out."

Winston left Venice a note on her desk as Arnelle waited for him in the front lobby. When he walked toward her, she felt his awesome magnetism. He stood over her and without any warning, he picked her up and hugged her. Arnelle hugged him back and tried to recover from his sudden action. He released her, reached into his jacket pocket, and pulled out a small card.

"Arnelle, if you ever need anything or you just want to talk, call me. This card has my home, cell, and private office numbers on it. Okay?"

Arnelle took the card from his hand and smiled. "Thank you, Winston."

She watched through the window as he walked in long strides out to his truck, climbed in, and drove away.

"Winston Carter, I will find out why you're acting like you don't know me; if it's the last thing I do. If Cyrus is involved, I'll never forgive him."

∞

Back in his office, Winston put his hand over his face. "What the hell is wrong with me?"

He couldn't believe he'd practically lifted Arnelle off the floor when he'd hugged her. It was a spontaneous reaction that reminded him how out of control he became in her presence. Walking around his office in a daze, he wondered who or what was the cause of Arnelle's tears. He'd never asked Venice or Craig if she was dating anyone. To tell the truth, he really didn't want to know. It would be too painful for him to know someone else was touching her in a way he wanted to. He thought he was going to be able to forget about her, but after holding her in his arms, there was no way he could walk away. The most surprising fact was that Arnelle had accepted his embrace. He hoped she would eventually sit down and tell him everything about their past and how they had met.

∞

Saturday came and went with Brandon. They had a great time at the NBA game. The 76ers won as usual, and Winston and Brandon filled up on all sorts of snacks at the game. Since it was over so late, Brandon spent the night at Winston's place. As they prepared for bed, Winston decided to quiz Brandon on Arnelle's personal life. He knew it was pathetic of him to quiz a child, but what the hell.

"Brandon, have you seen Miss Arnelle since we were all over at your house for dinner a couple of weeks ago?"

"She was at my house one day this week. She's so pretty, isn't she, Uncle Skeeter? She looks just like a Barbie doll."

"That she is, my man. Has she ever brought a friend over to your house with her?"

Brandon sat there looking confused, then answered, "Oh, now I remember. Yes, Uncle Skeeter, she brought a man with her a lot of times, but I don't know his name. You want me to ask her?"

"No, I was just wondering. Goodnight, Brandon."

"Goodnight, Uncle Skeeter, and thanks for taking me to the game. I really miss going to the ballgames with my daddy. It makes me sad sometimes that he had to leave me and go play football in heaven."

"I'm sure you miss him very much, but remember if he could've stayed here with you and your mom, he would've. Your dad loves you and your mom very much; just remember that."

Sighing, he said, "Yeah I know, but I still cry for him sometimes; mostly at night. I don't want my momma to know 'cause it'll make her sad. Having Pops around helps her a lot, though."

"I'm sure it does." He rubbed Brandon's head. "I'm proud of you, Brandon. I know your mom is proud of you, too."

"Thank you, Uncle Skeeter."

"Anytime, my man."

Winston's head dropped and his heart thumped against his ribs. He felt sad for Brandon and couldn't imagine what he had gone through with losing his dad. He hoped he had comforted him in some way. He felt another pain in his chest as he realized that Arnelle *was* seeing someone.

When he got back downstairs, he made a pot of coffee and decided to work on some of his case files. It didn't take long for his phone to ring.

"Hello?"

"Well, hello stranger. I was beginning to think you'd forgotten about me."

Skeeter smiled. "I haven't, Victoria. I've just been busy."

"So when are you going to spend some time with me? I know you're busy, but you have to take time out to have some fun. What are you doing tonight?"

He leaned back in his chair. "Well, I've been busy, and you're right, I could use some fun. Tonight is out because I have my friend's son spending the night with me. How's next weekend?"

"Well, I guess next weekend it is," she said in an airy voice, pouting. "Call me tomorrow, so we can decide what we're going to do."

"I will. Goodnight, Victoria."

Winston hung up the phone, not feeling his normal enthusiasm when talking to Victoria. She taught classes at a local university and for a professor, she was very uninhibited and very freaky. She was closing in on 30 and was starting to hint around about a commitment. He knew he was tired of running around with a lot of women, but he just couldn't see himself settling down with Victoria. She was intellectual, fine and beautiful. She just didn't ignite the passion he wanted in a mate. So far, only one woman had been successful in setting him on fire, and she didn't have a clue of the feelings she stirred up in him.

∞

It was nearing midnight when he decided he'd worked enough on a particular case file. He turned off the light in his office, checked on Brandon and retired to bed. Tomorrow, he would take Brandon to church, then back home. He had a standing pick-up game of basketball that he played every Sunday evening with friends at the local Y. He always looked forward to the games since it usually helped relieve a lot of stress. He took his shower, dressed in a pair of shorts and a T-shirt, and turned in for the night. Before closing his eyes, he thought about Arnelle. He didn't want to think about her too much because he knew what it did to his body. That was the last thing he wanted to deal with tonight.

CHAPTER THREE

Brandon sat in the front seat of Winston's truck Sunday afternoon during the drive to Craig's house. He was unusually quiet.

"Brandon, you okay?"

"Yeah, I'm okay." He sighed. "I was just thinking."

Winston glanced at Brandon, then back to the highway.

"You look like you got a lot on your mind. You want to talk about it?"

Brandon stuttered and said, "Well, I don't know. I don't want to get in trouble. I wasn't supposed to be listening to Momma and Miss Arnelle talking the other day. I accidentally heard Miss Arnelle tell my momma something that was making her sad. The next thing I knew they were both crying and hugging. I got scared so I ran to my room. I don't like to see my momma or Miss Arnelle cry."

Winston's grip tightened on the steering wheel of his truck. "Why didn't you ask your mom about it if it scared you so much? I'm sure she would understand you didn't mean to listen."

Brandon leaned back against the leather seat. "I can't, Uncle Skeeter. They always tell me to keep my nose out of grown folks' business."

"You want me to ask? I promise I won't get you into trouble."

Brandon took in a deep breath and released. "I just don't want my momma and Miss Arnelle sad. You can ask. Thanks, Uncle Skeeter."

∞

When they entered the house, Craig was still dressed in his Sunday attire, reading the paper. The twins were in their playpen, playing with their feet and various baby toys. When they entered the family room, Craig said, "Welcome home, Brandon. Did you have a good time?"

Brandon hugged Craig's neck and said, "Yes, Pops! We had the bestest time at the game, but I fell asleep in church."

Craig stood and said, "I'm glad you had a good time. Go on upstairs and change your clothes."

"Okay, Pops."

Before leaving the room, he went over to the playpen to look at his brother and sister; he needed to make sure they were okay. He then walked over to Winston, who picked him up. He gave him a big hug and whispered in his ear, "Don't forget to talk to my momma."

So Craig wouldn't know what was going on, Winston answered, "I had a good time, too, Lil' Man. We'll do it again real soon."

After he went upstairs, Craig asked, "What was that all about?"

"Nothing. Are you going to play ball this evening?"

Imitating his jumpshot, Craig said, "You know it. I can't let Venice beat me staying in shape. She still runs a couple miles a day."

"What you mean is you have to keep working out to keep up with her." Winston laughed.

"Forget you, Skeeter. I have no problem keeping up with Venice."

"Yeah, right."

Venice walked in with fresh diapers and asked, "I heard my name. What's up?"

"Skeeter, don't think I can keep up with you."

She was dressed in a black sports bra and snug-fitting sweatpants, revealing her shapely figure. She laughed as she bent over to pull one of the twins out of the playpen.

Craig froze and said, "Dang, Babe! Skeeter, man, you got to go, now! I'll see you on the court."

Winston laughed. "You're throwing me out, Bro? You're so sad. Don't you ever talk to me about being out of control again. I'll see you guys later. Have fun."

Venice sat across the room, changing one of the twins, not knowing that her husband was plotting to get some afternoon delight.

As Craig hustled Winston out of the room, Venice smiled and said, "Goodbye, Skeeter, and thanks for letting Brandon hang out with you this weekend."

"Anytime. He was great. I need to talk to you about something, but since your husband is throwing me out of the house, it can wait."

"It's going to have to wait." Craig laughed. "You can call her later."

"I'm going, I'm going. Damn, Craig!"

Craig hurried Winston out the door. "I'm sorry, Bro, but I'll catch you later. I need to give Venice some attention."

"Looks like you're the one starving for attention. You're worse than the kids, Craig."

Craig looked back in Venice's direction and said, "You'll be doing the same thing one day, and I can't wait to tell you I told you so. I'll see you at the Y."

"Goodbye, you pervert."

Craig laughed and closed the door. Winston smiled as he walked to his truck. His best friend had practically thrown him out of his house, so he could make love to his beautiful wife. He paused at his truck and daydreamed about the day he would kick Craig out to do the same thing. He hoped his wait wouldn't be too long.

∞

That evening, Winston returned to his house after what seemed like a million games of basketball. His body was numb from the bumps and bruises he had experienced on the court. He couldn't wait to hit the showers. It was about eight o'clock and his stomach let him know it was empty.

Before jumping in the shower, he checked his messages. He had one from his mother and another from Victoria. There were several other messages from women he had dated in the past. It seemed like they were coming out of the woodwork, almost like they sensed he was ready to settle down. His mother would be the first call he would return. He was happy her health had returned and she was back to being a nosey mom. He was an only child and his mom was somewhat overprotective.

He ran upstairs, stripped out of his sweaty clothes and stepped under the hot stream of water. He lathered his chocolate skin and let the water massage his strained muscles. After a short time, he stepped out of the shower, toweled off and lay across the bed, completely nude. Before he knew it, he had fallen asleep. The ringing of the telephone startled him out of his sleep. It took a moment for him to realize what day it was. He turned over, looked at the clock and saw that it was ten-thirty. He rubbed his eyes and reached for the telephone.

"Hello?"

"Oh, you can't call your mother back?"

"I'm sorry, Momma. I fell asleep."

Concern entered her voice. "Are you feeling okay, Winston?"

"I'm fine, Momma, just tired."

"Well, you need to take better care of yourself. You're wearing yourself down running around with all those women. It's time you grow up and stop that foolishness. Do you hear me?"

Winston lay back on the bed and closed his eyes.

"Momma, first of all, I am taking care of myself. Secondly, I'm not running around with a harem of women, so relax."

His mom started tearing up and said, "Baby, I just want you to be happy. I want you to find a nice girl and settle down. You're not getting any younger, and you need someone to take care of you up there."

Smiling, he said, "I know, Momma. Thank you and don't worry about me. How are you feeling?"

"Child, I'm fine. Well, it's late and I'm going to let you get some rest. I was worried since you hadn't returned my call. I love you and call me soon."

"I will, Momma. I love you, too. Tell Daddy hello."

"I will. Goodnight, Baby."

"Goodnight, Momma."

Winston hung up the phone and sat there absorbing his conversation with his mother. His stomach rumbled, and he knew he needed to eat something. He didn't like to eat late, but tonight, he had no choice. He slipped into his robe and slippers and headed for the kitchen. He decided on a ham and cheese sandwich.

As he made his sandwich, he turned on the small TV on the counter. Once again, his telephone rang.

"Hello?"

"See what I mean, Winston? You have forgotten about me."

Cradling the phone against his neck, he said, "I'm sorry, Victoria. I fell asleep, and I just woke up. I was going to call you, but I thought it was too late."

In a seductive tone, she said, "Baby, it's never too late for you. As a matter of fact, if you like, I could come over and give you one of my fabulous massages."

Winston stopped applying the salad dressing on the bread. It had been a long time since he had made love to Victoria or any woman. He knew if he let her come over, he would be in for a marathon of intimate activity. Before he could answer, an image of Arnelle popped in his head.

"It's late, Victoria," he finally said, "and you don't need to be on the road. Look, we're seeing each other next weekend. Right?"

"Okay, Winston. You win. So where do you want to go Saturday?"

Relief swept over him. "What about Jazzy's? You always like going there."

"Okay, Darling. Sounds good to me, so I guess I'll see you next Saturday. I can't wait. You do know it's been a while."

"Yeah, I know. Night, Victoria." When he hung up, there was no excitement. There was no looking forward to next weekend. His mind was too occupied with the secret Arnelle and Venice shared. He promised Brandon he would find out what was going on. Tomorrow, he would ask Venice out to lunch and try to find out what or who was troubling Arnelle. If someone had hurt her in any way, he just didn't know what he would do. He had never felt so reckless when it came to any woman until Arnelle.

CHAPTER FOUR

A rnelle had seen two patients this morning. One was an Eagles defensive end, who was suffering from a separated shoulder. The team doctors knew their reputation and loved sending the players to the Bennett Clinic for reinforced treatment. When Corey walked into the treatment room, he was stunned at the beautiful face staring back at him.

"Hello, Corey. How's your shoulder feeling today?"

He swallowed and said, "It's still sore. So you're my doctor?"

She motioned to him to sit on the table. "That I am."

"Corey, I'm Dr. Arnelle Lapahie." She extended her hand to Corey. "I will be treating you."

"Dang! Nobody told me you were fine, Doc."

Arnelle sighed and stopped writing on the clipboard for a moment.

"Corey, look, I'm your doctor…period. I am not to be treated like any of those chicken heads or hoochies you might be accustomed to. Understood? If this is going to be a problem for you, I can have your athletic trainer make other arrangements for you. I don't put up with any bullshit from any of my patients or you'll find yourself slapped with a lawsuit or worse. Do you understand where I'm coming from, Corey? I'm here to help you get back out on the field, nothing else. Understood?"

Corey threw up his hands in surrender. "I didn't mean any disrespect, Doc. It's not every day we have doctors that look like you and Dr. Bennett. I'm cool, and I apologize."

"Apology accepted. Now, let's get busy. We have to get you back out on the field."

"Just tell me what to do, Doc."

Winston and Venice arrived at the restaurant at the same time. After greeting each other with a loving hug, the waitress showed them to their table and brought them their drinks. She gave them a minute to look over the menu and they decided to split a tray of hot wings. Within minutes, the waitress arrived with their food and Winston immediately dug in. Venice took a sip of her drink and asked, "So Skeeter, what is it you want to talk about?"

He wiped his mouth with a napkin and said, "Brandon was a little upset at something. He didn't want to come to you because he was afraid he would get in trouble. He said he overheard you and Arnelle talking and then you both started crying."

Venice's eyes widened and she asked, "Did he tell you what was said?"

"No, he said he couldn't hear you, but it scared him. What's going on, Venice? I ran into Arnelle at your office the other day. She practically knocked me down, running out of her office in tears, and she's been making some strange comments about something happening between us. She apologized and everything. I'm clueless to what's going on."

Venice sighed and said, "I'm sorry, but I can't tell you, Skeeter. If Arnelle wants you to know, she'll tell you."

"So you do know what's going on with her? Venice, you know it's not like Arnelle to be nice to me. The woman cried her eyes out right in front of me. She let me hug her and everything, so whatever it is has to be big. Just tell me if anyone has hurt her."

Venice covered his hand with hers. "I'm sorry, Skeeter. I can't. All I can say is don't be so hard on her 'cause she's dealing with some deep issues right now."

"I've always been nice to her. She's the one who gives me a hard time."

"Look, just give her time. She'll come around. Why don't you ask her out or something?"

Winston picked up another hot wing and halted its disappearance into his mouth. "I don't know about that."

Laughing, Venice said, "Like I said, give her time. As far as Brandon, I'll talk to him tonight and let him know that everything is okay. Thanks for being so good with him. You know he really admires you."

"He's a cool kid."

"Yes. He's so much like his dad."

Winston stole a glance at Venice and noticed the sadness that swept past her eyes.

"You okay, Venice?"

"Yeah, I'm okay. I still miss him, you know?"

He held her hand. "I know. I can't imagine what that could've been like to lose your husband so suddenly. I know it must've hurt like hell. Brandon still misses him, too. He tries to be brave for you, but he misses his dad a lot."

"I worry about him sometimes. He tries to be a big boy for me, but I'm a little concerned about him."

"Why?"

"I don't think he really let his emotions out like he wanted to when Jarvis died, and I know it's because of me. During that time, I was a wreck, and I wasn't there for him like I should've been. I believe I failed my son."

"That's not your fault, Venice. I'm sure you did the best you could emotionally, under the circumstances."

"I don't know. He didn't take his dad's death as hard as I expected. I think he's still holding it in."

"Do you want me to talk to him?"

"Would you? I would ask Craig, but I don't want to make him feel awkward even though I'm sure he wouldn't have a problem talking to Brandon about it. God sent Craig back to me, and I'm so thankful to have him in my life, but Brandon is my heart, and I don't want him hurting inside."

"I'll talk to him and get back with you, and I'm also glad you and Craig found each other again."

"Thank you." Venice smiled. "I think Brandon will open up to someone outside the family and since he hangs out with you, he'll probably confide in you."

"Let's hope so."

Rubbing goosebumps from her arms, Venice stood and said, "Well, Winston Fredrick Carter, the third, I'd better get back to the clinic. Thanks for lunch and next time it's my treat. I really appreciate you being such a good friend to me."

"I feel the same way."

They smiled at each other in silence. Venice took a sip of her drink and said, "You know Lamar and Tressa's wedding is coming up. Are you going?"

Frowning, he said, "I don't know. Weddings make you women get kind of crazy, and I'm not sure I want to be in the middle of all that drama."

She hugged his neck and kissed him on the cheek. "Your clock is ticking, my love. Besides, Craig would be upset if you didn't come. He's best man and yours truly is a bridesmaid." She couldn't fathom him not supporting Lamar Fletcher, Craig's business partner and one of his best friends.

"I don't know, Venice. As far as my clock ticking, I can deal with that."

She laughed. "I know you will. Now get your butt back to work."

∞

Arnelle decided that this Saturday afternoon, she would treat herself to some pampering. After doing some shopping, she drove to her favorite salon for a manicure, pedicure and massage. She wanted the works. Her muscles and nerves were all balled up. Her workdays consisted of doing everything within her power to make others feel good. Now, it was her turn. She walked through the front door of the salon.

"Hello, Arnelle," the receptionist said, her voice chipper. "It's so good to see you. Raymond is waiting on you in the Rain Forest room."

"Thank you, Sicily."

Arnelle couldn't wait for Raymond to work his magic. He was the best, and that's exactly what she needed. When Arnelle walked out of the salon, she felt one hundred and ten percent better. It was around seven o'clock, so she decided to catch a movie, and then pick up some Chinese food for dinner.

By nine-thirty, she pulled into her garage and shut off the engine. She entered her kitchen and got a strange feeling in her gut. When she walked down the hallway, she noticed things were out of place. Drawers were opened, and things were scattered around every room. She started trembling, realizing that some-one had gotten past her security system and entered her house. She paused for a second, and then heard a noise coming from one of the other rooms. Backing up, she went back into the kitchen and picked up her cell phone. She dialed 911 but was put on eternal hold. Next she tried to call Craig and Venice, but she remembered they were having dinner at Ms. Camille's house. She didn't have Ms. Camille's number and couldn't remember any of their cell phone numbers. Sinking to the floor, she pulled Winston's card from her purse and dialed his number. There was no answer at his house, so she dialed his cell phone. She closed her eyes and scooted over to the corner of her kitchen. Her legs had given out on her and she couldn't move. The phone was on the third ring when she heard his welcoming voice.

"Hello?"

"Winston?"

He immediately knew something was wrong.

"Arnelle? What's wrong?"

Her voice was barely above a whisper. She started sobbing and fear swept over her body.

"Someone broke into my house, and I think they're still here. I'm so scared."

Cutting her off, he said, "Did you call the police?"

"Yes, but the 911 operators put me on hold. I can't find Craig and Venice…"

"Stay put. I'm on my way."

She covered her face and prayed that it wouldn't take him long to get there. What inspired her to call Winston next had her clueless. All she knew was that Winston made her feel safe the other day when she was upset and whether she wanted to admit it, she was drawn to him.

∞

Winston dialed 911 and grabbed his leather jacket. He hurriedly put it on as he waited for the operator to answer. As soon as someone picked up, Winston was placed on hold. He cursed as he continued to hold. After a few more seconds, he hung up the phone, disgusted. He and Victoria had just arrived back to her house from Jazzy's when Arnelle had called. She had just changed into some sexy lingerie and was about to give Winston a private dance. She entered the room with two wine glasses and asked, "Where are you going?"

"I'm sorry, Victoria," Winston said as he stared at Victoria and her barely dressed body. "I have a friend who's in trouble. I'll have to take a rain check."

Victoria sat the glasses down and said, "A woman no doubt."

"I don't have time for this. I'm sorry, but I have to go."

She dropped her lingerie to the floor and stood stark naked in front of him.

"Winston, you're going to walk out on all of this?"

He dropped his head and said, "I'm sorry, Victoria. You are a desirable woman, but I have to go."

"Winston," Victoria said, her voice firm, "if you walk out that door, don't expect me to ever let you in again."

He picked up his keys from the table and said, "Victoria, I can't believe you'd expect me to choose sex with you over helping a friend in trouble. Look, face it. We've had a nice time while it lasted. Thanks for showing me your true colors tonight. Goodbye, Victoria."

As he hurried out the door and to his truck, Winston heard Victoria yell, "You'll pay for this, Winston!"

Winston pulled his truck out onto the expressway and dialed Arnelle's number. A faint voice answered. "Hello?"

"Arnelle, it's Winston. Where are you?"

"I'm in my kitchen."

Winston gripped the wheel with one hand and put his foot heavy on the gas, exceeding the speed limit.

"Arnelle, I'll be there in a few minutes," he said. "Stay on the line until I get to the door. I tried to call 911 but they put me on hold, too."

"Just hurry."

He heard her sobs return as he drove even faster. Winston's heart was breaking, and he knew that if anyone harmed Arnelle, he would make sure the person didn't take another breath.

"Arnelle, have you heard any more noises?"

"I don't know. My heart is beating too loud."

Winston's heart thudded as a sense of helplessness consumed him.

Within minutes, he came to a screeching halt in her driveway. He jumped out and ran to her door.

"Arnelle, I'm at the front door," he said. "Come open it."

"I can't move, Winston."

He didn't want to break down her door, but he would if he had to.

"Arnelle, come on, Baby. You can do it. Come open the door."

All he could hear was her sobbing.

"Winston, there's a spare key under the small green flower pot."

"Where? Oh, I see it....got it. Hold on, Arnelle. I'm coming."

Winston retrieved the key and pulled his 9mm from his waistband. If anyone was still in the house, he wanted to make sure he was protected. He slid the key in the lock and turned the knob slowly.

"Arnelle, I'm coming in the front door. Where's the kitchen?"

"Down the hall to your left."

Winston cautiously walked down the hallway, glancing up the stairs as he passed them. When he turned the corner, he spotted Arnelle sitting in the corner with the phone cradled up to her ear. He put his cell phone in his pocket and went to her, pulling her up from the floor. She dove into his arms, and he held her tightly to his large frame. Arnelle completely broke down crying at that point.

He hugged her and said, "It's okay, Arnelle. Let me get you out of here so I can check the house."

"No, don't leave me."

"Arnelle, I'm just going to take you out to my truck so I can call the police again. Okay?"

She finally nodded in agreement. Winston led Arnelle by the hand and locked her securely in his vehicle before returning to the house where he checked every room thoroughly. He returned to his truck, climbed in and said, "Arnelle, whoever broke into your house is long gone now. How did they get past your alarm system?"

"I don't know." Arnelle wiped her eyes with a tissue she clutched in her left hand.

"Do you feel like going back in to see if anything is missing?"

She looked into his compassionate eyes and said, "Yes."

They returned to the house and went from room to room. Fortunately, nothing was missing, but her TV was unplugged and so was her DVD player.

"Don't touch anything, Arnelle. I finally got through to the police. They might want to see if there are any fingerprints on the electronics."

Wiping away a few more tears, she said, "Okay. I guess we can wait for the police downstairs."

Winston watched as Arnelle seemed to move around in slow motion. They went back downstairs and sat in the living room. It was there they tried to come to terms with what had happened.

"Arnelle, you must've come in before they had time to take your stuff. The back door was unlocked, so they must have gone out that way. I'm glad they didn't hang around and try to hurt you."

She wrapped her arms around herself and said, "I don't understand this."

Winston sat next to her on the sofa and asked, "What's going on, Arnelle? I know something's going on. You ran out of your office in tears, and Brandon saw you and Venice crying."

"He did? Oh, my poor baby."

"Yes, he did," Winston said as he leaned in closer, "and it upset him to see you two crying. He's okay now, though."

"I'm glad." She stood. "I don't ever want to do anything to upset Brandon."

Winston stood and looked down at her, searching her eyes for answers. He found her so fragile at that moment, he wanted to wrap her in his arms and protect her.

"He loves you, you know."

Smiling, she said, "I know. I love him, too."

He came closer and asked, "Can we talk now?"

"I glad you asked, Winston."

He smiled. "I hate the fact that I don't remember you."

"So do I, and Winston, I can understand why you want to forget me. I never meant to hurt you."

He'd taken all he could of Arnelle's mysterious conversations. He quizzed, "How did you hurt me?"

She stared at him. Something was wrong...very wrong. Wringing her hands, she answered, "I don't know where to start."

She needed time to think about what was going on. He was like a stranger to her and they were far from strangers; in fact, they knew each other very well.

He threw up his hands in disgust.

"Why not at the beginning, Arnelle?"

"I'm too upset to get into all of that tonight. Can it wait?"

Shoving his hands in his pockets, he looked away and answered, "I guess so."

She unexpectedly wrapped her arms around his neck and whispered, "Thanks for coming to my rescue, Winston. I'll never forget it."

He held her close and enjoyed the warmth and scent of her body. They held each other in silence for a moment. He released her when the police officer interrupted them when he rang the doorbell. He was glad because his body would've revealed the desire he carried for her.

The policeman did a walk-thru of her house and took a report of the burglary. Since her alarm system had been tampered with, he suggested that she stay elsewhere for the night before he left.

Winston walked the officer outside and when he returned, he said, "Arnelle, the officer was right. Until you find out how the burglar got past your alarm system, I don't think it's a good idea for you to stay here. Is there someone you want me to call for you? Your boyfriend, maybe?"

Arnelle dabbed her eyes with a tissue and asked, "What boyfriend?"

Winston fumbled with his words.

"The guy you bring with you over to Craig's house."

Arnelle started laughing hysterically. "Where did you get your information?"

"Brandon told me," Winston answered, lowering his head. He nervously fumbled with his words.

Arnelle shook her head, still laughing. "Winston, Brandon must be talking about Timmy Hughes. That's the only man I've ever brought to Craig's house."

"The high school All-American?"

"The one and only. We were installing new whirlpools at the clinic, so we used the one at their house instead for his physical therapy."

Arnelle saw the embarrassment in his face. Despite the humor, she stopped laughing. "I'm not dating anyone right now, Winston. Is it too forward of me to ask if I could stay at your house tonight? I'm a little nervous about sleeping here considering what happened. If it's going to be a problem with the woman in your life, I understand and can make other arrangements."

His gaze met hers lovingly. He smiled. "Well, Miss Arnelle, I'm not seeing anyone and even if I was, she would have nothing to say on who I can have in my house. There's no way I'll leave you alone tonight. I was going to invite you anyway."

"So you won't mind me hanging out at your place?"

"Not at all."

"Good. I can't sleep here tonight knowing someone has touched my things, especially my bed."

"Go pack, Arnelle. I couldn't ask for a better houseguest."

She smiled and turned to walk up the stairs. When she reached the door, she said, "Winston, I'm sorry for the way I've treated you."

"Apology accepted, but we do need to sit down and talk. Now hurry up and pack. I'll make sure everything is locked up."

∞

As she packed, she realized this was no longer a game. Winston really didn't remember her. So what happened to him? What she did to help Cyrus three years ago sealed her fate to Winston and he didn't even know it. Eventually, she would have to tell him everything. That was unless he remembered on his own. Once everything came to light, all hell would definitely break loose.

She stuffed the last item into her bag. She forwarded her calls to her cell phone and headed back downstairs. Winston stood at the bottom of the stairs, watching her descent. Nervousness crept up her body. She was going to sleep under the same roof with a man who once made her feel very uninhibited.

"You got everything you need?"

Handing him her bag, she answered, "Well, if it's not in there, I guess I don't need it. Thanks again."

He helped her with her coat. "Tomorrow, you need to call your insurance company and change security companies because the one you have is jacked up."

Arnelle laughed. "Is that how you talk in court?"

"Most definitely." He smiled. "Let's get out of here."

∞

Not even five minutes in to the thirty-minute ride home, Arnelle was sound asleep. Winston called Craig to let him know what had happened and told him to pass the information on to Venice.

"Bro," Craig asked, "are you going to be able to handle Arnelle tonight? I mean y'all two don't really get along."

"We'll be fine," Winston whispered. "Actually, we cleared up some of our differences. She's asleep right now."

"Well, be careful, my man. I know how you are when you're around her. Don't get yourself into a situation you can't get out of."

"I'll be cool. Don't worry. Besides, I might not want to get out of a situation with her. It's just for the weekend anyway, so I'm sure nothing will happen."

Craig laughed. "What do you think Victoria is going to say about this little arrangement?"

"She's history. I ended that tonight and should've done it a long time ago. She started tripping when I had to leave."

"Was she pissed?"

"That's an understatement. She didn't appreciate me leaving to help Arnelle. She got butt naked and everything trying to get me to stay. I told her she should want me to go help a friend. That was it for me, Man."

"Well, good luck. Holler if you need us."

"I will. Goodnight and kiss the kids and that bossy wife of yours."

Winston hung up and glanced over at a snoring Arnelle. *What a beautiful sight and sound*, he thought.

∞

He pulled into his three-car garage and turned off the truck. He unlocked the house and took Arnelle's bag inside. It was nearing midnight now, and he returned to his truck and picked up a sleeping Arnelle. She must have been exhausted because all she could do was wrap her arms around his neck and bury her face against his warm neck. The mere contact of her face against his neck caused a throbbing in his lower body. He carried her up the stairs with ease and placed her onto the large bed.

She stirred slightly. "Stay with me tonight?"

"I am with you, Arnelle."

She took his hand in hers and said, "No, I mean stay with me in here. I don't want to be alone."

"I don't think that would be a good idea."

She was hoping something would jar his memory. Standing, she wrapped her arms around his neck again and kissed him lightly on the lips. Winston's heart skipped several beats as she ran her tongue across his mouth and between his parted lips. He crushed her body to his and moaned as his body reacted swiftly to their exchange. Arnelle pulled him closer and looked deeply into his eyes. Searching for another way to jar his memory, she greedily tasted his sweet mouth. Breathless, she whispered, "Winston."

He kissed her lips, neck and cheek, then pulled himself apart from her. He wanted her so bad, but not like this.

"Arnelle, sweetheart, we should stop. You've had a traumatic evening, and it's been a long day. I don't want you to do anything you'll regret in the morning. Okay?"

She searched his familiar eyes and said, "I guess you're right. I'm sorry…"

"Don't be, Arnelle. That was the nicest feeling I've had in a long time."

She smiled. "Ditto."

"Anyway, you should be able to find everything you need. If not, I'm across the hall, so just holler if you need me."

"I'm sure I can find everything. Goodnight, Winston."

Backing out of the bedroom, he said, "Goodnight."

Winston closed the door behind him and leaned against it. After a moment, he slowly walked to his room.

∞

Arnelle unpacked and scolded herself. She had thought for sure he would remember her kiss.

What the hell is wrong with you? Winston doesn't have a clue. Who am I fooling?

She slipped out of her clothes and ran a hot bath, adding bath salts to the running water. As she sat on the side of the tub, she daydreamed about the man across the hall. She was ashamed of the things she had done to him in the past. She needed Winston to remember because she didn't have the heart to tell him. Cyrus was going to bug the hell out of her unless he got what he wanted. Hopefully Winston would recall before Cyrus drove her crazy. Now that she knew for sure that Winston wasn't pretending, she had to do whatever it took to help him remember.

∞

Winston sat on the edge of his bed going over the events of the day. Having Arnelle in his house would hopefully spark a

new beginning for them. It seemed as if she had disliked him
for so long and for reasons he didn't understand. Maybe this
weekend would allow him to give her a different opinion about
him. Still, he was puzzled with her recent comments. Getting
Arnelle to trust him was top priority. The fact that she kissed
him revealed that either she was thankful for his help or that she
liked him more than she pretended. His mind was becoming
exhausted from thinking. He discarded his clothes, showered
and went to bed even though he knew he wouldn't get any
sleep because Arnelle's perfume filled the air.

Arnelle tossed and turned into the wee hours of the morning. She woke to find her nightgown drenched in sweat. The
nightmare was the same she'd had for the past couple of years.
Pushing the covers away from her body, she stood and walked
over to the window. The night air was frigid, but temporarily
soothing to her hot skin. Her thick, wavy hair hung loose around
her shoulders. After closing the window, she padded across the
floor and pulled a locket from her purse. She opened it and
stared down at little MaLeah's face. It was almost like looking
into a mirror except for those eyes. The eyes she fell in love with
a few years ago. How could things have gotten so out of hand?
She had to make it up to MaLeah one way or another. This had
now become her mission in life....to make amends with the
person she had wronged at whatever cost. She looked back on
everything and tried to remember where things went wrong.
She had always heard the saying about being in the wrong
place at the wrong time and that's exactly what happened to her.

∞

Senior year in college, after cruising around with friends
after a party, the car in which she was a passenger was pulled

over by the police. Arnelle had no idea narcotics were stashed under the seat. Arnelle and her four classmates were taken to the police station since no one would admit to owning the drugs. She knew if her father, being a judge, found out, he would be devastated. Even worse, her chances of going to medical school would disappear after four years of hard work. She just couldn't do that to her family. At the police station, the students were able to make one telephone call. Her call was to the only person she knew could help them...Cyrus McDaniels. At the time, he was waiting to be drafted into the NBA and held a lot of clout in the city. He came down to the police station and vouched for all of the students, assuring officers they were unaware of the drugs.

The car did belong to another student who was not in the vehicle. On several occasions, that particular student would let various friends use it, so the police had no way of determining ownership of the drugs. After Cyrus's speech, all the students were released. Obviously shaken from her brush with the law, Arnelle was very grateful and even to this day, Cyrus refused to let her forget it. They went their separate ways after graduation but kept in touch. Arnelle went to medical school and Cyrus into the NBA. Things were peaceful until Cyrus ran into a little trouble years later and needed her help. She knew she owed him for helping her, but what he wanted her to do was unimaginable. She knew she would never forget the sound of his voice...

Arnelle, I need you to help me blackmail someone. My future depends on it.

Arnelle shook her head, trying to shake the sound of his voice from her mind. How in the world did he expect her to risk her career? What he did for her was petty compared to what he wanted her to do for him. Against her wishes, he wrote her a check for a hundred-thousand dollars in payment for her help. She never cashed it and to this day, she still had it in her possession. She was in medical school and her father had just talked to the family about his plans of running for mayor in the upcoming elections. This had been his lifelong dream and she knew she couldn't ruin it for him or embarrass her family. Now, all she wanted was for Cyrus to quit harassing her so she could get on with her life in peace. Her future depended on the handsome man sleeping down the hall.

CHAPTER FIVE

The next morning, Winston awoke to a heavenly aroma and the sound of music. He slipped out of bed and followed the scent and sound. When he walked into the kitchen, he saw that Arnelle had a full-course breakfast laid out on the table: coffee, orange juice, homemade biscuits, country ham, eggs, and pancakes.

She turned with a grin on her face and said, "Good morning, Winston."

"Good morning." Winston smiled and looked from the breakfast to Arnelle. "Where did you…"

She led him to his seat and said, "I went to the store because, Honey, your refrigerator was practically empty. I hope you don't mind me borrowing your truck."

"Of course not."

"How do you survive without food, Winston?"

He sat down, poured a cup of coffee and said, "I manage."

With a jealous tone, she said, "What you mean to say is you have women cooking for you all the time."

He looked at her seriously and said, "What I mean is I eat out a lot."

Arnelle was embarrassed that she showed her jealousy.

"I'm sorry, Winston. Your personal life is none of my business."

"Arnelle," he began while he buttered a biscuit, "I barely have a personal life, contrary to what you may think about me. You act like I'm a dog or something."

She sipped her orange juice. "What makes you say that?"

"Because I can't think of any other reason why you won't talk to me."

Arnelle dropped her head and softly said, "I can't, Winston."

He just stared at her because he knew she was hiding something. After a short silence, he said, "Breakfast is delicious, Arnelle, but you didn't have to go through all this trouble."

"It was no trouble at all. I enjoyed cooking for you."

"I see you have good taste in music also."

She closed her eyes and whispered, "There's nothing like Maxwell to soothe you."

"I agree. I take it you dig Maxwell."

"He's my favorite. The man has it going on."

Winston wanted to break Arnelle's solemn mood. He took a bite of his buttered biscuit and jokingly asked, "Are you trying to fatten me up, woman?"

"No silly." She laughed. "I'm just trying to keep you alive."

He placed his larger hand over hers. "I'm glad. Thank you."

"You're welcome."

They finished their breakfast while talking about various subjects in the morning paper. Arnelle forgot to bring Sunday clothes, so church was out of the question. It would be Monday before she could call a new security company, and the temperature outside was frigid and snow was still on the ground. The pair wound up in Winston's spacious family room.

"What about a movie?" he asked.

"Nah…What about shopping?"

"No way! You're not going to have me carrying your purse and all your shopping bags."

"Do you play pool?"

"Pool?"

"Yes, Winston…pool."

He sat the paper down and said, "Don't tell me you're a pool shark?"

"I dabble a little. So how about it?"

Winston took her hand and said, "I'll play pool with you if you go bowling with me."

"You have yourself a deal." She smiled. "Last one dressed pays for everything."

Arnelle jumped from the sofa and sprinted for the stairs, her giggles trailing behind her. Before she could get halfway up the stairs, Winston darted past her with ease. They dressed hurriedly and within minutes, Arnelle stood by the door waiting for Winston, dangling his keys. He didn't know she had taken her shower before she made breakfast. As he rushed down the steps, tucking his shirt into his jeans, he stopped immediately upon seeing her. She was a sight, leaning against the front door, dressed in a pair of snug faded jeans and a bright red sweater. She smiled as she dangled his keys at him. She walked over to him swaying her hips and said, "My, my, my, Winston. Must I do everything for you?"

Before he could respond, she reached around his waist and tucked a piece of his shirt inside his waistband. He blinked rapidly at the sensuality of her touch. He stared down at her as he fought for control.

"Be careful where you put your hands, woman. You're playing with fire."

Laughing, she said, "Yeah, whatever. Let's go, slow poke."

Does this woman not know what she's doing to me, Winston thought.

Arnelle dropped the keys in his hand and turned to put on her coat. He couldn't help but notice the fit of the jeans to her rear end.

"Mercy!"

She turned and asked, "What?"

"I said I'm not giving you any mercy."

She walked over to him once more and straightened his collar. She looked into his eyes and asked, "Is that a promise?"

She's flirting with me, Winston thought, *and for some reason, it feels so familiar to me.*

Meeting her challenging gaze, he said, "Cross my heart."

"We'll see who has who crying when it's over, Winston."

Winston was alert to all the sexual overtones Arnelle was throwing at him. But why now? If all it took was having her housebroken for her to be nice to him, he would've done that a long time ago.

"Actions speak louder than words. Let's go so I can teach you a lesson."

"Men!"

"Women!"

They continued their little discussion as they climbed into his truck and headed for the bowling alley.

∞

Back in Texas, Arnelle's dad, Judge Herbert Lapahie read the paper as a sleeping MaLeah lay in his lap. He was in his early fifties, and had served on the bench for twenty years. Zenora Lapahie was also in her early fifties, but you couldn't tell by looking at her. Her skin and hair was that of a woman in her early forties. Zenora is where Arnelle had gotten her personality and fiery temper. Her Navajo heritage was very prominent in her features. Arnelle had inherited her features and height from Judge Lapahie. He didn't let anyone run over him and always instilled that in his children. He fell in love with Zenora the moment he laid eyes on her. When Zenora entered the den, she asked, "Herbert, do you want me to take MaLeah?"

"No, she's fine. I'm going to miss her when she goes to Philly."

Smiling, his wife said, "Me, too. You do know you're spoiling her just like you did Arnelle."

"That's what daddies do to daughters, my love. Besides, you spoiled Keaton."

Zenora leaned down and kissed her husband's lips.

"You're right, Darling. Dinner will be ready in about fifteen minutes."

Keaton was Arnelle's older brother, who at thirty-four, owned a restaurant in Houston. He was single and vowed to keep it that way. As Zenora straightened pictures on the table, Herbert asked, "Zenora? Did Arnelle say anything to you about Cyrus being in trouble?"

"No, what happened?"

Judge Lapahie closed the paper. "He's mixed up in some type of money laundering scheme. His case is coming to trial soon. It's such a shame because he's a great ballplayer and a good kid. He's worth millions, but he'll probably lose it after this."

Zenora came and stood near her husband's chair. "That's a shame. He and Arnelle are very close. I'm glad she's not mixed up with him in all this. That wouldn't help your campaign one bit."

"I know, my dear."

"Do you think Cyrus is MaLeah's father?" Herbert asked after a moment of silence.

MaLeah stirred in her grandfather's lap to get a better position. They both stared at her to see if she would wake up out of her satisfied slumber.

Whispering, Zenora said, "No, I really don't think Cyrus is MaLeah's father. MaLeah looks just like Arnelle except for those eyes. Those are not Cyrus' eyes."

"I don't know why you didn't let me make her tell us who the father was three years ago," Herbert said, anger lacing each word. "We deserve to know who our granddaughter's father is."

Zenora frowned. "I agree, Herbert, but Arnelle's our daughter, not one of your defendants. Now lower your voice before you wake the baby." After a moment, she added: "Look Herbert, we talked about this. Arnelle is a good girl. She must have her reasons for not telling us. I'm sure in due time she'll eventually reveal the information because MaLeah needs to know her father."

Judge Lapahie frowned and placed the paper aside. He looked down at his sleeping granddaughter and softly stroked her cheek. Before rising from his chair, he placed a tender kiss on her chubby cheek.

∞

Since it was getting late, Winston and Arnelle decided to eat out for dinner. On the drive home, they stopped by her house to retrieve her car. He didn't want her separated from him, so he insisted they talk on their cell phones the entire ride back to his house. He said, "You know we're going to have to break this tie. You beat me at pool and I beat you at bowling."

"What do you suggest, Winston?"

"I'll think of something."

"I'm sure you will."

He maneuvered the truck into the garage and Arnelle followed in the space next to him. They shut off their engines. Arnelle quickly got out of her car and headed for the door.

"Arnelle."

She looked over her shoulder and asked, "Yes?"

"Thanks for hanging out with me today. It was really nice."

"Same here." She smiled.

As they made their way into the house, she said, "I'm a little tired, so I think I'll turn in. What time do you have to be at work?"

"Around nine. What about you?"

Arnelle walked through the hallway while removing her coat. "I usually go in at eight o'clock, so I need to be up by six-thirty. Do you have an extra alarm clock or will you wake me?"

He was afraid to look at her because she would see the longing in his eyes. He hung up their coats and said, "I'll make sure you get up, Arnelle."

She kissed him on the corner of his lips and said, "I'm counting on it." She turned and ran up the stairs to her room, leaving him frozen. His lower body had once again defied him, stiffening at the casual contact from her. He cursed himself for allowing his libido to run rampant.

∞

Arnelle sat Indian-style on the bed and wondered what to do next. Even though she had spent hours alone with Winston, nothing seemed to jar his memory. As she sat there, she reminisced about how everything had happened three years earlier. It seemed like only yesterday that she had agreed to help Cyrus. He'd found out that Winston would be the prosecutor on his case and felt he had no choice but to dig up dirt to discredit him. Arnelle understood what her job was and even though she was against the idea, she did owe Cyrus a favor. She flew to Los Angeles, where Winston was attending a week-long conference. She checked into the same hotel, dressed in a snug taupe dress and waited in the hotel lounge. She had no idea what he looked like, but Cyrus' other partner in crime, Robin, did. She had observed him and the other lawyers for a couple of days earlier, and the lounge was where they wound down after all-day meetings. Arnelle wore her hair loose, but wavy. It hung midway down her back and men of all colors couldn't help but proposition her.

Robin sat at the bar and the signal was to order an alcoholic beverage called a Screaming Orgasm when he walked in. Several men approached her table and eventually left after she told them she was waiting on someone, but one very persistent man refused to leave. Arnelle was afraid he would mess up the plan if he didn't leave soon. The man was clearly inebriated.

"Come on, pretty lady. I'm sure it's not going to hurt for you to have one drink with me?"

Arnelle squirmed in her seat and said, "I'm sorry, but I'm waiting on someone and I would appreciate it if you would leave."

Continuing his aggravation, he said, "Well, he's not here right now, so how about it?"

Arnelle was becoming even more frustrated and elevated her voice slightly.

"Look! I told you I was waiting on someone."

At that moment, she heard Robin order the signal drink. She strained to look over the shoulder of the irritating man, who was blocking her view. That's when he tried to kiss her. She leaned back and slapped him hard across the face.

He yelled, "You bitch!"

The drunk man then tried to grab her but his hands were blocked by a tall, handsome, gentleman who pushed him away from her. The inebriated man said, "Who the hell do you think you are?"

A lethal baritone voice said, "The man who's going to break you in two if you even think about laying a finger on this woman! Now get the hell out of here!"

The man stumbled over to friends who escorted him out of the lounge. Arnelle stood and said, "Thank you."

The handsome gentleman scanned her from head to toe and said, "It was my pleasure…Miss???"

"Giselle."

The fake name fell from her lips as if it was her given name. She wasn't about to use her real name because if things went bad, she didn't want him to be able to track her down. He held out his hand and said, "Giselle? That's a beautiful name. Winston Carter at your service."

It's him, Arnelle had thought. *My God, Robin didn't tell me he was gorgeous.*

Arnelle smiled and tried to compose herself.

"Would you like to join me for dinner? It looks like I've been stood up anyway and I feel like I owe you for helping me."

Winston shoved his hands in the pockets of his black designer suit and said, "He's a fool."

"Yes, he was drunk."

"No, besides that idiot, I'm talking about the person who stood you up."

Blushing, she said, "Oh! Thank you."

"Giselle, you don't have to thank me, but I am starving and dinner does sound nice right now, but I insist on buying."

"You're so kind."

Arnelle grabbed her purse, winked at Robin and exited the lounge. They entered the hotel restaurant and sat down to dinner. Winston couldn't keep his eyes off her. She was breathtaking.

"So, are you from Los Angeles, Winston?"

Her soft voice snapped him back to reality. He leaned back in his chair and said, "No, I'm here on business. What about you, Giselle?"

Sipping her water, she answered, "The same."

Arnelle took in every detail of his face. He had penetrating eyes, full lips and smooth chocolate skin. His closely cropped hair and smile topped off his handsome features. They enjoyed their dinner and casual conversation and Winston could already feel himself being drawn to this mysterious woman.

Admiring him, she said, "You have beautiful eyes, Winston."

He blushed and said, "Thank you, Giselle. They run deep in my family."

She continued to admire his unique eyes as she sipped on her beverage. They were piercing and very sexy. These were eyes she would never forget.

∞

After dinner, they walked together through the hotel lobby to the elevators.

"Do you mind if I see that you reach your room safely, Giselle?"

She linked her arm in his and said, "That would be nice, Winston; thank you."

Winston had been known as a ladies' man most of his life, but there was something about this woman. He wanted to get to know her better. He'd only met her a couple of hours earlier, but she made him feel so relaxed. When they entered the elevator, he turned and asked, "What floor?"

She tugged at her dress and said, "Seventh. Room Seventy-four, forty-seven."

He admired her as she continued to tug at her dress.

Smiling, he said, "I'm on thirteen in thirteen eighty-two."

They smiled at each other and rode the elevator in silence. When the doors opened, he allowed Arnelle ahead of him.

Good Lawd, his mind screamed. *This woman is fine!*

His body was trying to betray him. In the past, he'd always been able to control his body around women...until now. They reached her door and she turned and said, "Winston, I want to thank you for being my knight in shining armor tonight."

"It was nothing, Giselle. It would be nice if you would join me for breakfast out on the terrace in the morning."

Playing hard, she said, "I don't know. I've already taken up enough of your time."

"Come on. I've enjoyed every second of your company."

"Okay." She smiled. "What time should I meet you?"

"How does ten o'clock sound?"

She leaned in, kissed him on the cheek and said, "Ten o'clock it is. Goodnight, Winston."

It was on that first night that Arnelle had captured the heart of Winston Carter III and put Cyrus' idiotic plan in motion.

∞

Winston couldn't wait to get back to his room to call his best friend, Craig. While waiting for him to pick up the extension, he couldn't help but touch the area on his cheek her lips had kissed.

"Hello?"

"Yo, Craig, what's up?"

Yawning, he asked, "You tell me since you're calling so late."

"My bad." He laughed. "I forgot about the time difference, but this couldn't wait."

"What is so urgent that you couldn't wait and call me at a decent hour?"

Hesitating briefly, Winston sighed and said, "I met someone."

"A woman, no doubt. What's new about that? You're always meeting someone. A matter of fact, you meet a different woman almost every other day," Craig said while laughing hysterically.

Becoming irritable, Winston interrupted, "Damn, Craig! I'm serious! I met this incredible woman tonight. She is very intelligent, sweet and absolutely gorgeous!!"

"Really?"

Rubbing his head, he stood and walked out onto the balcony.

Staring out over the city lights, he said, "She's making me think some crazy thoughts and I've only been around her for a couple of hours."

"Like what?"

"I'm thinking about turning in my playa's card."

"Get the hell out of here!!"

Solemnly Winston admitted, "No shit, man. She's...she's perfect."

"Damn, Skeeter! You're making me nervous. You're not joking are you?"

He sat down in the balcony chair and whispered, "Nah, I'm not joking. Look, I just needed someone to talk to. I'm sorry I called so late. I'll see you when I get back to town. Goodnight."

"Yo, Winston, I'm happy for you and I can't wait to meet this woman."

"Yeah, I just hope she feels the same way about me."

"I'm sure she does," Craig said, grinning.

"Well, goodnight, Craig and thanks for listening."

"You bet. Goodnight and be safe out there."

"I will. Later."

Winston hung up the telephone and sat out on the balcony for hours in deep thought.

∞

Over the next few days, Winston couldn't wait to get out of his daily meetings to see Arnelle for various activities. They went on picnics in the park, drives down the coast and walks on the beach. Before Arnelle knew it, she had unexpectedly fallen deeply in love with Winston and she didn't even see it coming. There was no way she could go through with Cyrus' plan now even though he was putting a lot of pressure on her to complete her mission. Arnelle kept the fact that she had fallen in love with Winston to herself. She'd made up her mind that she didn't want to hurt him in any way and tried to back out of the deal. Cyrus had no problem reminding her about her father and his upcoming bid for mayor. Destroying Winston's career was not something she wanted to be a part of. He had been wonderful to her and now it had come down to the decision of choosing Winston or her father's career.

On their last evening together, Arnelle knew what she had to do and it made her sick. She loved Winston with all her heart and hoped that somewhere down the road, he would forgive her. As she stood daydreaming on his room's patio, Winston embraced her from behind and said, "I know how you feel, Sweetheart."

He turned her to face him and said, "These last few days have been magical for me. You have made me experience things that I've never felt before. I feel myself falling hard for you, Giselle."

She lowered her head and asked, "Winston, do you have a forgiving heart?"

"Why would you ask me that?"

She wrapped her arms around his neck and buried her face into the warmth of it.

"Just answer the question, Winston."

He soothed her by rubbing his strong hands up and down her back. He tilted her chin and said, "I'm a lawyer. Of course I have a forgiving heart."

Tears stung her eyes. "I'm going to hold you to that, my darling."

He lowered his head and greedily kissed her lips. She clung to his strong body and fought to get closer.

"Giselle, I don't want us to end here. I want to continue seeing you, Babe. If we keep this up, who knows where we'll end up?"

"I feel the same way, Winston."

His hands gathered the fabric of her dress as he continued the exploration of her mouth. Her moans escalated as his hands found warmth inside her satin panties. At that moment, there was a knock at the door. They reluctantly broke apart.

"I guess dinner is served."

When she opened the door, she was shocked when Robin wheeled in the food cart. Arnelle did her best to hide her surprise from Winston. Robin stayed long enough to set their plates. Before leaving, she winked at Arnelle and discreetly handed her a note. As Winston inspected the entrees, she quickly read the note which revealed her instructions.

She returned the note to Robin.

"Would there be anything else?" Robin asked as she handed him a small envelope.

Winston took it out of her hand and removed the ticket he had to sign. "No, everything looks fine. Thank you."

He handed the envelope back to Robin and turned his back to the women momentarily to sample the food. Arnelle noticed Robin was wearing white gloves as she quickly and discreetly slipped small packets of a substance inside the envelope and placed it in the pocket of Arnelle's robe. Obtaining his fingerprints was easy.

Once Robin left, Arnelle asked, "Are you hungry?"

He came to her and pulled her against his body. The contact of his body caused her breasts to harden against his chest. He kissed the curve of her neck and said, "Yes, my darling, I'm very hungry, but not for food."

"Oh, Winston."

He picked her up and carried her to the large bed. He had to get a hold of himself before he lost his mind. Arnelle closed her eyes as she felt him run his hands from her cheek, across her breasts and down her stomach.

In a whisper, he said, "Giselle...Damn, Girl!"

"Winston...I-I...Oh...God."

Those were the last coherent words she would say before he would relieve her of her dress. She practically trembled when she felt his lips trace the waistband of the satin undergarment covering her womanhood. He kissed his way back up to her bra, which he easily removed. Her long wavy hair fell across her chest as he took one ripened nipple into his mouth. Arnelle squirmed as he savored one, then the other. He lowered her panties over her hips and stared at her like a stalker to its prey.

"You are beautiful."

Arnelle's chest was heaving in anticipation and she could hardly stand it. She wanted him so much. Winston stood to remove his clothes. What he revealed to her was nothing short of magnificent. She noticed his aroused body and gasped at the mere size of him.

"I won't hurt you, Baby. I promise."

She reached for him, pulling him down to her soft body. He devoured her mouth, parting her lips with his tongue. He sprinkled kisses down the column of her neck. She moaned as his lips seared her skin. Going lower, he kissed her inner thighs and buried his face in her triangle patch, tasting her. Arnelle's body arched off the bed as she screamed out his name in passion. He worked his magic as he feasted on her womanhood. His body throbbed out of control; it was only Arnelle who could ever quench his flame. He moved up her body and kissed her deeply, allowing her to taste herself on his lips before he entered her moist body. Tears ran out of her eyes as she met each thrust. She loved him and there was no way she could turn back now. Winston moved inside her tight space, stretching her to accommodate him. He had never opened up like this before to any woman. He wanted to make sure she would spend the rest of her life with him. She wrapped her legs around his waist to give him full access. As he quickened his pace, she felt her body spiraling out of control.

"Winston…mercy!"

He groaned loudly as his body also gave into the effects of their lovemaking. His seed entered her body, and he realized this was the first time in his life that he didn't protect his partner. He collapsed onto her body, totally exhausted. Arnelle stroked his back and tried to come to grips with what she had done.

The room was filled with silence until Winston pulled her on top of his body and said, "Giselle?"

"Yes?"

"I didn't protect you, Sweetheart."

She snuggled closer and said, "Don't worry, Darling. I don't have any diseases."

He kissed her on the lips and said, "Baby, I would never put you at risk either, but I was talking about getting you pregnant."

Smiling, she said, "Babe, that means a lot to me, but I'm on the pill."

"I guess we should've had this conversation before we made love, huh?"

She kissed his lips. "You right. Now, are you hungry? Our food is getting cold."

"Let's take a shower first, and then we'll eat."

She kissed his chest and said, "Go start the water; I'll be right in."

They got up from the tangled sheets on the bed and kissed passionately before he entered the bathroom. After he closed the door and turned on the water, Arnelle used a dinner napkin to remove a different envelope from her purse. She placed it in Winston's briefcase and took the envelope Robin handed her out of her robe pocket and placed it in her purse. Cyrus may have won the battle but not the war, she thought. Running this blackmail scheme could ruin Winston's career. A career he had worked so hard to establish and she wasn't about to be a part of it.

"Giselle! Come on in, Baby, the water's hot!"

"I'm on my way, Sweetheart."

After making love once more in the shower, they finally made their way to their dinner. Miraculously the food was still warm.

He leaned forward and said, "You are a remarkable woman and I can't wait to see you again. I don't want to leave you tomorrow."

She dropped her head and said, "I feel the same way, Winston. Let's enjoy tonight and see what tomorrow holds. Okay?"

He saluted her with his glass and said, "To new beginnings."

"To new beginnings, Baby."

Shortly after sipping the wine, Winston complained of a severe migraine. Arnelle helped him to the bed as he became ill and then unconscious. She ran over to the bed and frantically called to him.

"Winston, Baby, wake up!"

Just as she was about to call for help, his telephone rang.

"Hello," Arnelle shrieked into the phone.

"Is he out?"

"What the hell do you mean is he out, Robin?" Arnelle asked. "What did you do to him?"

"Quit tripping. I just put a little something-something in his drink for the occasion."

Arnelle stroked his cheek and said, "You bitch! If you've done something to hurt him, I'll never forgive you or Cyrus. I didn't want any part of this shit anyway!!"

Robin calmly said, "Chill out, Girl...damn! I just gave him a little something to make him sleep for awhile. Now, did you make the drop?"

"Yes, I made the drop, you scandalous bitch."

"Whatever, Arnelle. Get dressed and get your ass out of there. The shit is getting ready to hit the fan."

"What do you mean?"

"Just get out of there!"

"You bitch!"

Slamming the phone down, tears ran out of Arnelle's eyes as she looked down at his helpless body. She had to make sure Robin didn't harm him severely. She left Winston's room in a hurry, packed her bags and checked out of the hotel. Before leaving the lobby, she placed a call to the hotel receptionist and reported that a guest might be sick in room thirteen eighty-two. It was the least she could do because she wouldn't be able to live with herself if something terrible happened to Winston. What she didn't know was Robin expected Arnelle to back out of the deal, so she backtracked to Winston's room and switched out the envelope Arnelle had placed in his briefcase.

On the way to the airport, she cried as her heart broke.

I hate you, Cyrus was Arnelle's repeated thought.

She loved Winston and prayed he was okay because she would never be able to see him again…ever.

Weeks later, Arnelle realized she was pregnant. Her family wasn't upset with the pregnancy as much as the secrecy surrounding who the father was. Her father was clearly disappointed as well as her brother, Keaton. Her mother, Zenora, was the only one she could go to for comfort. The child she carried belonged to the only man she had ever loved, and she could never tell him. Curiosity got the best of her as she surfed the Internet to find possible news articles on their scheme. It only took a few minutes for her to find an article related to the events.

High Profile Lawyer Denies Drug Use Allegations

Arnelle's heart stopped beating as she continued to read the article…

Winston Carter III is scheduled to appear in court later this week to face charges of possessing a controlled substance. A statement released by Mr. Carter explained that he was the victim of a robbery attempt and has never abused drugs. He plans to fight these allegations to the end. The Bar Association has yet to comment on the case.

∞

When she finished reading the article she was able to breathe. Stunned, she was clueless on how he was arrested and charged. She'd switched the envelope containing the drugs with one filled with powdered sugar to prevent this from happening. Devastated, she cried until she couldn't cry anymore.

MaLeah was a blessing and came into the world right on time several months later. Arnelle ached knowing she had robbed Winston of the opportunity of seeing his daughter born. MaLeah was the spitting image of Arnelle, with the exception of having Winston's unique eyes.

∞

It was now that she realized the drug Robin put in his drink must have severely affected his memory. After reliving that horrible term of events, Arnelle grabbed her pillow and sobbed. The only thing good that came out of the whole situation was MaLeah. She stared at the door, wondering what MaLeah's father was doing in his room this very moment across the hallway.

∞

Monday rolled around and Arnelle let Winston arrange for his security company to install a new system in her house while she was at work. She planned to work only a half-day because she needed to get back to her house. She hated to admit it, but she really had enjoyed Winston's company over the last few days. She also hadn't felt this safe since she lived at home. Feelings for Winston had come flooding back with a vengeance. She still loved him. As she checked the equipment in the exercise room before leaving for the day, she heard Venice call out her name.

"Arnelle?"

"In here!"

Venice walked in, smiling. "Well?"

"Well what, Venice?"

"You spent the weekend with Skeeter, so what happened?"

Arnelle sat down on a weight bench, smiled and said, "We had a great time. We went bowling and played pool. I cooked breakfast for him. I have to admit it was nice."

Venice sat next to her. "So, what's next?"

"I don't know. Venice, I still love him. I do know that. I was angry because I thought he was playing me off, but he really doesn't remember me. I remember that Cyrus' friend put some kind of drug in Winston's drink and that did something to him, affecting his memory. I have to see if I can get him to fall in love with me all over again. I pray when he finds out the truth, he won't walk away."

Venice hugged her and said, "Well, good luck and don't worry. I believe everything will eventually work out. I just wish you'd go ahead and just tell him the truth."

"I can't, Venice. Not yet."

CHAPTER SIX

C raig Bennett's business partner, Lamar, was marrying the beautiful Tressa Roan in two days. Winston still hadn't decided if he wanted to attend their wedding because they really weren't his favorite functions to attend. He knew Craig would be upset if he didn't show up to witness him serve as best man. Bennett and Fletcher Architectural would have a lot of prestigious guests in attendance and if he got anything out of showing up, it would be obtaining some profitable networking.

Later, as he sat in his office library doing research, his receptionist came to the door and said, "Mr. Carter, you have a guest at the front desk."

He wasn't expecting anyone and was curious to see who had come to see him unannounced. He put on his jacket, straightened his tie and curiously walked down the hall toward the reception area. When he turned the corner, he couldn't believe his eyes.

Arnelle.

She stood there admiring various awards on the wall. She had on a short black dress, and he worried that if she had to bend, even the slightest, his colleagues might get an eyeful. He stood there, unable to move for a moment as he drank in her beauty. Her long shapely legs caught the eyes of several fellow colleagues as she tossed her wicked black hair over her shoulder. He gave them the territorial glare to let them know this woman was hands-off.

"Good afternoon, Miss Lapahie. What a nice surprise."

Turning, Arnelle smiled and said, "Mr. Carter. It's so nice for you to see me on such short notice."

The receptionist listened to their exchange and sensed they were already acquainted. Their eyes revealed what their conversation didn't.

"My office is this way."

She picked up a large basket, which he happily carried for her. "What's this?"

She leaned in close to his ear and said, "Something delicious."

Chills ran down his spine as her warm breath caressed his ear. Entering his office, he closed the door and sat the basket on a nearby table.

"Winston," Arnelle began, "I hope you're hungry."

He removed his jacket and said, "You didn't have to go to all this trouble."

Arnelle smiled with pride as she removed sandwiches, fruit, juice and other goodies from the basket. She handed him a plate with a sandwich and fruit along with a glass of juice and noticed his face light up like a kid on Christmas morning.

"Yummy," he said.

Her eyes met his and she asked, "The food?"

"Everything."

"Sit, you naughty boy," Arnelle said as a blush crept on her cheeks.

At a small conference table in his office, Arnelle placed a tablecloth and they sat down and enjoyed their lunch.

"You're off today?"

Dabbing the corner of her mouth, she said, "Only a half-day. I had some things to take care of, remember?"

"Oh yeah, the security company was scheduled to come today. Did they get everything set up?"

"Yes, thanks to you."

He sampled some of the fruit. "You're welcome."

"So, how has your day been so far?"

Sighing, he said, "Busy. I have a big case coming up in California soon, so I'll be out of town and I don't know for how long." Winston noticed a hint of sadness in Arnelle's eyes. "Have you ever been before?"

"A long time ago."

"While I'm out there, you should come for a visit. We could hang out."

Arnelle's thick lashes lowered and she said, "I don't know. We're kind of busy at the clinic."

"Well, just so you'll know, the offer stands. I'll miss you."

Their eyes met for a moment, then Arnelle said, "I'll miss you, too, Winston. You know, you're not as bad as I thought and for a lawyer, you do know how to have fun."

He smiled, and then playfully flicked water from his cup in her face. Arnelle stood and flicked water back at him, laughing.

"Don't make me soak you in that nice suit, Perry Mason."

He slowly walked over to her, holding the full cup high in the air. Backing up, Arnelle pointed her finger at him and said, "Don't you dare, Winston!"

She still had a half cup and threatened to toss it at him if he didn't stop. Winston only grinned and continued his slow pace toward her. In seconds, he had her body pinned against the wall. While holding the cup over her head, he softly asked, "Scared?"

She looked up at the cup nervously and said, "Winston."

Laughing, he lowered the cup, took a sip and said, "Sweetheart, when I decide to get you wet, I guarantee you'll enjoy it."

He turned on his heels and returned to the table. Arnelle, however, couldn't move. It was a few seconds before she realized she had been holding her breath. His statement caught her off-guard and turned her legs to jelly. What he said held hope that Winston liked her more than she thought. His statement held intimate promises, and she hoped he would keep that promise very soon. She loved him and it was getting harder to hide it from him. She smiled and returned to the table, where they finished their lunch and cleaned up.

He walked her out to her car and put the basket in the trunk. Turning to her, he leaned down, kissed her lovingly on the cheek and said, "Thanks for lunch. I guess this means next time it's my treat?"

She held his hand. "You have yourself a date, Mister. Oh, I forgot. Are you free this Saturday? I don't want to go to Lamar and Tressa's wedding alone."

He tightened his grip on her small hand and said, "Arnelle, I don't know."

"What are you afraid of? You're not the one getting married."

He folded his arms. "I know, but people act weird at weddings. I usually stay clear of them."

"Please. Come on; I don't like begging."

His penetrating gaze fused with hers and he said, "We'll see about that."

He had her blushing again. She didn't want him to know she was aware of his sexual comment.

"So will you go with me?"

He stroked his goatee and said, "Okay, I'll go, but I'm not getting out there to catch any garters. Understood?"

Hugging him excitedly, she said, "Thank you, Winston. Now, the wedding is at five, so you can pick me up at four."

"A'ight. Well, I'd better get back to work. Thanks again for lunch."

She eased into her car, allowing him to close the door for her. She rolled down her window and said, "Thanks again for going to the wedding with me. I'll make sure you have a good time. I would hate for you to be standing around pouting like a chastised child."

Smiling, he said, "You're lucky I don't have a cup of water right now, Woman. Get out of here and drive carefully."

"I will. Goodbye."

∞

The days passed and Arnelle and Winston had been so busy, the only time they spoke was to confirm their date for the wedding. They hadn't seen each other since they had lunch together and Saturday had rolled around quickly. Arnelle got an early start because she wanted to get her hair and nails done. She went to her closet and pulled out the gold beaded gown she planned to dazzle Winston with. Her doorbell chimed and she curiously went to the door. When she looked through the peephole, she screamed, "Keaton!"

She swung the door opened and jumped in her brother's arms. "Hey, Sis!"

"What are you doing here?" She hugged him hard.

"I'm glad to see you, too, Little Sister."

Pulling him inside, she said, "You know what I mean. Why didn't you tell me you were coming?"

Hugging her again, he said, "I wanted to surprise you. I decided to take a few days off from the restaurant since I've been working nonstop. I haven't seen you in about a month, so I figured I'd fly up. I went by the house last weekend and spoiled my niece a little. She's really growing up."

Arnelle smiled. "She is getting to be a big girl. I can't wait until we can be together every day."

"She misses you."

"I know. That's my baby, but it won't be much longer before she's up here with me."

He sensed her sadness as he watched her eyes fill with tears. "Well, I'm here to hang out with you for a few days. I needed a break."

"I'm glad you're here, but I have a wedding to go to tonight. Did you bring any dress clothes?"

Keaton sat down in the recliner and grabbed the remote. "Knock yourself out, Arnelle. I came here to chill, plus you know weddings are not my thang."

Arnelle hit him in the back of the head and said, "What is it with you men and weddings?"

Staring at the television, he said, "Weddings are for women, Sis."

"Whatever. Are you hungry?"

"Nah! I'm going to shower and crash. I need to catch up on a little sleep."

Arnelle leaned down and kissed him on the cheek. "Well, you know where everything is. I need to get dressed before my date gets here."

"What date?"

"Don't start and mind your business."

Laughing, he said, "I'm just messing with you, Giirl. I'll holler at you later."

Arnelle checked her watch and decided to take a hot soak in fragrance bubbles to relax herself. She ran the water, discarded her clothes and eased into the warm water. She couldn't help but wonder if her date was just excited as she was.

Winston stepped upon Arnelle's porch right on time. He was dressed in an Armani suit and for some reason, he was glad this day had come. He hadn't seen Arnelle all week except in his dreams. After taking a deep breath, he rang the doorbell. As he straightened his tie, he was startled when Arnelle's door was answered by a man dressed in faded jeans, a 49ers football jersey and bare feet.

"Yes?" the man asked.

"Is Arnelle in?" Winston asked, a frown furrowed on his face.

Protectively, Keaton asked, "Who are you?"

In the background, Winston heard Arnelle yell, "Quit playing, Keaton, and let him in."

Keaton stepped aside and let Winston enter. He looked him up and down and said, "Nice suit."

"Thanks."

"Have a seat, Man."

Keaton flung his body back in the recliner and grabbed his beer off the table. Frowning, he decided he wasn't about to take it upon himself to make any introductions. That was Arnelle's job. Winston sat on the sofa nearby and noticed Keaton was watching a game he was taping. He cleared his throat, knowing it would be rude to ask him to change the channel so he wouldn't see what was going on. He sat there feeling the heat rising up his neck.

Arnelle said she wasn't seeing anyone, he thought. *Who is this man sitting here like he owns the place?*

Keaton took a sip and glanced over at Winston. He continued to look and it eventually turned into a stare. His eyes widened as if a light bulb went off in his head. He sat his beer down and said, "Excuse me."

Keaton burst into Arnelle's bedroom as she put on her earrings. He stalked over to her and asked, "Who is that guy out there?"

"He's my date. Why?"

"I think you know why. MaLeah has his eyes."

Arnelle stared down at the gold earring in her hand and said, "Not right now, Keaton."

Trying to keep his voice down, he asked, "Is that MaLeah's dad?" When Arnelle didn't respond, Keaton yelled, "Tell me, Arnelle."

She looked up at him with tears in her eyes and said, "Yes, but he doesn't know about her."

Keaton placed his hands over his face in anger. "I'm going to kick his ass!"

Arnelle grabbed his hand. "Keaton! It's not his fault. He doesn't know about MaLeah because something happened. He doesn't even remember me."

Keaton sat on her bed and asked, "What the hell do you mean?"

"Something happened to his memory. I don't understand it completely myself, but I'm trying to find out."

Keaton sighed, confusion in his eyes. "So how did you hook back up with him?"

"Coincidence, act of God, fate. Call it whatever you want. Whatever it is, I have to help him remember, but my way. Okay? Stay out of this, Keaton. I mean it! Now go back in there and keep him company. I'll be out in a minute."

Keaton stood. "I'll do what you ask, but if things get out of hand, even an inch, I'm all over this. Do you understand me, Arnelle?"

"I understand, Keaton."

As he was about to close the door, he said, "You look beautiful, Arnelle, and I hope you know what you're doing."

"Thank you, Keaton, and so do I."

He closed her door and went back into the den. When he sat down, he said, "Arnelle will be right out."

Winston looked at his watch and said, "That's fine. We have time."

Arnelle finally walked into the room and both men stood. She went over to Winston and gave him a kiss on the cheek. Keaton glared at them and noticed that Winston stood an inch or two taller than him.

"Wow, Arnelle," Winston said. "You look beautiful."

Her dress fit snug to her curves, but with elegance. The gold color accented her brown skin tone and eyes. Her long black tresses had deep waves and covered the open back of her dress. Winston couldn't help but slowly take in her beauty. On her feet were gold shoes, matching perfectly to her gown.

Feeling the heat from Winston's eyes, Arnelle blushed. "You're looking mighty handsome yourself. Have you two introduced yourselves?"

Keaton extended his hand to Winston and said, "Sorry about before, Man. I'm Keaton, Arnelle's brother."

As if air had been let out of a balloon, Winston let out a breath and said, "Nice to meet you. I'm Winston Carter."

The two men shook hands as a peace offering. Arnelle got her coat and as Winston helped her into it, Keaton said, "Take care of my sister."

With a serious expression on his face, Winston said, "With my life, Keaton. Goodnight."

Arnelle turned and hugged her brother.

"Don't wait up," she whispered. "If I'm not coming home, I'll call. I love you."

"Okay. Have a good time. Don't worry about me. I'm going to watch the tube most of the evening."

Arnelle's heart swelled as Winston escorted her outside into the cool air. He opened the door of his silver Lexus and said, "Miss Lapahie, I hope I don't have to defend your honor tonight. You are stunning."

When he eased behind the steering wheel, Arnelle looked over at him and smiled. "Thank you, Winston, and I won't think twice about taking my earrings and shoes off to defend your honor as well."

They looked at each other, and then burst out laughing before he pulled out of her driveway.

∞

The wedding was beautiful as expected and the reception was in full swing. The bride and groom as well as their guests were finishing a delicious dinner when the band started playing. Venice was glowing in her teal chiffon bridesmaid's gown.

She walked over and gave Arnelle a hug. "Girl, you know you look like a model in that dress!"

"Thanks, Venice. You look great, too."

Venice sat down next to her. "Thanks, but these shoes are killing me. I have got to take them off."

They laughed and Venice asked teasingly, "Where's your date?"

"I don't know, probably somewhere hiding. He said he doesn't care for weddings."

"Men."

About that time, Craig came over and kissed Arnelle on the cheek.

"Well, good evening, Witch Doctor."

"Don't start with me, Craig," Arnelle said as she punched him on the arm.

He laughed. "Where's my boy?"

"Probably in a corner, crying. Why is he so afraid of weddings?"

Craig played with Venice's hair and said, "I guess he has his reasons. In any case, as long as I've known Skeeter, he's never been afraid of anything."

Arnelle watched the guests as they danced away at tunes the band played.

"Venice, my sweet...would you like to dance?"

Venice smiled. "Of course, Bennett."

Craig took her hand and led her out onto the dance floor. Arnelle searched the dimly lit room for Winston, but to no avail. A fair-complexioned gentleman approached and kindly asked

Arnelle to dance to a slow ballad. Winston stepped back into the ballroom and immediately spotted his date on the dance floor, in the arms of another man. He had only stepped outside for about fifteen minutes to clear his head and to get a breath of fresh air. He swallowed hard and watched as the man smiled and spoke into Arnelle's ear. Jealousy leapt into his heart and the vein on his forehead throbbed. He stood against the door frame and watched as the man's hands went lower than necessary on her back. Arnelle readjusted her position, causing the man to remove his hands.

Having danced song after song, the stranger escorted Arnelle back to her table and sat down next to her. The vein continued to throb as Winston watched their exchange from across the room.

She's your date, not your woman, he kept telling himself. The words rang out in his head loud and clear, and it angered him. Did he really want Arnelle or was it just lust?

"If I didn't see it with my own eyes, I wouldn't believe it," Craig said as he snuck up alongside Winston.

"What are you talking about?" Winston asked.

Craig shook his head. First, the Fat Boys break up...now this."

"What the hell are you talking about, Craig?"

"Man, you are sinking like the Titanic. You are so in love with Arnelle, it's sickening."

"Craig, you're full of it."

Patting Winston on the shoulder, Craig looked over in Arnelle's direction. "Bro," he said, "it shows all over your face. The only time that vein pops out on your forehead is when you're pissed. All I'm going to say is don't forget where you are and I got your back."

Craig disappeared into the crowd, hoping Winston didn't make a fool of himself. Winston couldn't take his eyes off Arnelle and the man who was keeping her company. He had taken enough, so he walked to them.

"Excuse me. Arnelle, could I talk to you for a second?"

The gentleman frowned and asked, "Can't you see I'm talking to the lady?"

Arnelle saw and believed she felt the heat from Winston's gaze.

"Bro, I don't think I was talking to you and this lady happens to be my date; and another thing, if I ever see you put your hands on her again, your ass is mine."

The man stood, thinking he was going to intimidate Winston, but it didn't work. Arnelle stood and began to get nervous.

"Winston, please don't. Derrick, it's okay. I'll talk to you later."

The gentleman turned to look at her and said, "Arnelle, it's been a pleasure. I look forward to seeing you again."

He reached into his jacket pocket and handed her a small card. She smiled as she took the card.

"Thank you, Derrick. Goodnight."

Before walking off, he looked at Winston one last time and said, "Later." Winston didn't even acknowledge the gesture. He looked at Arnelle, clearly upset and took the gentleman's card out of her hand, making sure Derrick saw him.

Surprised, she asked, "What is wrong with you?"

"I said I need to talk to you."

Disgusted, she yelled, "I can't believe you would embarrass me like that."

Taking her by the arm he said, "Not here. Follow me."

He led her into a secluded hallway and that's where she lit into him. He closed his eyes and leaned against the wall. He knew she was upset, but he didn't care. He just didn't want another man to put his hands on her…ever.

"Who in the hell do you think you are?" she screamed. "You can't tell me who I can and cannot talk to. What was so important that you want to talk about? You're acting like you're sixteen, Winston. I was only talking to the man, dang!"

He opened his incredibly sexy eyes, noticing that her skin had taken on a bronze tone. He softly said, "I'm tripping, Arnelle. Okay? I mean...well...I haven't had a chance to dance with you all night and I didn't like it that you were dancing with someone else. Will you dance with me, Arnelle?"

She started laughing and said, "I don't believe you. You almost got into a fight because of a dance?"

"Is that so hard to believe, Arnelle? I didn't like the way he was touching you."

She studied his expression and realized his sincerity. Winston didn't blink an eye, and his heart thumped against his ribs as he heard Craig's words ringing in his ears: *She's your date, not your woman.*

"It is customary to dance with your date at least once, Miss Lapahie."

She put her hands on her hips and was unable to speak. She knew he was right. She hadn't danced with him all night.

No wonder he's angry. I would've felt the same way had some woman been pawing at him, Arnelle thought. *Could it be that he's starting to have feelings for me? I would've saved every dance for him, if only he had asked. Why did you wait, Winston?*

She looked down at her perfectly manicured toes, and then back up at Winston. "Why, Mr. Carter, I would love to dance with you. All you had to do was ask.. Lead the way."

He leaned down and kissed her on the cheek. "I apologize for embarrassing you, but I'd do it again if I had to. You're lucky I didn't throw his punk ass across the table; now let's dance."

Taking her by the hand, Winston led her to the floor and they danced a slow, sensual rhythm to the O'Jays ballad, "Stairway to Heaven." Winston felt like he was in heaven as he held Arnelle's warm body close to his. Her fragrance was caressing his senses seductively and what they were doing felt so familiar and so right. He couldn't explain it, but for some reason, he felt like they had danced this way before. When the song ended, he said, "Thank you. That was very nice. Now, are you ready to blow this joint?"

With her arms still around his neck, she answered, "What do you have in mind, Winston?"

He placed his lips to her ear and said, "It's a surprise so stop being so nosey. Do you want to go or not?"

"Yes. After we say goodnight to our friends, then I'm all yours."

He pulled her tighter to his body and said, "Be careful for you wish for, my dear; you might just get it."

I'm counting on it, Darling, Arnelle thought.

They said their goodnights, retrieved their coats and left. Winston drove swiftly through the streets.

Arnelle turned to him and asked, "Where are we going?"

"Relax. You're going to have fun. I promise."

Within minutes, he pulled up to a small club called Nino's.

Arnelle looked out the window curiously as she noticed a steady flow of patrons going in and out the door. He pulled up front and hopped out, handing the keys to the valet.

"Come on, girl," Winston said, his face glowing with excitement and sensual desire. "Let's party."

They entered the club and a heavyset gentleman grabbed Winston in a bear hug. He introduced Arnelle to the owner who told him he had his best table reserved for him. Arnelle followed the gentleman to the table and allowed Winston to seat her. She took in the décor of the beautiful club and was instantly taken in by the atmosphere.

"Winston, this is so nice. You come here often?"

He unbuttoned his jacket and said, "I used to. I haven't been here in a while."

Within minutes, the DJ played an old school dance song.

Arnelle screamed and said, "Oh Winston! That's my song. Come on!"

She grabbed his hand and pulled him to the dance floor. They danced several fast songs back to back. Winston had Arnelle laughing and in tears as he demonstrated his rendition of the Robot and poplocking.

"Stop it," she squealed in between pants. "I can't breathe!"

He finally stopped his old school dances and laughed along with Arnelle. They returned to their table where he ordered drinks. Arnelle had to retrieve a Kleenex from her purse to dab the tears and sweat from her face. "You are so stupid! What made you do that?"

He smiled. "I wanted to show you I still had it."

"Well, you need to lose it again. I need to go to the restroom. You've made my bladder weak."

He stood. "You want me to go with you?"

She looked at him sarcastically and said, "Thanks, but no thank you. I think I can handle this without you."

He picked up a glass of water and gave her the eye. She pointed her finger at him, laughing. "Winston, I'm not playing any water games with you tonight. Behave! You're so silly to be so old."

He put the glass back on the table. "Chicken! Hey, who are you calling old?"

"Where are the restrooms?" she asked, avoiding his question.

He pointed her in the right direction and watched her make her way across the room. So did a few other men. He sat back down and waited for her return.

∞

When Arnelle came back, the pair enjoyed a nice and easy conversation with each other. Before they knew it, midnight had rolled around and it was time to go home. He had noticed Arnelle yawning a couple of times and finally asked, "Last dance?"

"I guess it is getting late. Yes, last dance."

He didn't think this DJ could beat their last dance song at the reception, but he did. Arnelle held Winston's hand as Luther Vandross' silky voice started singing "Superstar/Until You Come Back to Me." Chills ran down Arnelle's spine as she listened to the words in the song. The wine she had consumed relaxed her more than she had expected. As Winston swayed with her, she snuggled even closer. She felt her guard coming down as she buried her face against his neck. He tightened his grip and embraced her protectively. He couldn't help but touch that thick, black hair of hers. It was as soft as cotton and smelled of scented perfume. His lower body betrayed him and he knew Arnelle was aware of it. Instead of being startled, she squirmed to get even closer. Winston didn't know what this meant, but what he did know was that he wanted…no, needed to kiss her, right there before another second passed. He grabbed a handful of hair and pulled gently, causing her face to tilt up to his. His eyes scanned every detail of her lovely features. Her eyes were filled with tears as he said, "Arnelle, I'm going to kiss you. If you deny me, I might explode right here before your very eyes."

She couldn't speak. The tears ran down her cheeks as she leaned in and met him halfway. He kissed her softly, sampling every inch of her mouth. She parted her lips and tasted his sweetness. Somehow, tonight, in this club, dancing to Luther Vandross, made her want to scream out her love for him. She wanted to let him know that no man had touched her in any way since he had. Feeling his body straining for release, he was thankful the song ended.

He whispered, "Ready to go?"

"Yes," she responded softly.

∞

The ride home was quiet. There was even a time he thought she had fallen asleep but she couldn't. Her mind, body and soul were spiraling out of control. She had to do something quick. His trip to California would be coming up soon, and Cyrus was getting even more anxious to get his hands on the package Arnelle had in her possession. Hopefully by then, Winston would be in love with her again and remember the passion they once shared. MaLeah needed her father, and Arnelle needed the love of her life back.

Winston pulled into Arnelle's driveway and shut off the engine. He got out and opened her door. In silence they walked through the front door. Arnelle expected Keaton to be waiting up for her, but he must have been too tired. She leaned against Winston's body and removed the shoes from her feet.

"You want to sit down?"

He shoved his hands in his pockets and said, "Nah, I'd better get home."

She walked over to him and pressed her face against his neck. He hugged her in silence.

"Thanks for going to the wedding with me, Winston, and for taking me to the club. I had a great time."

He angled her chin up and said, "It was my pleasure. Maybe we can go again sometime."

"That would be nice."

He lowered his mouth to hers and once again savored her intoxicating kiss. Arnelle moaned as his tongue parted her lips. His hands roamed over her luscious body, pressing her hips against his rigid groin. He had to stop himself again before he threw her over his shoulder and took her up to her bed. If her brother had not been in the house, he would've taken her right there in the foyer. He broke the kiss and said, "Arnelle?"

She lowered her head. "Yes?"

"Sweetheart, I have to go…now!"

She looked into his dreamy eyes and said, "I understand. Goodnight, Winston, and drive safely."

"Goodnight."

He gave her one last kiss on the cheek, walked out to his car and drove away. Arnelle locked the door and made her way up the stairs, knowing she was headed straight to her bathroom to take a cold shower.

Winston, on the other hand went straight to his twenty-four-hour gym. He always kept a packed gym bag in his car. Arnelle was turning him out and he hadn't even made love to her. He needed to work off his frustrations, and the only thing that would work for now was several games of racquetball.

CHAPTER SEVEN

In the office, Arnelle went over her schedule for the week, and oddly it was blank.

"What is wrong with this computer?" she said aloud.

After trying unsuccessfully to pull up her schedule, she paused to smile. She couldn't help but remember the wonderful night out she had shared with Winston a couple of weeks earlier.

Venice poked her head in the door and watched Arnelle's sappy expression.

"Arnelle," she said, "I'm giving you notice. You are officially on a two-week vacation, starting now. Go visit your family or Winston or whatever you want to do."

"What are you talking about?"

Venice came into the room and said, "Look, I've make all the proper arrangements for your patients. Leon's coming in to help out while you're on vacation. You need some time off so you can handle your business."

Arnelle stood and said, "No wonder I couldn't pull up my schedule. Are you sure about this? I mean I could go home next month."

Venice walked over and sat in front of Arnelle's desk. "I'm sure. You know Leon has it going on."

"Yes, he is good and the clients like him."

"Now, how was your date with Skeeter the other week? We haven't had a chance to talk about it."

Blushing, she said, "We had a good time. We're supposed to go out again."

"Good, I can tell by the smile on your face you're getting along. I wish you two nothing but the best, Arnelle."

Arnelle came around her desk and hugged Venice. "Thank you, Girl," she said.

"Did your brother have a good time while he was in town?" Venice asked.

"Yeah, we promised to get together at least once a month."

"That's great." Venice clapped her hands and stood. "With that said…get out of here. Be safe and tell the family hello."

"You sure?"

"Get out."

Arnelle laughed, turned off her computer and grabbed her purse. "Yes, Ma'am," she said, saluting Venice.

∞

Winston had clothes everywhere. He was trying to pack for his trip to California and get his mind together for the big trial he had been preparing for. He was a little reluctant about going back to a city that held some unpleasant memories for him. He himself had a brush with the law while visiting years prior. Thanks to statements by a couple of hotel employees, there wasn't sufficient evidence to officially charge him with the offense. After the case was dropped, Winston convinced police to keep the details out of the public in hopes that the assailants would eventually come out of hiding because he still didn't know why he was targeted. So far, it had been quiet, but he would never give up looking for the person or people who almost ruined his career. Especially after doctors revealed that his memory had been affected by the drug slipped into his drink.

He was headed to California to try the case of Cyrus McDaniels, a high-profile pro-basketball player who was arrested a few years earlier for laundering drug money. His career had already taken a blow from the publicity surrounding his arrest. The trial would bring even more publicity. He was used to litigating large cases, but this one would really put him on the map. After a couple of years of motions and postponements, the trial date was finally set.

He sat down and tossed a shirt on the bed. He thought of Arnelle and how much he was going to miss her. They hadn't had a chance to go out since the wedding because of his trial preparations, but they had spoken on the phone several times. He hoped he could make it up to her in a big way when he got back from California. However, he thought that because this was his last night in town, there was nothing he would enjoy more than spending time with Arnelle. Leaning over, he picked up the phone and dialed.

"Bennett Clinic."

"Dr. Lapahie, please."

"I'm sorry; Dr. Lapahie has already left the office. May I take a message?"

He ran his hand over his head. "Dr. Bennett, please."

The receptionist put the call through to Venice.

"Dr. Bennett here."

"Hello, bossy woman."

Venice laughed. "Hey, Skeeter, what's up?"

"Where's Arnelle?"

Venice twirled around in her chair. "I made her go on vacation this morning, no questions asked."

"Oh, well, I'm leaving day after tomorrow to go to California. Take care of my boy and the kids while I'm gone."

"What about Arnelle?" Venice giggled.

"You're so funny."

"Well, in any case, good luck, my dear."

"Thanks."

"Hey! Watch your back out there."

"Don't worry, I will."

Winston hung up and dialed Arnelle's number. Her answering machine picked up, so he left her a message, inviting her to dinner at his house. He prayed she hadn't left town already. He hung up smiling in anticipation of her call. He hoped to make this a night to remember for both of them. First, he had to see what he had in the refrigerator. He looked at his watch and hurried downstairs. Opening the cabinets and refrigerator showed him he definitely lived a bachelor's life. Grabbing his jacket, he hopped in his truck and headed to the store.

Arnelle entered her house with bags in hand. She had stopped at the store on her way home with the intention of cooking a nice dinner for Winston before he left for California. She really didn't know what he liked, but who could go wrong with steaks. He knew he wasn't a vegetarian because she had seen him eat meat.

She sat the bags down and noticed that she had messages on her answering machine. She pushed the button and started putting the food up. The first message was from Keaton and the second was from MaLeah, her mom and dad. The third was from Winston, and his voice shook her to her core.

"Hello, Dr. Lapahie. This is Winston Carter, the third, calling to invite you over to my house tonight, so I can cook dinner for you. I can assure you that you will not be disappointed. Please call me and I'm sorry for the short notice. Talk to you soon, Doc."

Arnelle screamed and clapped with excitement. He was thinking about her just as much as she was thinking of him.

She picked up the telephone to return his call. On the second ring, he answered, breathless.

"Hello?"

"Well, well, well, Mr. Carter, what has you so out of breath?"

"Not what I wish it was."

Arnelle gnawed at her nails, knowing exactly what he meant. She composed her nerves and said, "I got your message. When do you want me to come?"

She quickly realized what she had said. Winston didn't let any sensual remarks get past him. With a serious tone, he said, "Why don't you let me handle that?"

"Winston."

"They're forecasting snow tonight, so I'd feel better picking you up. I'll be there at seven," he said, laughing, "and be ready, woman."

"I will and thank you for inviting me."

"The pleasure is all mine. See you soon."

Arnelle finished putting up her groceries and noted that she had a few hours to relax. She would take the time to return the calls from her family. She spoke briefly with MaLeah, who had a cold. Arnelle assured her she would come home soon and take care of her. After talking to her parents, she decided to take a nap and a long bubble bath. She didn't know what the night held for her, but whatever it was, she would accept it with no regrets.

A couple hours into her nap, the telephone rang. Still groggy, she answered, "Hello?"

"Arnelle, I'm still waiting on you to help a brotha out."

She sat up. "Cyrus, I told you, I'm not going to stir all of that up again. It's been quiet and we need to be thankful. Why can't you face this thing because my ass is on the line, too?"

"Because my career and life depend on it. I can't take a chance of getting convicted."

Placing her hand over her face, she said, "You weren't worried about Winston's career and *him* getting convicted. He's going to do his job regardless of any blackmail scheme."

"I don't believe you, Arnelle!"

"No, Cyrus! You're going to have to think of another way."

"Arnelle, there is no other way. That package is my only hope!"

She tightened her grip on the phone. "Cyrus, are you guilty? Tell me the truth…please. I have to know."

"No, I'm not guilty, but I can't take any chances with this. You have to help me."

She stood with tears stinging her eyes. "Cyrus, are you being honest with me? Did you do this?"

"I can't talk about this anymore over the phone. It's not as simple as it looks. Arnelle, I thought I was your boy. You've had your chance to help me, but I see who my real friends are."

"Cyrus, I *am* your friend and I've always been your friend. I've done a lot of shit to help you out over the years. I still don't know why I agreed to do that idiotic thing to Winston. Please, don't do anything you'll regret. I already have."

He softly said, "Arnelle, we could've been so good together. I hate I let you get away."

Arnelle rubbed her temple with her free hand; she felt a migraine coming on.

"Cyrus, what we had was just a little rendezvous," she said. "You could only be a friend to me. We were young and adventurous, and we learned from all that foolishness. You didn't want me."

"I wish MaLeah was mine. She's so beautiful."

"Well, she's not, Cyrus, and leave my daughter out of this."

"Arnelle, I have to go. I hope you'll have a change of heart and give me the package. Goodbye."

"Cyrus!"

He was gone. She hung up the phone not knowing what Cyrus would do next. She sat down and wondered if she should go ahead and tell her dad what Cyrus was holding over her. At least Cyrus didn't know Winston was MaLeah's father. She was dating someone else at the time, and they eventually broke up. If he knew Winston was MaLeah's father, there's no telling what he would do. She just prayed he would stop this foolishness. Looking at the clock on her nightstand, she knew it was time to get ready for her dinner with Winston. She wasn't going to let Cyrus ruin this night for her. She entered her bathroom and turned on the tub, filling it with hot water. She slowly eased into the water, closed her eyes and leaned back into the suds. She replayed her conversation with Cyrus in her head. He was her friend, and she had to come up with a way to help him.

Winston was unexpectedly nervous. He had prepared shrimp alfredo, salad and cheese bread. For dessert, he had chosen peach cobbler and ice cream. He wanted this night to go perfectly since he planned to ask Arnelle to visit him in California. She wouldn't have an excuse since she was on vacation. He had dressed in black slacks and a thick ivory sweater. He applied a small amount of cologne before grabbing his black leather jacket and heading out the door to pick up Arnelle.

Arnelle had changed outfits three times.

Why am I nervous? Arnelle had asked herself several times. *Maybe it's because I'm having dinner with my daughter's father, and he doesn't know she exists.*

She stopped for a moment, then said, "Arnelle, get yourself together. Okay, this is the last outfit."

She pulled from her closet a long black skirt, boots and a red sweater, casual and comfortable. Looking at the wall clock, she realized Winston would be there soon. She laid the clothes out on the bed and looked in the mirror, trying to decide how to wear her hair. Up or down? Braided or loose? She stopped stressing over her hair and got dressed. She eventually decided to wear her hair down. After hurriedly dressing, Arnelle tried to catch her breath as she waited for Winston in her den. Just like clockwork, he was on time. The doorbell chimed and what she saw through her peephole made her heart flutter.

She opened the door and said, "Hello, Winston, come in."

He stepped through the door and kissed her on the cheek.

"Arnelle, you're looking fine as ever."

Twirling, she said, "Why thank you, Mr. Carter. You're looking debonair yourself."

"Only for you. You ready to go?"

"Let me grab a couple of things and I'll be ready." He watched her retreat further into her house, and when she returned, she held out a bottle of white wine.

He accepted it. "You didn't have to, Sweetheart. Thank you."

"I know, but I wanted to. It's the least I could do."

Laughing, she pulled her other hand from behind her back and handed him a bottle of antacid. He took it and said, "Real funny, Arnelle. I'm going to prove to you that I am a very good cook."

She leaned in and kissed him on the cheek and said, "I was just teasing you, Winston."

He pulled her hard against his chest and said, "You're going to pay for that little joke, woman."

Before she could respond, he lowered his mouth and covered

hers with a soul-stirring kiss. He released her as if the kiss meant nothing and said, "Now where's your coat?"

Arnelle was still trying to recover from the heat of his lips. She pointed to her hall closet because she couldn't form words. He helped her into her coat and said, "Let's ride." He took the key from Arnelle and locked up before escorting her to his awaiting truck.

As soon as they pulled off, Arnelle's cell phone rang. She turned the ringer down and smiled at Winston.

When Winston and Arnelle walked into his house, the succulent smells hit them in the face.

Arnelle removed her coat and said, "Winston, dinner smells wonderful."

"I told you I could cook."

"Man, it smells so good in here, my stomach is acting up. I'm starving!"

Winston hung up their coats and followed Arnelle into the kitchen. She rubbed her hands together and asked, "What can I do to help?"

He walked over to the stove. "I have everything under control here. Let me show you to the table."

He took her by the hand and led her through the hallway and out into his sunroom. He had decorated the room with soft light and white candles. As Arnelle admired the scene, he started lighting twenty candles of different shapes and sizes. The table was set with gold plates and utensils. The centerpiece was a half-dozen white roses. Winston had taken the time to move his other furniture out of the room except for a large ivory sofa and coffee table with a glass top and gold legs. Arnelle loved the view to his huge backyard. It was landscaped with a variety of trees and flowers. Down the walkway was a man-made waterfall and small pond. Since it was winter, the water was not running. She stood in awe and said, "I can't wait to see your waterfall in the spring."

Still lighting candles, he looked up and asked, "Do you think you can put up with me that long?"

She turned and faced him, a smile radiating on her face. "It's going to be a hard job, but someone has to do it."

He couldn't help but return a smile. He knew in his heart, no other woman could fulfill him as much as Arnelle had in a few short weeks. It was hard to believe they could hardly stand to be in the same room together at one time.

"Winston, are you a romantic?"

"When I have to be. Why do you ask?"

"I just never thought of you as a flowers and candles kind of guy."

She sat down and tilted her head in curiosity, staring at him.

He sat across from her and asked, "What do you want to know, Arnelle?"

She leaned toward him. "Do you have a forgiving heart, Winston?"

He leaned back and lowered his head in thought. Arnelle went into a slight panic. Did he remember she had asked that same question a few years ago? Her eyes widened as they locked with hers.

"I hope we never have to address that issue, but I'm a lawyer so I have to have one, to some degree." He stood. "I'll be right back with dinner."

She nervously took a sip of water and started breathing heavily. She gnawed at her nails and wondered what was keeping him and whether he remembered.

∞

Winston moved around in the kitchen like a robot. He thought and thought to himself what was it about this woman that made him fall apart anytime he was in her presence. Was she really as different from other women like Craig said? He couldn't understand why he was drawn to her, why he felt so comfortable and possessive. He'd never been like this with any of the others. Even lately, his dreams consisted of beautiful walks on the beach, picnics and just holding each other. His dreams had never been this vivid before and yet when he dreamed of Arnelle, it couldn't be more real.

"Can I help?"

He turned toward her voice, startled out of his daze. He stuttered and said, "You can take the salad if you want to."

She walked over to him and said, "I didn't mean to startle you."

"You didn't," he said, his pride kicking in. "I was just in deep thought."

She took the bowl out of his hand and sat it on the counter. She wrapped her arms around his neck and pressed her body against his.

"Thank you, Winston."

He hugged her waist and stared down into her eyes.

"For what?"

"Everything. I'm going to miss you."

She planted a soft kiss to his lips, then pressed her face against his neck.

"Arnelle?"

"Yes?"

He gently ran his hand over her back and said, "Unless you plan on skipping dinner, you'd better stop while you're ahead. Right now, I'm not a man with a lot of control."

She looked up into his eyes and said, "Then I guess we should have our dinner, huh?"

His hot gaze met hers.

"That's totally up to you."

He had called her bluff. Now would she play her hand?

Her thick lashes lowered and she answered, "The night is young. Let's eat."

"Take the salad and I'll be right behind you."

He watched her hips sway as she walked out in silence. Arnelle *was* different. She was a challenger, and he should've expected it. It was in her Navajo/African-American blood.

Joining her at the table, they enjoyed his delicious meal. Arnelle was thoroughly impressed with his gourmet skills. He took pleasure in feeding her the huge shrimp. Seeing her lick her lips stirred him unexpectedly. Winston's selection of Will Downing and other jazz artists set the aura.

"Arnelle, I have a confession."

"What?"

He laughed and said, "You know you used to be real mean and nasty to me. You were so bad, I gave you a nickname."

Her eyes tightened and she pointed her fork at him.

"What nasty name did you give me?"

He took a sip of wine, laughed and confessed, "Devil Woman."

"Devil Woman? I wasn't that bad!"

"Bull!"

She looked at him apologetically and said, "I'm sorry I was so mean to you, but I had my reasons."

Curious he leaned in and asked, "And they are?"

"I'll tell you about it one day."

She lowered her head, and he stared at her for a few seconds.

"Wanna dance?" he asked.

She looked up at his empathic eyes and said, "Sure."

They danced to several songs after clearing the table. Unconsciously, he stroked her long, thick mane.

"Do you like my hair, Winston?"

He looked at her. "Yes," he whispered. "It's so soft, but it wouldn't matter if your hair was short. I just like touching it and you."

"Winston, are you flirting with me?"

"I'm beyond flirting, Arnelle. I don't know what it is about you that makes me act the way I do."

They stopped dancing but continued to embrace.

"Is that a good thing or a bad thing?" she asked.

He kissed her ear and started dancing again.

"Oh, it's definitely a good thing, almost too good. You make me ache."

"Winston!"

"Well, you do. You asked and I answered."

She closed her eyes and leaned into the strength of his arms. The song ended and Arnelle held on tighter. They could feel their hearts dancing to the same rhythm. They knew the inevitable would eventually happen.

"Arnelle?"

"Yes?"

"Would it be okay with you if we went upstairs?" Winston felt his insides turn warm and liquidy. *Damn*, he thought. *Why am I nervous? I've bedded many women before. I usually tell women what I want. Why is Arnelle so important to me that I asked?*

She nuzzled his neck and said, "Lead the way."

He really didn't expect it, but she had agreed and he was pleased. He took her hand and in silence, they blew out all the candles before going upstairs.

∞

Upon entering his bedroom, Arnelle became nervous. She knew she was still quite in love with Winston, but not having contact with him after all these years made her feel like a virgin. Winston looked at her expression and pulled her into his arms to comfort her.

"Nervous?" he asked.

She nodded. "A little. Winston, look, it's been a while for me."

"What's a while, Sweetheart?"

She took a deep breath. "Over a year."

He looked at her with that penetrating gaze.

"If you don't want to, we don't have to."

She cupped his face in her hands and said, "But, I do want to, Winston. I want to very much."

He almost lost his mind, hearing her proclaim her desire for him. She kissed him, praying he could feel the depth of her love. He was her daughter's father and he meant everything to her. She would do whatever it took to keep Cyrus from hurting him, her daughter's dad. He pulled her protectively into his arms and kissed her hard on her soft lips. She couldn't stop the breathless moan that was escaping as his tongue and mouth assaulted hers. He slowly and gently laid her on the bed, making sure she didn't leave his arms. He pulled her sweater over her head and removed her red lace bra. His large hands covered her swollen nipples.

"Beautiful."

Arnelle blushed and felt heat radiating from this sensual contact. He ran his tongue across her lips and sprinkled kisses along the column of her neck. She cried out and arched her body into his as his mouth covered her sensitive breasts. Winston's kisses trailed lower until he reached the waistband of her skirt. He never broke eye contact with her as he unbuttoned and slid the skirt over her hips. He stared at the lacy material covering her and swallowed hard. He ran his hand slowly down her body, noticing goose bumps appearing on her skin. He slid his hand into her panties and stroked her, before inserting his finger.

"Winston!"

He kissed her and said, "I have to make sure I don't hurt you, Sweetheart, and I would never hurt you."

Shyly, she answered, "I know."

He watched her skin change colors before his eyes as he methodically prepared her for him. She was unable to mask her expressions of passion as he continued. Stopping briefly, he pulled his sweater over his head and lowered the lights to a minimum. He wanted her as relaxed and comfortable as possible.

On his way back to her, she called, "Winston?"

"Yes?"

"Can we use the candles instead?"

He smiled and said, "I'll be right back." He must have run because he was back within ten seconds. Arnelle lay upon the bed and watched Winston's movements. He was so relaxed. She calmed herself by remembering her confidence of years earlier. Then, it was just two of them. Now, MaLeah was part of that equation. He lit the last candle and asked, "How's that?"

Turning on her side, she said, "Perfect."

He came to her and sat on the bed to remove the rest of his clothes. Arnelle was in awe...total awe. She couldn't help but remember what Brandon had said about Winston's male form. She was very familiar with every inch of him, even though he didn't remember her. There weren't many places on his body that she hadn't explored in the past. He pulled back the linens on his bed and pulled her into his arms.

"Winston Carter, will you respect me in the morning?"

He ran his hand up her thigh and over her hips, squeezing the roundness of her derriere. She let out a loud sigh as his hands once again went to her lower body. He watched her expressions lovingly.

"Can't you tell I already respect you?" he asked, his voice tight. "I haven't ripped your undergarments off even though I've wanted to all night."

He kissed her and sampled her aching nipples once more,

gently biting them. Scooting back on his knees, he lowered her panties.

"Arnelle, you are one special lady. I know because I've never had these kinds of feelings before."

She raised herself on her elbows and asked, "What kind of feelings?"

He shook his head unable to look into her eyes, afraid he would tell her he loved her. It was too soon even though he knew he did.

"It's hard to identify. That's what makes it so…different. I'm trying to understand them myself."

She took his hand in hers and said, "Winston, you're feeling the same things I'm feeling. I've only felt this way one other time in my life."

He closed his eyes and said, "I really don't want to hear about you being with another man, Arnelle."

Little did he know, she was talking about him and their relationship, the one he couldn't remember. She rose to her knees, unfolded his arms and laid her head against his beating heart. "I thought you wanted to make love to me?"

He looked into her eyes. "I still do." He stared deeper. "Why me?"

"Why you what?"

He stroked her cheek. "If it's been a while since you've shared your body with anyone, why me…why now?"

"Because it's you who makes me toss and turn at night. It's you who puts this smile on my face and makes my body burn for your touch. Winston, it's you I want. You and only you."

Her words hit him like a sledgehammer. She had just confessed to the exact same desires that he had for her, but she was able to form them into words when he couldn't. He pushed the thick masses of hair away from her face and confessed, "Well, thanks to you, I haven't gotten much sleep either. You're also lucky your brother was in town the other week or you would've been in a lot of trouble."

She leaned forward, kissing the side of his neck and said, "For all you know, you might've been the one in trouble, handsome."

He lowered her onto her back. "Are you on any birth control?"

She shook her head to let him know she wasn't. He pulled out his drawer and then several condoms. Her eyes followed his movements as he placed the foil packets on the nightstand.

"You sure that's enough?"

His eyes darkened. "It'll do for starters," he said, smiling.

She became nervous again as she watched him apply the condom. He removed her undergarments and covered her body with his.

"Relax, Arnelle," Winston said. "I don't want to hurt you, okay?"

He wasn't bragging; he was being honest. If Winston had known it had been three years since Arnelle had made love, he might not go through with it tonight. He planted kisses on her lips, neck and finally her breasts as he parted her thighs. Arnelle's breathing had become heavier with anticipation. She closed her eyes and felt his flesh push against hers.

"Relax, Baby," Winston whispered. "I've got you."

Arnelle pulled him down to her and drowned in the pool of desire as his kisses became her life support. She clung to his tight, muscular body as he gradually filled her space. Winston was amazed at the snug fit, believing it was the result of a year of celibacy. Arnelle bit down on her lower lip and held her breath as he slowly moved within her body.

"Breathe, Sweetheart." Winston's breath tickled her neck. "Relax."

It was taking the strength of ten-thousand horses to keep

Winston from taking Arnelle's body fast and hard. She could feel her body stretching to accommodate the fill of him. He balanced his weight so that she could get familiar with him. He noticed her passionate expressions change as he gradually picked up his movements, making sure he could prolong their love-making. Arnelle must have become comfortable with their fit. She had started to move her hips against his in a rhythm designed only for them. Winston had to close his eyes because what he was feeling was too much ecstasy for him to sustain. Arnelle's body was nothing short of heaven. His hands and mouth were everywhere, and Arnelle found herself moaning loudly. This didn't help Winston because he knew their first encounter wouldn't last very long. He wanted her too much. It wasn't until Arnelle felt comfortable enough to wrap her athletic legs around his waist that Winston gave into his crazed state of desire. He had never lost control before. She made him lower any guard he had shielded his heart with. She made him cry out like never before. He whispered her name seductively in her ear and pro-claimed, "Sweetheart, I'm not going to last much longer."

She grounded her hips into him vigorously and dug her nails into his back as she arched into the curve of his body. Their mouths and tongues intertwined between the whimpers, which had consumed them as her body was rocked hard with release. Winston's name echoed throughout the house in a cry of uncontrollable satisfaction. He followed her screams with cries of his own as he collapsed on top of her body which still shiv-ered uncontrollably. He buried his face against her sweat-drenched neck to make an attempt to gather his thoughts and breath. Kissing her tenderly, he looked down at her face, which was covered by her hands. He became concerned and removed her hands. He had to see her eyes, and what he saw were tears.

"Sweetheart? Are you okay? Did I hurt you?"

Winston was still inside her, so he eased away gently and turned her face toward him. He cupped her face, kissing her tenderly. "Arnelle? Baby, I'm so sorry. I didn't mean to…"

"I'm fine, Winston. You didn't hurt me."

He ran his thumb across her lips and asked, "Then why are you crying? You really did scare me this time."

She wrapped her arms around his neck. "I love you, Winston, and I know in my heart I always have and always will."

She didn't expect a response from him right then and it was okay. She had just dropped a bombshell on him, and she knew he needed time to decipher it. He leaned down and kissed her tears away before kissing her lips. He rolled over onto his back, pulling her on top of his chest.

He looked into her eyes. "Arnelle, I know it took a lot of courage for you to tell me you loved me. I have feelings for you also that I been trying to explain for several weeks now. I haven't been able to sort them out yet, but if it's not love, I don't know what else it could be. This whole evening has been magical for me, and I wouldn't change a thing. Do you understand what I'm saying?"

She snuggled closer and kissed his cheek. "Yes, Winston. I understand. Now hold me."

"You don't have to tell me more than once. Come here, Baby."

Satisfied, the two cuddled and talked about his trip. He didn't want to go into the details of the trial; he just said he would be happy when it was over. She ran her fingers ever so lightly over his chest and thought about Cyrus.

"I'm going home in a couple of days," she said. "I haven't seen my parents in a while. I also told Keaton that I'd come see him for a few days also."

He brought her hand up to his lips. "You're going around to visit everyone, and you can't come keep me company for a few days?"

"Winston, I'll just be in your way. Don't you need to keep your head on straight for this trial?"

"Having you there with me is all I need to keep me focused." He ran his hand down her spine. "At least say you'll think about it."

"I'll think about it, counselor." Arnelle broke into a grin as she eyed the two remaining packets on the nightstand. "Now," she said, almost purring, "we have one down and two to go. Are you *up* for it?"

He smiled and rolled her over onto her side playfully. "I'll let you be the judge."

He took her hand and positioned it between his thighs.

Arnelle giggled. "You're so bad, Winston," she said as she smacked his thigh. "My ruling is you're more than ready. Can I do it this time?" Having her touch him there was ecstasy. Allowing her to apply their protection was going to cause him to lose any and all restraint he had left.

He handed her the condom. "Help yourself, Doc."

Hours passed and it was sometime around one a.m. when they ran out of condoms and the candles had burned down. Winston kept telling her she was going to be sore in the morning, but Arnelle wasn't about to stop giving her love to him. Before she succumbed to a deep sleep, he assured her he would pamper her with loving care in the morning as well as a nice soak in his massive tub.

His last day in Philly was tomorrow, and Arnelle was the only person he wanted to be with. That wasn't going to be possible because Craig and Venice made him promise to come over for a "Bon Voyage" dinner. Watching Arnelle sleep so comfortably in his arms put to rest any doubt of his true feelings for her. He loved her, and he was almost to the point of being addicted. He marveled at how his feelings for Arnelle had exploded in such a short period of time.

It was puzzling why he couldn't express his love hours earlier. He figured he was just scared—scared that he had never told a woman he loved her. Arnelle wasn't like the *love 'em and leave 'em* type of women he had dated in the past. He vowed from this moment on that Arnelle would be *his* woman and he knew he needed to tell her how he felt. First, he wanted to convince her to come visit him in California. It would be there that he would show her just how much he loved her. She had to come… she just had to.

CHAPTER EIGHT

The next morning, Winston did everything he had promised. He pampered Arnelle to no end. They slept in until nine o'clock. He made breakfast and served her in bed. Sore was an understatement of the condition of Arnelle's body. She had no idea she would have trouble walking, but she did. Winston ran a steaming hot bath in his garden tub and eased her into the water. She leaned back against him and closed her eyes.

"Baby, I'm sorry you're hurting, but I warned you."

She massaged his powerful legs. "I can't believe you actually tried to kill me."

"Don't even try it, Doc." Winston laughed. "You did that to yourself. What's a man to do? Anyway, I think those last couple of times you took advantage of me."

She pinched him. "Quit acting like you were helpless. If I go home walking with a limp, my dad is going to wonder."

He licked her earlobe and said, "You don't want Daddy to know how freaky you are, do you?"

That casual contact caused her to suck in a breath and her nipples hardened; Winston's eyes instantly noticed.

"Don't worry, Baby; when we get out of the tub, I have something that will make you feel all better."

She eyed him suspiciously. "What is it?"

He grinned. "You'll see."

∞

On the drive back to her house, Arnelle stared at Winston as he hummed to a tune on the radio.

"Winston Carter, I can't believe you."

He laughed. "You loved it so quit acting like you didn't. I know I enjoyed myself."

"That was torture and you know it."

He pulled up to a red light. "If that was torture, you're the best victim I've ever tasted."

"Winston!"

He laughed and continued to sing along with the radio. She turned away from him to hide her eyes. The intimacy they shared after their bath was remarkable and still affected her. Winston took great pleasure in hearing her moan his name repeatedly. He also took delight in seeing her body spasm continuously from his sensual assault on her inner thighs. He knew exactly what it was like to be totally out of control because last night, she took him there. This morning, he took her there and far beyond.

He pulled into her driveway and asked, "Do you have any plans for dinner?"

"Not really, I just have to pack for my trip. Why?"

"Craig and Venice invited me over for dinner, and I want to take you with me."

"I don't know. They might want to spend some time with you by themselves before you leave."

He laced his fingers with hers and lowered his head.

"Please, Arnelle. It's my last night in Philly for a while and I want to see you."

She leaned over and kissed his cheek. "I'll go with you, Winston. Now, see me inside so I can start packing for my trip home."

"Thank you. I'll pick you up at six o'clock."

She smiled. "Why don't I meet you there? I have some last-minute errands to take care of."

"If you insist."

Arnelle had to force herself out of Winston's grip and him out of her house. He had an awesome allure about him and sometimes it overpowered her, leaving her panting. She checked her messages and returned a call from Keaton.

"What's up, Bro?"

"Well, it's about time you returned my call. Where have you been?"

Arnelle fell back onto her bed, smiling. "Mind your business. What's up?"

"Have you told him yet?"

The smile left her face. "Keaton, I told you to let me handle this. I'll tell Winston when I think the time is right."

"You're going to be sorry if you keep on waiting around."

"Keaton, I love you. I'll be home in a couple of days. I'm on a two-week vacation so hopefully, you won't be too busy to hang out with me for a while."

"I always have time for my sister."

As she stepped out of her clothes, Arnelle asked, "Are you seeing anyone right now?"

"Why?"

"'Cause you're all up in my business and you are a little uptight. You need to get that off you, Darling."

"Don't you worry about me. I have friends. I don't need the drama of a relationship right now."

"Whatever Keaton," she said, laughing. "Goodbye. I have to pack."

"Don't forget what I said. If he gets out of line, I'm on his ass."

"You're a trip! Later."

∞

Brandon met Arnelle at the door later that night and gave her a big hug.

"Hi, Miss Arnelle," he squealed.

Arnelle hugged Brandon tightly. "How's my favorite man?"

"I'm great now that you're here."

Looking around the room, she asked, "Where's your mom?"

"In the kitchen. Pops is upstairs changing C.J. and Clarissa. I'll go tell them you're here."

Brandon ran down the hallway. "Momma, Pops! Miss Arnelle's here!"

Venice stepped out the kitchen and yelled, "Brandon, stop all that hollering! Hey, Arnelle. Skeeter told us you would be coming. Come on into the kitchen so we can talk."

Arnelle raised her eyebrows. "I brought some wine for us and grape juice for Brandon."

Venice took the bag from Arnelle. "Thanks, Girl, but you didn't have to do that."

In the kitchen, Arnelle asked, "Can I help with anything?"

"Nope, just have a seat and keep me company. So…how are you and Skeeter getting along?"

"Fine."

Venice turned and eyed her partner carefully. Arnelle looked away and started playing with a baby toy on the table. Venice continued to stare, and then put her hand over her mouth. "Ooh, you gave him some, didn't you? I knew it!"

Arnelle jumped up and looked toward the hallway.

"Be quiet, Venice!"

Craig walked in and asked, "What's going on?"

The two turned and looked at him in silence. Arnelle grabbed a bowl and said, "Nothing. How are you, Craig?"

He looked at the two women. "I just walked in on something juicy, didn't I?"

Venice said, "Quit being paranoid, Babe. We were just talking girl talk."

He slid his hands in his jeans. "Whatever. The rugrats are asleep. Witch Doctor, we're glad you could make it. Skeeter called and told us he invited you over. Where is he?"

She opened the refrigerator and innocently said, "I don't know. He knew what time to be here, didn't he?"

"Uh-huh. I'll guess he'll be here shortly. I'm going to build a fire. Holler if you need me."

Venice smiled. "I will."

Craig turned and left the room. Venice gave all her attention to Arnelle and was about to start quizzing her again when the doorbell chimed. Arnelle's heart rate accelerated and she was glad no one could tell. She tried to make herself busy as they heard Brandon yelling, "Uncle Skeeter!"

Seconds later, Winston entered the kitchen, carrying Brandon on his back. Craig followed, carrying a dessert Winston had brought along with two bouquets of flowers. Skeeter eased Brandon off his back and took the flowers from Craig.

He walked over to Venice. "For you, bossy woman." He kissed her on the cheek after placing the flowers in her hands.

Smelling them, she said, "Thank you, Skeeter. They're beautiful."

"You're welcome."

He turned toward Arnelle. He smiled and marched toward her slowly. Her breath caught in her throat not knowing what he was going to do. He walked over, held the flowers out to her and said, "For you."

She breathed a sigh of relief and accepted the flowers.

"Thank you, Winston."

He leaned down and kissed her on the cheek. Whispering in her ear, Winston said, "You can thank me later, Devil Woman."

Heat ignited her face as all eyes were on them. Venice saw the panic on Arnelle's face and saved her by saying, "Let's eat, guys. You men go on into the dining room. We'll bring the food to the table."

Arnelle looked at Venice and gave her a silent thank-you.

Winston found it hard to sit next to Arnelle and not touch her. He picked up on the fact that she wasn't ready for their friends to know they were intimate. For the moment, he had to act as if they were still just friends.

"Venice, I can't eat another bite," Winston said. He grabbed his stomach. "Dinner was da bomb, as usual."

"Why thank you, Skeeter," Venice responded before standing.

Winston followed suit. "Sit down, Venice," he said. "I'll do the dishes and Craig will help me." Craig's head shot up in surprise because Winston had never volunteered to do the dishes.

Venice and Arnelle took Brandon upstairs and checked on the twins. The men worked in silence as they cleaned the kitchen. Craig put away a dish and asked, "What's up with you two?"

"What do you mean?"

Craig placed another dish on the shelf. "I know you, remember? Why are you two acting like nothing's going on between you?"

Winston sighed. "Craig, come on, man. You're starting to act like that nosey wife of yours. Look, we hung out after Lamar's wedding and had a good time, that's all. We're just taking things slow right now. A'ight? We've covered a lot of ground over the past few weeks, and that's all I'm going to say right now. Cool?"

Craig laughed and said, "It's a'ight with me, but I can tell you're in love with her. I don't think Venice is going to let up on the questions though."

"Well, her twenty questions will fall on deaf ears as far as I'm concerned."

"You know Venice has been waiting for you two to get together for a while."

Turning to inspect their work, he said, "I know. Well, I'm out of here. My flight leaves at one p.m. I need to get home and go over some last-minute work I'm leaving for my colleagues. Thanks again for dinner. I'll give you guys a call from the West Coast."

Craig folded his arms and leaned back against the sink. "So are you ready for this trial?"

"As ready as I'm going to be. Man, I don't see how these guys come from nothing, make it in the pros, and then throw their lives away. It's sad."

"Yeah, I know. Hey! How do you feel about going back out there? I mean, some serious drama went down with you out there."

Sighing, Winston answered, "I know. I still don't know why someone tried to plant drugs on me."

"Yeah, and what about the mysterious woman you told me about? I wonder what happened to her? They way you were talking, I expected you to bring her back as your wife."

Hanging up the dish towel, Winston's eyes dimmed.

"Well, from what you told me that I said, I probably would've. I've never met a woman I wanted to marry before. Wouldn't you know the very time I do, I get jacked and lose my memory. I wish I would've told you more about her."

Craig patted him on the shoulder and said, "Don't stress over it, man. I'm sure with time, your memory will come back."

"I can't believe I don't even remember what she looks like. Wait! You don't think Arnelle...."

Surprised, Craig closed a cabinet door and said, "Nah! Surely not! You said, you'd remember a woman like her."

Winston nervously asked, "But what if she is the one? She said we've met before."

Frowning, Craig asked, "Are you seriously thinking she could be the one?"

"I don't know, man. I just wish I could remember. I might try to quiz her a little bit and see how she reacts. I've been trying to get her to tell me where we met before, but she keeps evading the question. That makes her more suspicious."

"Just make sure you stay focused on this trip."

"You don't have to tell me. Well, let me go tell everyone good-night, and I guess I'll see you when I see you."

As Winston walked out of the kitchen he felt a sense of relief after talking to his best friend.

∞

Upstairs, Winston said goodnight to Brandon and told him to expect a surprise in the mail from California. Brandon was very excited and told Winston he couldn't wait until they could go to another ballgame together. Skeeter hugged him and as usual, told him to look after his brother and sister. Down the hall, he heard Venice and Arnelle talking softly. When he walked into the nursery, each held a baby, rocking gently. He walked over, took C.J. from Arnelle's arms and held him close.

He smiled. "I can't believe how much they're growing."

"They should be driving in a few weeks," Venice joked. "They eat like teenagers."

Arnelle laughed. "Venice, I'd better get going. I still have a few more things to do before I start my vacation."

She stood and kissed C.J. on the cheek. Winston walked over

and placed the baby in his crib but not before giving him a kiss. His mind couldn't help but yearn to do the same ritual with his own children. Arnelle leaned down and kissed Clarissa as Venice held her. Winston walked over and said, "Let me hold my princess for a minute."

Venice gave Clarissa to Winston, and the baby smiled up at him as usual. They had a special bond, which was obvious by looking at them. He spoke softly to her as he walked around the room, away from the women. Arnelle watched their exchange and knew he would've been just as affectionate with MaLeah. She sighed and said, "Well, Venice, give me a hug. I guess I'll see you in a couple of weeks."

"I hope you have a nice vacation." Venice hugged her back. "Call me and let me know how things are going, okay?"

"I will."

Winston turned and handed a sleeping Clarissa back to Venice.

"How do you do that?" she asked. "She always falls asleep within minutes after you hold her."

He kissed Clarissa's chubby cheek and whispered, "I can't give away all my secrets."

He leaned in again to give Venice a kiss on the cheek. "I have to go also. I've got a lot to do before tomorrow. I told Craig I'll call you guys from California."

"Okay," Venice said. "Have a safe trip and be careful driving home."

"Well, Winston," Arnelle said, "you can walk me to my car since we're leaving at the same time."

Winston stood over her and gazed into her eyes. "I wouldn't be a gentleman if I didn't."

As they walked out of the room, Venice grinned and said, "Goodnight, you two."

"Goodnight," they said in unison.

Once in the hallway and out of sight, Winston couldn't help but link his arm around Arnelle's waist, pulling her close.

"You're coming home with me, right?"

Arnelle looked at him in surprise. "I thought you said you had a lot to do tonight since you're flying out tomorrow."

He gently kissed her cheek. "I do have a lot to do but it doesn't have anything to do with packing."

An electric current ran through her body.

"Winston," Arnelle whispered, "I don't think I could survive another night with you."

He looked down the hall to see if anyone was coming and kissed her again, this time firmly on the lips.

"Then we can just hold each other. One thing I'm sure of tonight, I want to fall asleep lying next to you."

Arnelle sighed and lowered her head. "Go home, Winston. I'll be there shortly."

"Thank you, Devil Woman." He smiled and gave her a wink.

"You keep that up and you will be sleeping alone tonight."

Laughing, he said, "I'm just playing with you. You are my Devil Woman."

"Oh, am I?" she asked, walking ahead of him down the stairs.

Following closely behind for a view of her hips, he answered, "Most definitely."

∞

Judge Lapahie tucked MaLeah in and felt her forehead. She wasn't running a temperature, but she was having a hard time fighting this cold. Zenora had put a vaporizer in MaLeah's room to help her stuffy nose. MaLeah was still in good spirits, but her nose irritated her on occasion.

"MaLeah," the judge said, "your momma will be home to help take care of you in a few days. Okay, Sweetie?"

"Momma!" MaLeah yelled. She smiled at her grandfather as if she knew exactly what he had said. Judge Lapahie held Arnelle's picture up so MaLeah could see it.

"Yes, Baby," he said. "Momma's coming home."

MaLeah smiled at the picture and giggled. "Momma!"

He patted her head, and then kissed her.

"Goodnight, MaLeah."

He turned out the light and closed her door. He walked into his bedroom to find Zenora walking out of the bathroom.

"Herbert, that baby doesn't seem to be getting any better. Maybe we should take her to the doctor tomorrow. I don't like that cough she has."

"It's just a little cold. As long as it doesn't get in her chest, she'll be fine. Relax, Grandma." He crawled into bed and added, "I'm sure MaLeah will be just fine."

He kissed his smiling wife and pulled the comforter over his body.

∞

Arnelle rung Winston's doorbell about an hour after saying goodnight to the Bennetts.

He swung the door opened and asked, "What took you so long? I was about to worry."

Arnelle handed him her overnight bag and caressed his cheek.

"That's so sweet. You can stop worrying now because I'm here."

He took the bag and closed the door, locking it as she walked into the foyer. She turned to him with her hands behind her back and noticed his luggage sitting by the door. He sat her bag down and went to her, pulling her into his arms. He just stared.

"What is it, Winston?"

Looking into her eyes, he said, "I don't know. I can't put my finger on it. There's something about you."

Her heart started beating rapidly as she wondered if he were remembering. Hoping he was, she asked, "What do you mean?"

He just shook his head and hugged her. She rested her head against his chest and closed her eyes.

"Arnelle, sometimes I feel like I've known you in another life. Weird, huh?"

She looked up into his eyes. "I don't think that's weird."

"You hungry?"

"After all that food at Venice's house? Please!"

He picked up her bag and grinned at her devilishly.

"Well, I guess the only thing left to do is go to bed."

She held his hand. "Hmm, I guess not. Let's go."

∞

The two shared a nice conversation while lying across the bed.

"Will you drive me to the airport?"

She smiled as she applied lotion to her legs.

"If you want me too, I will."

He crawled across the bed on his knees until he was in front of Arnelle. "Let me do that."

Handing him the bottle, she lay back and allowed him to massage the lotion on her legs.

"There's no one else I'd rather see before getting on that plane."

Blushing, she said, "And to think, Venice is taking me to the airport."

"I hope you're still considering coming to California to visit me."

He looked up at her as his hands went under her nightgown. She sucked in a breath and said, "Yes, I'm still thinking about it."

"Is there anything I can do to convince you?"

His hands went even higher, until he reached her center, brushing against her flesh ever so lightly.

"Winston Carter!"

He laughed as he removed his hand. "I'll never stop trying."

"I believe you and thanks for your nasty little massage."

He towered over her. "The pleasure was all mine. Now, is there anything I can get you before lights out?"

"Just your arms around me."

He pulled her against his body. "Done. Anything else?"

"A goodnight kiss."

He pressed his mouth against hers in a way to pledge his ever-lasting love. The heat from the kiss alone moistened her lower body.

"Done. Anything else?"

She put her arms around his neck and sprinkled his neck and bare chest with kisses.

"Make love to me, Winston."

He smiled as he covered her body with his. It wasn't until later that he rolled off her hot, sweaty body that he said, "Done. Anything else, Baby?"

With her chest heaving and eyes stinging with tears, Arnelle said, "I love you, Winston."

"I love you, too, Baby. Goodnight."

Winston couldn't believe how easily those words had slipped out of his mouth. He could've said it weeks ago, but now he was sure of it. He really did love Arnelle. It was something he'd never felt for any other woman before or would from this moment on. He loved the feel of her lying in his arms and the rhythm of her breathing. He couldn't help staring at her as she slept. Even her snoring was a welcoming sound in his normally quiet surrounding.

CHAPTER NINE

S eeing Winston walk down the tunnel to his airplane was heartbreaking. Arnelle's lips still stung from the kiss he had given her before walking away. She had never felt like this about any man. She had to find a way to help Cyrus without ruining her chances for happiness with Winston and MaLeah. Glancing at her watch, she walked out of the airport and to her car. As she drove off, she remembered how good it felt to finally hear him tell her that he loved her. She couldn't help but smile and cry tears of joy as she drove home.

Later that night, she tossed and turned in her bed. Winston had called her earlier to let her know he had arrived safely and to give her his hotel information. He still prayed she would come visit him, and he hoped his prayers would be answered. She told him she would call to check on him from Texas. Her plane was leaving first thing in the morning. Her heart ached as she cried herself to sleep. Her first priority was MaLeah. She hoped her trip home would clear her mind and lead her in the right direction to make things right.

∞

Winston arrived in court early to get his game face on. He'd spent his first two days in California preparing for this huge case. His former law partner greeted him with confidence and assurance that they would win this case hands-down. It wasn't long before Cyrus and his dream team entered the courtroom. He watched the successful basketball player adjust the tie that accompanied his thousand-dollar suit.

How much longer would society have to witness these high-dollar athletes throw away their lives, Winston thought.

After all parties had arrived, the court was called to order and the opening arguments were presented. Winston couldn't help but watch Cyrus as he constantly scanned the audience as if he were looking for someone. A family member, he presumed.

Cyrus turned and whispered into his attorney's ear. He lowered his head and thought to himself, *Where are you, Arnelle? I need you here.*

∞

Later that night, Winston showered and fell across the bed, mentally and physically exhausted. His phone rang and he rolled over to answer it.

"Hello?"

"Hey, Sexy."

"I was just thinking about you."

"I'm sure you were."

"Seriously, I'm lying here butt naked and..."

"Never mind, Winston. I just wanted to call and tell you goodnight."

He laughed. "Is that all?"

"Well, I miss you, too."

"That's better, Devil Woman."

"Winston," Arnelle said, pretending to be angry, "don't make me come out there."

"Is that all I have to do to get you here?"

"No... I'll be there in three days. Can you wait that long?"

He sat up. "Not really, but I guess I don't have a choice. Give me your flight information and I'll have a car pick you up since I'll probably be in court. Okay?"

Her heart swelled with affection as she answered, "I can't wait."

"Me neither. Rest up, Sweetheart. You're going to need it."

Giggling, she said, "We'll see. So, how did things go today?"

"It went okay. Today was just opening statements, but it still was a long day."

She sighed as she thought of Cyrus. "I'm sure it was. Well, hopefully things will be over quickly."

He yawned. "That's what I'm hoping for. How's your family? I'm sure they were happy to see you."

She smiled as she thought about MaLeah and said, "Yes, they missed me and I missed them."

"I hope I get to meet them one day soon."

"You will, Winston; I'm sure of it. Well, I'm not going to keep you up any longer. Goodnight, counselor."

"Arnelle?"

"Yes?"

"I love you, Doc."

"I love you, too, Winston."

Winston hung up the phone and the only thing that floated in his mind was the sweet vision of his Arnelle.

∞

After hanging up with Winston, Arnelle dialed Cyrus. He picked up and said, "Hello?"

"Cyrus, it's Arnelle."

Excitedly, he said, "Hey, Girl! I'm so glad you called. I was hoping you hadn't given up on me."

"Cyrus, you know I will never desert you, but I'm not able to come to your trial. Not yet. You are my friend and I will help you, but my way. No lying and I have to know everything and I mean everything."

Solemnly, he said, "I know you're my friend, Arnelle. Probably the only true friend I have. I'm sorry about talking crazy to you all this time and I'm sorry I messed up your life."

"You didn't mess up my life. I did what I did to help you and believe it or not, I did get something out of it. Cyrus, I'm in love with Winston Carter. I fell in love with him years ago and we've run into each other again in Philadelphia. We're seeing each other and it's looking serious, but there's a problem. Robin put something in his drink that night and it affected his memory and he doesn't even remember me."

Cyrus yelled, "For real? Damn. I'm sorry, Arnelle, if…"

"Don't be. God saw fit to send him back into my life, and I'm not about to mess it up, so you see the position I'm in?"

"I know you won't let me down. You're my girl! I saw him today in court. He looks pretty cool. I can see you guys together. I hope everything works out for you."

She stood and walked over to the mirror and leaned against the dresser. "I'm in Texas right now, but I'll be in California in three days to visit Winston. I'll call you so we can meet. Just be cool."

"I will and thanks."

"You're welcome. I'll holler."

"Goodnight. Kiss MaLeah for me and tell your folks hello."

"I will. Goodnight."

∞

Craig helped Venice cook dinner for Lamar and Tressa. This would be their first dinner together since their wedding. As Craig tended to the steaks, Venice said, "Babe, can I talk to you about something?"

Smiling, he said, "Sure, Sweetheart. What's up?"

Turning, he saw the stress on his wife's face and was concerned. "What's wrong?"

Wiping her hands on a dish towel, she said, "It's about Winston and Arnelle."

"What about them?"

"Arnelle is the woman Winston met in California that time when he was drugged."

Dropping the utensil he held in his hand, he asked, "What did you say?"

Sighing, she sat down and covered her face.

"Arnelle made me promise not to say anything. She said she was going to tell Winston everything as soon as she could find a way. She didn't drug him, but she knows who did. She was in love with him then and she's in love with him now."

Craig shook his head in anger and sat down across from her. "Wait! Wait! Wait! So you mean to tell me Arnelle was involved in that shit that went down?"

"Yes, but she didn't expect anything like that to happen. No one was supposed to get hurt. She loves him."

"I'll be damned! Winston was beginning to suspect Arnelle was the woman he met, but only because she's been avoiding telling him where they met in the past. I can't believe this! Venice, Winston has a right to know this!"

Touching his hand lovingly, she said, "I know, Babe, but I promised. I don't want to have any secrets between us and they are our friends."

Covering his face, Craig sighed. "Tell me everything."

Venice began to explain, and most surprising was the part about MaLeah and that Arnelle was planning on telling Winston everything when she visited him in California. Craig's heart ached for his friend because he knew how heartbreaking it was going to be for him when he discovered the truth. Once Venice finished telling him the whole story, Craig stood and walked over to the window and stared outside in silence. He stood there suspended in deep thought for what seemed like an eternity, then said, "Venice, if Arnelle doesn't tell Skeeter before he gets back to Philly...I will. The man has a right to know what happened to him and the fact that he has a child."

She walked to him and hugged him tightly. Laying her head against his chest, she answered, "I agree, Babe. They're in love and that baby needs her parents."

Kissing her cheek, he said, "Let's finish dinner."

Wiping away a tear, she smiled. "Okay."

∞

The next two days, Arnelle and MaLeah spent time with Keaton. They planned to surprise him at his restaurant. When they walked in, the aroma of entrees hit Arnelle in the face. They were seated and given menus. MaLeah laughed and giggled in her highchair.

"Do you need a minute to look over the menu?" the waitress asked.

"No, I know what I want."

Arnelle ordered their food and handed the menus to the waitress. Before she walked off, Arnelle asked, "Is Keaton Lapahie in?"

"Yes, he is."

"Could you tell him I would like to see him?"

The waitress frowned. "Is anything wrong?"

"Oh no," Arnelle replied before smiling. "I just want to say hello to him."

"I'll get him."

MaLeah chewed on a cracker as Arnelle scanned the dessert menu. A few minutes later, MaLeah clapped and smiled, seeing her uncle approaching.

"Hey, Rugrat!"

Keaton pulled MaLeah from the booster seat and planted kisses on her chubby cheeks. Arnelle looked up and smiled at the two. Keaton leaned down and gave Arnelle a kiss before sitting in the seat across from her.

"So," Keaton began as he held MaLeah in his lap, "what brings you guys to town?"

"We thought we would come up and hang out with you for a day or two."

"That's great."

"Are you sure we're not cramping your style?"

He leaned back and looked at her sarcastically.

"Why, are you going to try to hook me up? Again?"

Arnelle reached over and held his free hand. "Dear, brother, you are handsome, intelligent, and just a nice guy."

"Thanks, Sis, but I'm too busy for that right now."

"Please, Keaton. What's that girl's name you've been hanging with?"

Laughing, he asked, "Are you talking about Syria?"

"Yeah, that's Miss Thang's name."

"She's okay."

Arnelle looked him in the eyes and said, "She's too high maintenance for you, and I don't like her snobby attitude."

"She's not the only woman I date. Besides, I don't have time to be tied down to one woman right now. I don't need anyone upset with me because I can't give them the kind of quality time they want."

Arnelle smiled. "Big Brother, you are going to get blindsided by love one day, and you're not going to know what hit you."

He laughed. "Yeah right." He tickled MaLeah and added, "MaLeah, your mommy is delirious."

MaLeah let out a loud squeal of laughter and gave her uncle a wet kiss on the cheek mixed with crackers.

Keaton wiped his cheek and said, "MaLeah, you're my only love!"

Arnelle rolled her eyes and watched her brother and daughter enjoy each other's company. Keaton told the waitress to give him Arnelle's ticket. Arnelle protested and told the waitress to refuse. The waitress was caught in the middle, so she laid it on the table and walked away.

"Bro, I want to pay for my food, thank you. You do have a business to run."

"You're family; now give me the ticket."

He yanked the ticket out of her hand and said, "Don't make me get ghetto in here, Arnelle."

She laughed. "I'll let you win this time, Keaton."

"I'm not hearing your noise, Arnelle."

They laughed and Keaton fed MaLeah as Arnelle ate her dinner.

∞

In his office, Keaton held a sleeping MaLeah as Arnelle stretched out on the sofa.

"Sis?" he said softly.

"Yeah?"

"Have you come clean with MaLeah's dad yet?"

Arnelle sat up, her back rigid. "No, Keaton; I haven't. I'll tell him soon enough."

"You should, Arnelle. He needs to know he has a daughter. You are wrong for keeping that from him."

She stood and took MaLeah from his arms, clearly agitated at Keaton's meddling.

"I don't need you to remind me every minute, Keaton."

He folded his arms. "Oh, so you're mad at me now?"

"Keaton, I came here to have a nice visit with you, not to argue. I said I would handle Winston, so let me handle it, okay?"

Keaton stood and walked to Arnelle. Concerned was etched in his face. "Arnelle, if I didn't love you and MaLeah, I would keep my mouth shut. As a man, I would be pissed if a woman kept something like this from me. Tell the man and tell him now."

He rubbed MaLeah's pigtails and looked at Arnelle. Tears started to form in her eyes as she said, "I'm going to tell him, Keaton. I'm going to see him in California day after tomorrow."

"Good. Are you going to try and see Cyrus while you're out there?"

"Yes, but Winston doesn't know Cyrus and I are friends."

Keaton locked gazes with her again and asked, "You haven't told him? Arnelle, what the hell are you trying to do? I thought you wanted a relationship with Winston."

"I do, Keaton!"

He put his hands over his face and said, "Arnelle, my dear sister, Winston is going to freak the hell out if he finds all this information out from anyone except you."

She lowered her head. "I'm scared, Keaton."

"It'll be fine; just tell him the truth. All of it."

Arnelle took a breath and sat down. "Keaton, there's something else I have to tell you."

"What?"

She proceeded to tell Keaton the whole story. When she was finished, all Keaton could do was stare at her.

He stood and walked over to the window. "Arnelle, how in the hell did you let things get so out of hand?"

"I don't know. Winston is going to hate me."

"Do you want me to talk to him?"

"No, Daddy's campaign can't afford a scandal involving this or Cyrus."

He took MaLeah from Arnelle's arms and said, "Let's go. We'll finish talking about this at my house. Don't worry, Arnelle. Everything will be okay."

Arnelle followed him as he carried his sleeping niece out of the restaurant and to his car. Once they arrived at Keaton's house, he didn't try to judge his sister for the things she had done. Instead, he tried to reassure her that everything would be okay. Everyone has that one thing he or she regretted. Arnelle was no different.

CHAPTER TEN

The plane ride to California wasn't as long as Arnelle had hoped. Everything Keaton told her was true. She needed to come clean and be honest with Winston even if it damaged or ruined their relationship. The fact was he needed to know he was a father.

As she walked through the tunnel into the airport, she was met by a gentleman holding a sign with her name on it. She smiled, remembering Winston saying he was going to have someone pick her up.

She walked up to the gentleman and said, "I'm Arnelle Lapahie."

"Good afternoon, Ma'am. Let's get your luggage. Mr. Carter will be pleased to know you have arrived."

"Thank you, Mr. ..."

"Charlie, Ma'am. You can call me Charlie. Mr. Carter hired me to be at your disposal while you're here. I'll take you wherever you need to go. Welcome to Los Angeles."

"Thank you, Charlie."

Charlie retrieved Arnelle's luggage and escorted her to the waiting limo. Arnelle froze and said, "He hired a limo for me?"

"Yes, Ma'am."

Arnelle smiled and said, "Now if I have to call you Charlie, you can at least call me Arnelle instead of Ma'am, okay?"

He closed the trunk. "Okay, Arnelle."

"Much better."

Charlie smiled and opened the car door for her. Inside was a bouquet of peach roses and a note. Arnelle slid inside the car and opened the note.

Welcome to LA, Devil Woman!

I hope your trip was pleasant. These flowers are for you because they represent your beauty, both outer and inner. You are truly a breath of fresh air in my life. I can't even put into words what you mean to me. Now that you're here, I plan to make all your dreams come true for you are my dream come true.

See you soon.

Love Ya!

Winston

Arnelle crushed the note to her heart and said a prayer, one of courage to do what she came to do, which was to tell the truth. It was going to be very difficult, but she vowed to get through it one way or another.

The driver pulled up to the front of the hotel. The door swung open and a smiling hotel employee said, "Welcome to the Maserati."

Arnelle stepped out and looked up at the tall building. Charlie gathered her bags and followed her inside.

She was heading to the check-in desk when Charlie said, "Arnelle, this way."

"You already have a key?"

"Mr. Carter made it a point to see to your comfort."

The elevator ride was swift and within minutes, the doors opened. She followed Charlie down the hallway. He opened the door and as they stepped in, Arnelle knew Winston spared no expense in regard to comfort. The massive living area was shining with gold fixtures. Charlie continued into a back room which she presumed was the bedroom. She followed and was left breathless at the huge bed. Thoughts raced through her mind of she and Winston tangled in the sheets.

Charlie snapped her out of her daydream when he asked, "Would there be anything else, Arnelle?"

"Oh no, Charlie. Thank you so much."

He walked over to her and gave her a cell phone.

"All you have to do is push '2' on this phone and you'll reach me. The '1' button is reserved for Mr. Carter if you need him while he's out."

Arnelle shook Charlie's hand and said, "Thank you so much. I guess Winston didn't leave anything out."

"No, he didn't and I can see why. You are a very lovely young lady."

"Thank you, Charlie, and I guess I'll see you tomorrow."

He tilted his hat and said, "Good evening, Arnelle, and have a great time in L.A. Mr. Carter should arrive in approximately two hours."

Arnelle closed the door and turned around to take in the beauty of the room once more. She slid her hands in the back pockets of her jeans and sighed.

"Well, Arnelle, you have two hours before Winston walks in. You can do this, girlfriend. Damn it! I'm talking to myself."

She cursed herself and walked back into the bedroom. On the bed was a large box she hadn't noticed. She moved closer to inspect it. On top was another note in Winston's handwriting.

Hello again, Babe,

Do not open this box until later. I picked it out especially for you. When I saw it, I knew you had to have it. See you soon. Relax and if you get hungry, order whatever you want. I left instructions to make sure you have the hotel and staff at your disposal. Oh yeah, I love you.

Love Always…

W

Arnelle lay across the bed and played with the bow atop the box. She picked up the phone and dialed Cyrus' house. When his answering machine came on, she said, "Cyrus, it's me. I'm in L.A., and I need to see you. Call me on my cell so we can get together. If I don't answer, leave me a message. Hang in there, Bro; we'll get through this. I promise."

When she hung up, she called her parents to let them know shehad made it safely. They didn't know whom she went to L.A. to visit. She just told them a friend, but in their hearts they figured she was visiting Cyrus. Keaton, however, knew everything. She called him and told him where she was staying in case he needed to reach her. She hung up and within twenty minutes, her cell phone rang.

"Hello?"

"Hey, Girl!"

"Cyrus, where are you?"

"Court dismissed early, but I'm still at the courthouse. I checked my messages before leaving. When can we hook up?"

She looked at her watch and said, "I don't know. I just got here and Winston is probably on his way if you finished early. Look, I'll work it out somehow. It's going to be hard to go somewhere without him wanting to tag along."

Cyrus laughed and said, "You guys are really in love, huh?"

Smiling, she said, "Yeah. I can't mess this up."

"Okay, Arnelle. Just call me and tell me where, and I'll be there. Thanks for coming."

"You're my boy. I told you I would never leave you hanging."

"Thanks, Arnelle. I'll holler later."

"Goodbye."

Arnelle hung up the phone and checked the time. She didn't know how long it would take Winston to get back to the hotel. She hurriedly grabbed a change of clothes from her suitcase and headed for the bathroom.

∞

Winston climbed inside the rental car and headed for the freeway. It would take him almost an hour or so with traffic to get to the hotel. He couldn't help but smile with anticipation, knowing the love of his life was waiting on him. Even though they had only been separated a few days, he still missed her terribly. He checked his watch and weaved in and out of traffic, hurrying to get to his woman.

∞

Arnelle stepped out of the bathroom and checked her appearance in the mirror. She didn't know what Winston had planned for the evening, but for now, she had set the tone in her lavender satin lingerie. It fell long around her ankles and the open back plunged down to her hips. After fluffing her thick, raven hair, she lay across the bed next to the mystery box and waited.

∞

Winston opened the door and immediately, he picked up Arnelle's familiar fragrance. Smiling, he hung up his jacket and walked into the room. As he stepped into the bedroom, he thought he was dreaming. She looked like an angel curled up across his bed sound asleep and snoring. He sat down next to her and gently stroked her hair. She was dressed so sexy and the negligee she wore had risen up to expose her muscular legs. He leaned down, kissed her softly on the cheek and whispered, "Arnelle."

She didn't move. He planted a kiss on her ear and whispered, "Arnelle, Baby, wake up."

She stretched and yawned, then slowly opened her eyes.

Startled, she rose up and asked, "What time is it? I didn't mean to fall asleep."

He smiled and said, "You look beautiful lying across my bed. Now shut up and kiss me."

She smiled and linked her arms around his neck.

"I missed you, Winston, and I love you."

"I love you, too, Baby."

She pulled him down and savored the feel of his lips as he kissed her with a simmering passion. Winston was feeling as if his heart would explode as he listened to Arnelle moan just from his kisses. She reached up for his shirt, ripped it open and began to sprinkle kisses over his chest and neck.

"Oh, Winston, you mean everything to me."

Her heart was now pounding in her chest as Winston removed her negligee. He just stared at her as she lay before him.

"Winston, I..."

He placed his finger over her lips to silence her and continued to stare. She wasn't sure why he was staring, but she hoped he was remembering the passion they shared years before as well as recently. He swallowed hard and with glassy eyes said, "Don't move, Arnelle. I'll be right back. I need to take a shower."

Stuttering, she said, "I-I'll be here when you get back."

He walked into the bathroom and closed the door. Never in his life had a woman had this kind of power over him. He felt wild and out of control. He threw his shirt on the chair and removed the velvet box from his pocket. He opened it and took one last private look at the four-carat diamond ring he was going to place on her finger. No other woman had or would ever stir his heart, mind and soul as she had. He closed the box and finished taking off his clothes. He stepped under the hot steaming spray of water and cleansed his body.

∞

Arnelle could still smell his cologne on her body as well as feel the effects of his kisses. She heard the shower cut off and knew he would be back at her side momentarily. She loved him, and she had decided if their love was strong enough, it could survive anything, even the truckload of news she had to tell him.

Winston re-entered the bedroom with a towel wrapped around his waist. Arnelle rolled onto her side and said, "Why, Winston, you have me at a disadvantage. You have on more clothes than I do."

He grinned at her in silence and dropped the towel where he stood. Once again, she enjoyed admiring his beautiful body. She closed her eyes for a moment and then said, "Winston, you are beautiful. Come here, Baby."

He came to her. "Not as beautiful as you, Devil Woman."

She laughed and scooted over to give him room in the bed.

"Winston, can I open my gift now?"

"Not yet, nosey. Later."

Those were the last words he spoke before he disappeared under the bed covers. Arnelle gasped as he found what he was looking for. He reappeared later with a big grin on his face after Arnelle screamed out her love for him. He kissed her trembling lips and smiled.

"You okay, Baby?"

"No! Give me a minute, counselor. I feel like my heart is about to burst out of my chest."

∞

The afternoon had turned into night. Winston lay next to a sleeping Arnelle who was snoring with satisfaction and clinging to his warm body. He was surprised he wasn't in a coma-like sleep also. He and Arnelle had made love in every position known to man and then some. They had skipped dinner and now his stomach was growling. He reached over Arnelle's soft body and picked up the phone to order room service. She squirmed and snuggled even closer, but didn't wake up. He played with the strands of her long black hair before sliding out of bed. He picked up the empty condom wrappers and padded to the bathroom. It was there he picked up the velvet box and quietly crawled back into bed. He pulled her into his arms and waited for room service.

∞

The knock on the door woke Winston out of his catnap. He put on his robe and quietly slipped out of the bedroom. The waiter wheeled in the cart with all types of covered dishes. Winston tilted his head because this scene seemed familiar.

"Would there be anything else, Sir?" the waiter asked.

Winston tipped him and said, "No, thank you. Have a nice evening."

After the waiter left, Winston raised the covers to inspect the delicious entrees. He poured two glasses of wine and strolled back into the bedroom. Upon entering, he noticed Arnelle had awakened and was in the shower. Winston smiled and set the glasses down. He entered the bathroom and opened the glass door to the shower.

"Winston!"

He scanned her soapy body and said, "Don't be afraid. It's only me. I came to tell you that dinner was here."

She laughed. "You're so bad. Come on in. The water's great."

He dropped his robe and stepped inside the hot, steamy shower. He pulled her body to him and said, "Woman, you're going to be the death of me."

She kissed him possessively. "I'm a doctor, remember? I won't let anything happen to you, Sweetheart."

They talked and washed each other's body, trying not to give in to the sensuality of the moment. It eventually got the best of them and once again, they took each other on a hot, passionate ride.

Once they finished, they dressed in plush robes, sat at the dinner table and stared at each other lovingly.

"This looks delicious, Winston."

"I knew you would like it."

He poured her another glass of wine and asked, "Do you realize what we just did?"

Nervously, she answered, "Yes, but according to the calendar, we should be safe."

"It's all my fault. I knew better, but for some reason, you make me lose my senses."

"You weren't alone in there, Winston."

He covered her hand with his and said, "I want you to know that I'd never leave you, especially if I've gotten you pregnant. Understand?"

She took a deep breath, looked away and said, "I understand."

"What do you want to do this weekend?"

"I want to go to the beach, eat junk food and lie in your arms."

Smiling into her dark eyes, he said, "I think that can be arranged, Doc."

"Now after church on Sunday, an old friend from college wants me to come by for a visit. That'll give you a chance to catch up on work or rest before Monday."

He leaned forward and asked, "Are you trying to get rid of me?"

She kissed his nose. "Baby, I'd never leave you. You're in my system. Understand?"

He laughed and came around to her seat and knelt down. He took her hand into his and said, "Arnelle, you are the only thing that has been right in my life. I never dreamed a woman with your spirit, beauty, love, hot temper, stubbornness and big mouth could win my heart as you have."

Tears formed in Arnelle's eyes as she touched his cheek, smiled and said, "You sure know how to flatter a girl."

Winston reached into his robe pocket and pulled out the velvet box. Tears were now running down Arnelle's cheeks.

Winston looked up at her, opened the box and said, "Arnelle Lapahie, will you please put me out of my misery and marry me?"

Arnelle stared down into his sincere eyes unable to believe the words she had just heard. He looked so scared and full of emotion. Arnelle finally looked at the brilliant diamond ring he held before her. She was amazed at the glittering gems.

He loves me, she thought. *He really loves me.*

She cupped his face, kissing him passionately and said, "Yes, Winston. I'll marry you."

He pulled her from her chair and hugged her tightly before slipping the ring on her finger.

"Thank you, Baby. You just made me the happiest man on earth."

With her arms around his neck, Arnelle looked deep into his eyes and said, "Winston, you have no idea how deeply I love you."

"I sort of have an idea."

"Thanks for my ring, but it's much too extravagant."

"Nothing will ever be too much for my woman," he said, giving Arnelle an extra squeeze. "Now, let's eat."

"Whatever you say, counselor."

∞

After making love again to seal the proposal, Arnelle lay awake staring at the huge diamond on her finger. Winston finally allowed her to open her surprise gift, which was a white silk gown with a matching robe. It was very revealing and she knew it would always be for his eyes only. Winston was her past and now her future. That is, if everything worked out the way it was supposed to. She kept hearing Keaton's warning in her ears. She eased from the bed and walked onto the balcony. Out there in the warm California night, her emotions overtook her. She was so afraid of losing him. She couldn't stop the tears from falling from her eyes.

"What's wrong, Arnelle?" he asked as he approached her with a concerned look.

Startled, she turned in his direction and wiped away her tears. He walked over to her and pulled her into his arms to comfort her.

"I'm okay, Winston. I just had a nightmare."

"It was only a dream, Baby. I'm here."

If he only knew the truth she concealed from him.

"I don't know what I'd do without you, Winston."

With sincerity, he answered, "I'd never let anything or anyone harm you, Arnelle. Nightmares are what they are...nightmares. Come on, let's go back to bed."

Turning back to the skyline, she sighed and said, "I love it out here."

Seizing the opportunity, he asked, "Have you ever been out here before?"

"Yes, a long time ago."

Tilting her chin, he asked, "If you love it out here so much, why are you looking so sad?"

"The last time I was here, it was beautiful and ugly at the same time."

He frowned. "What happened?"

She looked up into his eyes. A lone tear slid down her cheek.

"Something happened out here that I'm not proud of. I hurt

someone that I care about and I've been trying to find a way to fix what I messed up for a long time."

He kissed her and asked, "Is there anything I can do to help?"

She hugged him and said, "I hope so. I'm sleepy. Can we go back to bed?"

"Sure."

Taking her hand into his they made their way back to the bedroom and under the covers.

Arnelle knew it would be a matter of time before she would have to be straight with him. She just had to find a way to do it without the risk of losing him.

CHAPTER ELEVEN

Saturday, the newly engaged pair got up to do just what they had planned: spend a leisurely day on the beach. Arnelle put on a red halter top, khaki shorts and sandals. Winston dressed in navy shorts, a white T-shirt and comfortable canvas shoes. Every now and then, Arnelle couldn't help but gaze down at the ring resting on her finger.

"You ready?" Winston asked.

"In a minute."

Winston turned and looked at Arnelle, his face full of concern. "Are you sure you're okay? I mean last night that nightmare had you pretty shaken up."

"I'm okay," Arnelle replied. She turned to him. "Thanks to you."

"I'm here for you, Sweetheart."

"I'm sorry I woke you up."

Winston ran his hand through Arnelle's hair. "When I saw you on the balcony, I didn't know what to think. Arnelle, if something's bothering you, please come to me. Whether it is a nightmare or whatever. I'll do whatever I can to make things better, okay?"

"Thank you." She kissed his chin. "Now, I'll be ready in a moment. I still have some primping to do, so I'll meet you in the lobby in five minutes."

He grabbed his keys. "All right. I'm going to time you, so hurry up."

She blew him a kiss. "I'm right behind you."

Winston closed the door and Arnelle quickly called home.

"Daddy?"

"Good morning, Sweetheart. How's California?"

"It's beautiful as ever. My friend and I are getting ready to go to the beach. Where's MaLeah?"

"Right here on my lap. Hold on."

Judge Lapahie held the telephone up to MaLeah's ear and said, "It's Mommy."

MaLeah grinned, and then coughed.

"Mommy?"

"Wow; that's a nasty cough. I miss you, and Mommy loves you very much. I'll be home soon, and I might be bringing you a surprise. I have to go now, but I'll see you soon. I love you, MaLeah."

"I wove you, Mommy. Bye-bye!"

"Arnelle," the judge said, "how much longer are you going to be out there?"

"Just a couple more days. I should be back home by Tuesday. I see MaLeah's cough has gotten worse."

"Yes, but your mother's keeping a close eye on her. She's been putting vapor rub on her, and she's running the vaporizer in her room. If she's not any better in the morning, we're taking her to the doctor."

"Daddy, I'm coming home. I don't like the way she sounds."

"Arnelle, I'm sure it's just a nasty cold. Don't shorten your trip unnecessarily. We'll see you in a few days."

"I don't know, Daddy. I don't feel right staying here when my baby's not feeling well."

"MaLeah is still playing and getting into trouble. I'll call you in the morning and let you know how she's doing."

"Okay. Tell Momma I love her."

"I will. She's at the supermarket right now."

"See you soon, Daddy."

Arnelle paced the floor and checked her watch. She punched in another number.

"Hello?"

"Good morning, Cyrus," Arnelle answered. "Look, I don't have but a minute, but I'll meet you tomorrow after church."

Cyrus sighed with relief. "Thank God. Where do you want to meet?"

"You tell me, Cyrus."

"Just catch a cab to my house."

"Okay, I have to go, Cyrus. Winston's waiting on me downstairs. I'll see you tomorrow."

"Thanks, Arnelle."

"No problem." Arnelle hurriedly grabbed her purse and sunglasses, and raced out the door.

∞

Sunday service was uplifting and touching for both Winston and Arnelle. Winston held her hand throughout the whole service. After the eight o'clock service ended, they went back to their hotel room for a champagne brunch. Anything you could ever want for breakfast and then some was available. Arnelle was partial to the omelets. Winston was a country ham and eggs man. He did venture out to taste the spicy omelet Arnelle was eating.

"So, Devil Woman. Did you enjoy church?"

Arnelle narrowed her eyes at Winston and said, "You'd better stop calling me that."

He laughed. "Nope. You earned that nickname fair and square."

She looked around to see if anyone was watching, and then she playfully flicked water at him.

He looked up, surprised and said, "A'ight, Arnelle. Don't start something you can't finish."

She looked at him and pretended to be scared.

"Look at you," he added. "You just left church and now you misbehaving. God don't like ugly."

Arnelle leaned in, grinning mischievously. "So I guess what you were doing to me this morning is okay with the man upstairs?"

Winston froze, his fork halfway from his plate to his mouth. He looked up at Arnelle. "That's different. I was…was uh…"

"Yes, Winston?"

Winston put his fork down and said, "Sweetheart, I'm a civil servant, and I was just doing my civic duty to please that booty."

"You're so nasty, Winston," Arnelle said as she leaned back in her chair.

"You like it."

Yes, Winston, she thought. *I like you very much.*

They finished their breakfast, went back in their room and lay down for a nap. Arnelle set her alarm for her three o'clock meeting with Cyrus. Winston held her possessively and minutes later, they were asleep.

∞

The cab pulled up to the security entrance of the gated community.

Static resonated and then a guard asked, "May I help you?"

Arnelle rolled down the window and answered, "Arnelle Lapahie to see Cyrus McDaniels."

The guard checked his clipboard and said, "Go right ahead, Ma'am."

The cab pulled into the circular driveway and stopped. Cyrus opened the door with a smile and came out to help Arnelle from the car. He hugged her and said, "Hey, Girl. You found it."

Arnelle smiled and said, "Dang, Cyrus, I didn't know you were balling like this. Your house…I mean your mansion is awesome!"

"Cut it out, Arnelle. Come on in."

He paid the cab driver and escorted her inside. When Arnelle stepped inside the foyer, she was in awe.

"Cyrus, this is so beautiful!"

He folded his arms and said, "I'm glad you like it. Come, let me show you around."

Cyrus took Arnelle's hand and led her from room to room. Once the tour was over, they sat out on his patio and sipped lemonade. Arnelle lay back in the chaise lounge and put her sunglasses over her eyes. Looking at Cyrus, she could see the stress on his face. He was an unbelievably handsome man, all six-foot-seven inches of him. His dark brown eyes and long lashes were quite attractive on him, and when he smiled, women swooned. Arnelle and Cyrus had been close friends for years and even experimented with intimacy but realized they could never be more than friends.

"How did you get away from dude?"

Arnelle took a sip of lemonade. "I told him the truth. I told him I was going to visit an old friend."

"He didn't try to come with you?"

"Nah, he said he had some work to do anyway." Arnelle looked up from her glass and directed all her attention to Cyrus. "Cyrus, what happened? Are you ready to tell me the deal so I can try and help you?"

Cyrus stood and walked over to his pool in silence.

"Baby Girl, I really got myself in a jam."

He walked over to Arnelle's seat and sat before her. It was obvious he was struggling with his words.

"Cyrus. It'll be okay. What happened?"

He told her how he had started a relationship with his accountant. Things were going really good between them, and he trusted her with his money.

"Arnelle, before I knew it," Cyrus said, "things had gotten out of hand. I found out she was laundering money for her drug-dealing brother through my accounts. When I confronted her, she reminded me that I had signed every paper showing a transaction, and if I took her brother down, I would go down, too."

Arnelle grabbed Cyrus' hand. "What did your attorney say?"

"He said it's going to be hard proving that in court. It's my word against hers. So you see, it's up to your boy."

Arnelle hugged Cyrus' neck and said, "We'll work something out, Cyrus. Now, let me have some of that delicious-looking fruit."

"Arnelle, what's that big rock on your finger?"

She stretched out her hand and said, "He asked me to marry him."

"No shit? Congratulations! I'm happy for you. Hey, I have two court-side tickets for the Lakers game tonight. Why don't you take your boy out? He likes basketball, right?"

She smiled. "Yes, he does and thanks, Cyrus."

"Does MaLeah like him?"

Her eyes widened. "He doesn't know I have a daughter. I haven't told him yet."

"Well, you'd better hurry and tell him." Cyrus cleared some of their dishes. "Whatever happened to MaLeah's dad?"

"I don't want to talk about that right now," she said before clearing her throat. "Okay?"

"Whatever you say, Baby Girl."

They sat at the table and enjoyed fresh fruit with lemonade.

∞

Winston had gone over his notes a dozen times. He knew he was ready for court, but since his mind constantly strayed to Arnelle; he had to be sure. He twirled his pen between his fingers and wondered if he should've gone with her. He checked his watch again and realized she had been gone for almost three hours. He paced the floor trying not to worry. Just when he was about to call her, Arnelle walked through the door with a big smile. He sighed with relief and tried not to show his concern.

"I take it you had a good time?"

She threw her arms around his neck. "Yes, my darling. I had a great time."

"So who is this friend? Do I have any reason to be jealous?"

She laughed. "Winston, I love only you and you have nothing to worry about. I just went to visit an old friend from college."

He studied her expression and relaxed, seeing the depth of love in her eyes.

"Woman, don't ever make me worry like this again."

"You were worried about me?"

He embraced her possessively and said, "You better believe it. Now kiss me."

"Winston Carter, I'm going to..."

He cut off the rest of her sentence as he covered her lips with his. When he released her, she was glowing.

"I have a surprise for you," she stuttered.

"You do?"

Arnelle reached inside her purse and pulled out the Lakers game tickets. Winston studied them and asked, "Where did you get these?"

"A gift from my friend."

He kissed her again. "You amaze me every day. Tell your friend thanks."

"I'll let you tell him yourself tomorrow."

"Him?" he asked, his voice slightly elevated.

"Silly, I do have male friends. He's harmless and you'll get a chance to meet him tomorrow, okay?"

"Okay. Now let's get out of here and take in some sights before the game."

∞

Charlie took them from one end of Los Angeles to another.

"Arnelle, since you surprised me earlier, I have a surprise for you also."

"You do? Winston, tell me!"

He caressed her hand. "Patience, my love."

Within minutes, Charlie pulled up to a large office building and parked.

"Where are we, Winston?"

"You'll see." He kissed her cheek. "I guarantee you'll like it."

They entered an office and Winston was greeted by a huge, caramel-skinned man. Arnelle couldn't hear everything they were saying, but she knew they were talking about her. Winston turned and introduced them.

"Nice to meet you, Arnelle," the man said before shaking her hand.

"Likewise."

He was carrying a two-way radio, and a voice boomed from the other end.

He answered, "Cool! We'll be right in." He looked at them and said, "This way."

Winston and Arnelle followed him into a dimly lit room and at that moment, R&B singer Maxwell entered. Arnelle covered her mouth with her hand and let out a low squeal. She looked at Winston and took in the big grin on his face.

She pinched him on the shoulder and said, "Are you trying to give me a heart attack? Do you know who that is?"

"Yeah, Arnelle. Dang, that hurt."

She rubbed his shoulder. "I'm sorry I pinched you, Baby."

Maxwell approached with his manager. He hugged Winston. "What's up, Carter? Who is this lovely lady?"

Maxwell took Arnelle's hand into his and kissed the back of

it. Winston eased her hand away from Maxwell and said, "Back up, Pretty Boy. This one belongs to me. Arnelle, I'd like you to meet Maxwell. Max, my fiancée Arnelle Lapahie."

"Congratulations. It's about time. It's a pleasure to meet you, Arnelle. You are a beautiful woman and if Winston wasn't my boy, I'd steal you from him."

Arnelle was still speechless. She stood mere inches away from one of her favorite balladeers.

"It's a pleasure to meet you also," she finally managed to get out. "No offense, but I think I'll stick with Winston."

Maxwell grabbed his heart, pretending to be wounded. "No offense taken. Well, you have a good man, Arnelle. Winston and I go back a few years, and you couldn't have chosen a better man for a husband."

Her heart swelled and she choked back tears. Linking her fingers with Winston's, Arnelle said, "Thank you. Can I tell you that you are my favorite artist?"

Maxwell smiled. "Thank you, Arnelle. Winston, it's great seeing you again. Thank you for introducing me to Arnelle and don't be a stranger."

Winston hugged him. "It's great seeing you, too. You take care of yourself."

"I will."

Maxwell turned to look at his staff. "Hey, guys, take a picture of us. I'm sure Arnelle wouldn't mind."

She was in awe.

"Come on, Winston. I guess I'll let you get in the picture, too."

Winston smiled. "Just watch where you put your hands on my woman."

One of Maxwell's assistants snapped the picture.

"Well, I have to get back to work."

Winston shook hands with Maxwell. "Thanks, Max."

Before walking off, Maxwell gave Arnelle a hug and kissed her on the cheek.

"Nice meeting you again, Maxwell."

"Same here, Arnelle. Goodbye."

As they walked away, Arnelle asked, "How do you two know each other?"

"His lawyer is a friend of mine. We went to law school together so I got invited to a couple of his CD release parties. We've been friends ever since."

"I'm impressed, Winston. This was a priceless surprise. I'll never forget this day."

"You're welcome," he proudly answered as he kissed her cheek.

∞

At the game, Winston and Arnelle yelled and screamed like most of the fans in attendance. Arnelle noticed the wives and groupies sitting and waiting to get close to the millionaire players. The game was close, but the Lakers ended up winning. All avenues of Hollywood were at the game.

On the way back to the hotel, Winston asked, "You feel like stopping to get something to eat?"

She snuggled up to him. "I'd rather eat in our room if it's okay with you. I'm kind of tired."

He kissed the top of her shiny hair. "Your wish is my command."

Charlie pulled up to the front of the hotel and opened the door for them. They bid Charlie goodnight, and Winston took Arnelle by the hand and guided her inside the hotel. They stopped to place their dinner order and a bottle of wine. The elevator ride to their room didn't take but a few seconds.

Upon entering, Arnelle asked, "Do we have time for a soak?"

"You bet. Lead the way, Babe."

The precision of how Winston washed her body was the most stimulating experience Arnelle had ever had. She leaned back against his chest and closed her eyes. The only sound was the rhythm of their breathing and the beating of their hearts.

He whispered close to her ear, "Arnelle, are you asleep?"

She stirred. "I think I did doze off for a moment. I guess we better get out, huh?"

"Yeah. Dinner will be here shortly, and I know you're hungry. Let's go."

He helped her out of the tub and dried her body lovingly. She did the same to him. Once they put on robes, they entered the living room. Dinner arrived within minutes, and they sat down to enjoy their meal.

"I'm going to miss you after you leave."

Arnelle took a bite of her food. "I'm going to miss you, too, Babe. I'm going back home for a while before returning to Philly."

"When do I get to meet your parents? You *are* my fiancée."

Nervousness crept over Arnelle's body. "Soon; real soon."

"When do you want to get married, Arnelle? I'd do it right now if you were up to it."

She locked gazes with him and said, "That's so sweet, but a girl does have to plan. You men."

"Yeah, we're cavemen and want to get straight to the honeymoon."

"You're so silly. What time do you have to be in court tomorrow?"

"Ten o'clock and I hope it's a short day so I can spend more time with you."

She stroked his hand. "Business before pleasure, Baby."

"You finished?"

"Winston, I can't eat another bite. This hotel has some of the best food I've ever tasted."

He gathered their dishes. "Yes it does." Winston glanced

Arnelle's way and she picked up the suggestive vibes. "Ready for bed?"

"You're so bad, Winston."

They entered the bedroom and the heat their bodies generated was explosive.

Winston took Arnelle on the ride of her life. He felt her body give into the effects of his lovemaking and it was unbelievable. He had never in his life opened his heart the way he had with Arnelle.

As he slowly ran his hand over her soft skin, Winston couldn't help but feel at home. He daydreamed about the faces of the children they would have together. Arnelle had filled a void in his life he thought would take longer to find. She would become his partner for life. He pulled her sleeping body into his embrace before drifting off into a sound sleep.

The events in court the next day were stressful. Winston was waiting for Cyrus to be called to the stand. It would be there that Winston would make Cyrus confess to the crime for which he had been charged. Winston couldn't help but notice that Cyrus seemed to be more relaxed than he had been the other day. He also noticed that Cyrus seemed to be staring at him on occasion.

As witness after witness was called to the stand, Winston realized that Cyrus wouldn't be called that day. He would have to wait a while longer to have his day in court. The judge finally dismissed court, so Winston called Arnelle once he reached the lobby. She told him that her friend would meet them in an hour at his house for dinner. Arnelle had spent the day trying to get her courage and thoughts together for tonight would be the night she would tell Winston everything.

CHAPTER TWELVE

Later, in the hotel room, Arnelle fielded questions from Winston about her "friend."

"Arnelle," Winston said, "what is your friend's name?"

"You'll see."

"Are you okay?"

"I'm fine, Winston." She really wasn't. Her insides were twisting in knots. This was the hardest thing she would ever have to do. "Now hurry with your shower or we'll be late."

What she wanted to say was that she prayed he wouldn't hate her for the rest of her life after tonight.

When Charlie pulled the car up to the security gate, the guard asked, "How may I help you?"

Without speaking, Arnelle handed the guard a card. He checked his clipboard and said, "Go right ahead."

Winston looked at Arnelle suspiciously. "Arnelle, what are you up to?"

She held his hand and closed her eyes for one last prayer.

"Winston," Arnelle whispered, "do you have a forgiving heart?"

Winston looked at her nervously and swallowed hard. She had asked him that the night they had dinner at his house. It seemed familiar then and it seemed even more familiar now. He was positive. He had heard that remark before. Something was too familiar and Arnelle fit right in for some strange reason.

"What's going on, Arnelle?"

Charlie opened their door and Arnelle stepped out without answering. Winston joined her at the door and she rang the bell. Within seconds, Cyrus swung open the door.

"Hey, Arnelle. I'm glad you two could make it."

"What the hell is going on here?" Winston asked. His eyes grew large as he stared at Cyrus and then Arnelle. "How do you two know each other?"

"Winston, please come in," Cyrus replied quickly. "Arnelle and I have a lot of explaining to do."

Arnelle couldn't look into Winston's eyes. If she did, she would see the hurt.

They followed Cyrus into a huge room. "Have a seat," Cyrus said. "Can I get you something to drink?"

"I'd rather stand, McDaniels," Winston replied, "and no, I don't want anything to drink. Now will someone please tell me what the hell is going on here? Arnelle?"

Arnelle went to him and looked him in the eyes. "Winston, I'm so sorry. There are some things in my past that you need to know about. Please, Baby, sit down so we can explain."

Winston was furious and scared. He prayed that Arnelle hadn't had an intimate relationship with Cyrus. He didn't know if he could handle knowing that. He decided to sit and prepare himself for whatever they were going to tell him. Cyrus poured himself a glass of bourbon and handed Arnelle a glass of wine.

"Winston, I guess by now you've figured out that I'm Arnelle's friend from college," Cyrus began. "I want to assure you that all we are to each other is friends. That's all we've ever been. I know the two of you are engaged and you couldn't be so lucky. As long as I've known Arnelle, there's nothing I wouldn't do for her. She feels the same about me. A couple of years ago, that dedication was finally put to the test."

Winston looked over at Arnelle who was silent and said, "Go on."

Cyrus stood and walked over to the window. He took a sip of bourbon. "Winston, you have to understand. When I was arrested for laundering money, I thought my life had come to an end. I didn't know what to do or who to turn to so I concocted what I see now was a stupid, idiotic plan."

Winston leaned forward. "What does that have to do with me?"

Cyrus walked over and sat down across from them. He continued, "When I found out that you would be one of the prosecuting attorneys, I called Arnelle. Carter, I'm not guilty. My ex-lover and former accountant laundered the money for her drug-dealing brother. I had no idea what was going on, but unfortunately, my signature is on every transaction."

Winston asked, "Why should I believe you?"

"Because I'm telling the truth. Drugs killed my younger brother, and I would never get involved with anything like that. If you knew me, you would find that I have several programs in place to combat drugs, not promote them."

Winston was feeling like he was being pulled in a hundred different directions. He looked over at Arnelle who sat in silence.

Winston frowned. "Arnelle, how are you involved?"

Tears had filled her eyes and were running down her cheeks.

"Winston, I now realize that you don't remember some things from a few years ago," Arnelle said, her voice trembling. "The night I met you at the hospital when Venice had the twins, I thought you were so angry with me, that you pretended not to know me."

"What do you mean pretended? I didn't know you when we first met."

"Sweetheart, we met a few years ago here in California. It was my job to meet you, seduce you and...well."

"And what?" Winston asked through clenched teeth.

"Cyrus thought that if he had some dirt on you, he could blackmail you into dropping the charges against him. Even though he wasn't guilty, he felt trapped. We didn't know what we were doing, and I didn't expect to fall in love with you."

He looked at her angrily and asked again, "What did you do?"

Gritting his teeth he stood and realized the unthinkable. "You were the ones who framed me with those drugs?"

Arnelle looked up at Cyrus with her tear-filled eyes.

"Cyrus, could you give us some privacy, please?"

He walked toward the door. "I'll be in the kitchen."

Winston sat in silence. Arnelle didn't know where to start. She explained how Robin had him handle the envelope with the hotel receipt so they could get his fingerprints. She went further by telling him how she was to put the drugs in his briefcase, but switched it out with sugar instead.

Jumping to his feet, he yelled, "Goddamit, Arnelle!! I didn't have sugar in my briefcase; I had cocaine in my suitcase!!"

"I didn't find out until later that Robin went back to your room. She told me she didn't trust me so she took the sugar out and put the cocaine back in its place." Sobbing, she whispered, "I never meant for anything to happen to you, Winston."

Getting up in her face, he screamed, "Do you have any idea what you did to me??"

"I'm sorry, Winston. I love you; that's why I didn't put drugs..."

"It doesn't matter now, does it? I was arrested for possession because of you...you... Get the hell away from me!!" he yelled as he pushed past her and headed toward the door.

"Winston!"

He stopped and without turning, he asked, "How could you, Arnelle? I honestly can't believe that you could've ever loved me when I see the things you're capable of."

The tears continued to run down her face as he turned to face her.

With his voice barely above a whisper, their eyes met. He asked, "How could you leave me in that room like that?"

"I do love you, Winston. I loved you then, and I love you now. I made sure no harm came to you. I called for medical assistance."

The room grew quiet except for their heavy breathing.

"Well," Winston said, "obviously I was harmed since I have no recollection of you or that night. Arnelle, people don't do things like this to the people they love. I thought I knew you, but I was wrong."

"Winston, no! You have to understand. I was helping a friend. That's why I never gave Cyrus the envelope with your fingerprints on it. I convinced him to fight his case the right way."

"How gallant of you," Winston said sarcastically.

"When I ran into you at the hospital that night, I almost passed out. I never thought I would see you again. When Lamar introduced us, I thought you were just being stubborn, so I went along with your little game."

"Is that why you were so mean to me?"

"Yes. It wasn't until later that I realized you really didn't remember me. That's when I came to the conclusion that the drug Robin gave you must've caused memory loss. I was hoping that spending time with you would've made you remember me...us."

Winston was clearly hurt. She could see his heart breaking right before her eyes. He backed away from her.

"You had a lot of nerve to be angry with me when it was you that did me wrong? Don't you realize I could have all of you charged with assault? Hell, maybe that's exactly what I should do!"

Arnelle grew scared. "I was confused, Winston!" she yelled. "I know I should've told you right away, but I was scared."

Winston shook his head and muttered, "This is some foul shit! When I got out of the hospital, I did some investigating on my own. The police thought I overdosed on that shit. When they couldn't find my fingerprints on any of the drugs, they dropped the case due to lack of evidence. I almost lost my job over this bullshit!!"

Arnelle tried to approach him, but he held his hand up for her to stay away. He gritted his teeth and said, "You're the woman the bellhop saw me with. Since I didn't remember anything, I thought he was mistaken. When I tried to get access to hotel security tapes, they were mysteriously missing. I guess you and your crew thought of everything, huh? Damn you, Arnelle! I have to get out of here. I'm sorry I ever met you. I'll send Charlie back for you so you can get your shit and get the hell away from me."

Arnelle ran toward him in desperation.

"Please, Winston, don't leave. There's more I haven't told you..."

Winston raised his hand. "Arnelle, stay away from me, okay? I can't stand the sight of you right now."

He practically ran out the door. Arnelle followed, screaming, "Winston, please! I need to tell you about our..."

Her pleas were ignored. All she saw were the taillights as the car sped away from the house.

Arnelle sobbed and sank to the floor as her world came crashing down. Everything she wished to keep silent had fallen upon her with a vengeance. Winston had walked out on her before she had gotten the chance to tell him about MaLeah.

Cyrus ran into the foyer and asked, "What happened?"

"He hates me, Cyrus! I've lost him!"

Cyrus lifted a hysterical Arnelle and took her upstairs to a guest room.

"Arnelle, calm down," he said. "He's just shocked right now. I'm sure once he cools down everything will be okay."

"No, it won't! He's gone, don't you understand? I messed up the only chance I've ever had for MaLeah to get to know her father."

Cyrus tilted his head. "Wait. You mean to tell me that Carter's MaLeah's dad? Man, I don't know how I missed that one. Arnelle, he doesn't know?"

"He ran out before I could tell him."

Cyrus hugged Arnelle, realizing it was now his turn to help her.

"Everything will be okay, Arnelle. Let me get you something to drink so we can talk. You've always been in my corner; now it's my turn to be here for you."

∞

Winston had Charlie drop him off at a nightclub not far from the hotel. He had to get himself together. He had never felt as lost as he did at the moment. He didn't even know if he had done the right thing by walking out on Arnelle. His manhood told him yes because no man should allow a woman to disrespect him like Arnelle had done.

"Can I get you something?"

Winston looked up and saw the waitress waiting for his response.

He thought for a moment. "Scotch and water."

"I'll be right back, Sir."

"Wait! Make it a double."

"Yes, Sir."

Winston put his hand over his face in despair. *What the hell have I gotten myself into*, he thought. *Arnelle, why did you have to lie to me?*

The waitress returned with his drink, and Winston quickly threw the brown liquid to the back of his throat. He felt it burn as it went down and ordered another before the waitress could walk off.

∞

A couple of hours later, he found himself drunk and miserable. He returned to the hotel room and was glad Arnelle wasn't there. Her things were there, but she was nowhere to be found. He had no idea what he would say or do if he saw her. What made him so angry was the fact that he had trusted her. He poured himself another drink and after taking a sip, he threw the glass against the wall and sank down on the bed.

"Damn you, Arnelle!"

He dropped onto the bed and fell into a drunken sleep.

∞

Arnelle sat down on the bed of the guestroom, dressed in one of Cyrus' oversized shirts. A glass of Cristal was in her hand.

"Arnelle, are you sure you don't want me to drive you back to the hotel? I mean Winston must've cooled down my now and you guys need to talk about MaLeah."

She took a sip of her champagne. Her hands trembled as she drank.

"I don't think Winston ever wants to lay eyes on me again, and I can't blame him."

Cyrus turned to walk out of her room and said, "It'll be okay, Arnelle. Get some rest. What time does your flight leave to-morrow?"

"Three o'clock." She sniffled into her glass, tears still falling.

Cyrus came back to her and pulled Arnelle into a hug. "If I'm out of court in time, I'll take you to the airport, okay?"

She nodded and blew her nose. Cyrus left the room, and Arnelle sat on the bed, looking dejected and feeling as if her whole world had come to a disastrous end.

CHAPTER THIRTEEN

The next morning, Winston walked into court and made unavoidable eye contact with Cyrus. He wasn't feeling like himself, mostly from the hangover he was suffering from. His eyes were bloodshot and he had a migraine. The alcohol he had consumed did allow him to get some sleep, but when he woke up, his thoughts went to Arnelle. Immediately, he felt sick. The judge called the court to order and they began another day of testimony.

∞

Arnelle let herself into the hotel room reluctantly. She hurriedly gathered her belongings so she could leave before Winston returned. About that time, her cell rang and she froze. She took several deep breaths and answered. "Hello?"

"Arnelle, where are you?"

"I'm still in L.A., Keaton. What's wrong?"

"MaLeah's in the hospital. She has pneumonia. You need to come home right away."

Arnelle's body went numb. "I knew I shouldn't have left her," she whispered. "My baby is sick."

"Arnelle, she's okay, but she's very sick. Have you told Winston about her yet?"

Through her tears, she said, "We had a fight and I didn't get a chance to tell him. Look, I'll talk to you when I get there. Tell my baby I'm on my way home."

"Okay and be careful."

Arnelle frantically packed her clothes. Before walking out, she left a note in an envelope on the bed. This was her last gesture to show Winston that she really was sorry. After leaving Cyrus a message on his phone, she hurried to the airport and took an emergency flight home.

∞

When Winston made his way back to the hotel room, he walked in and immediately picked up Arnelle's scent. He walked into the bedroom and noticed that all her belongings were gone. He felt an instant emptiness in his heart along with the hurt. Had he acted hastily and chased her away? He sat down and wondered what to do next because he didn't have a clue. Out of the corner of his eye, he noticed the envelope on the bed. He opened it, and slowly read the note. When he was finished, he cursed out loud and balled up the paper. Standing, he walked over to the garbage can and tossed it in. He changed his clothes and decided to go work out in the hotel exercise room. Hopefully it would clear his mind.

∞

Cyrus entered his house and immediately checked his messages. Arnelle's hysterical voice greeted him.

Cyrus, it's Arnelle. I had to go home earlier than expected. Keaton called me this morning and told me MaLeah was in the hospital with pneumonia. I have to go. I love you and I pray everything works out for you. Please say a prayer for my baby, too. Goodbye.

Cyrus knew what he had to do. He jumped into his Range Rover and headed to the hotel where Winston was staying. Thirty minutes later, he walked into the lobby and spotted Winston walking toward the elevator.

"Yo, Winston!"

He turned and saw Cyrus approaching. He punched the button on the elevator and asked, "What do you want, McDaniels? Haven't you and Arnelle done enough to me?"

"I need to talk to you, Carter. It's not about me right now. It's about Arnelle."

"Are you her messenger now?" he sarcastically asked as he stepped inside the elevator.

Cyrus followed and sighed. "Something's happened."

"More drama I'm sure," Winston mumbled in anger.

"Not really. Is there somewhere we can talk?"

Winston laughed as he stepped off the elevator and walked to his room.

Opening the door, he announced, "I'll give you five minutes; then I want you to get the hell out of my room."

Cyrus followed in silence. "Aren't you even concerned about her?"

"Yes. Just as concerned as she was when she set me up. Look, if she sent you over here to be some type of peacemaker, you're wasting your time."

Winston placed his keys on the table and looked at his watch. "You have three minutes left."

Becoming agitated, Cyrus walked over to Winston and calmly reported, "Carter, you didn't give Arnelle a chance to finish talking to you last night. She had something else very important to tell you."

Winston poured himself a glass of orange juice. "I think I've heard and seen enough from you and Arnelle."

"I don't think so. Don't you still love her?"

Covering his face momentarily, he answered, "At this moment, I don't know what I feel."

Cyrus turned and walked over to the balcony in silence. As he looked out over the Los Angeles skyline, he whispered, "Arnelle is scared and in a lot of pain right now."

"Tell her to join the club!"

Making eye contact, Cyrus revealed, "She went home to see about MaLeah who's in the hospital with pneumonia."

Winston looked at him with confusion. "Who's MaLeah? Her mom?"

Cyrus looked him square in the eyes and said, "No, MaLeah is *your* two-year-old daughter."

"What the hell did you say?" Winston asked, his fingers clenching the glass.

"I said MaLeah is your daughter. You and Arnelle have a daughter. That's what she was trying to tell you when you walked out last night. MaLeah has pneumonia and Arnelle went to be with her. I didn't know you were MaLeah's father until last night. Look, I just felt you had a right to know."

Winston was speechless and in shock. Cyrus walked toward the door and as he reached for the knob, he turned and said, "Carter, Arnelle hasn't dated anyone seriously since you. I was too caught up with my own life to put two and two together. Now that I know, I think you should go a little easy on her. Your daughter is just as beautiful as her mother and she does have your eyes."

Winston looked at his watch and solemnly asked, "What time did she leave?"

"I don't know."

"Do you know the name of the hospital?" he asked as he tried to swallow the lump in his throat.

Cyrus shook his head. "She didn't have time to tell me. She did say she would call me later at let me know how MaLeah was doing. Why?"

"I don't know yet. I have to get my head together. Damn it! Why didn't Arnelle tell me about the baby a long time ago?"

"Arnelle has always felt guilty about what we did to you. That's why she never tried to contact you. You said it yourself...you could bring all of us up on assault charges. She didn't want to risk having MaLeah taken away from her if you pressed charges. Arnelle was against the plan from the start but I pushed her. She really does love you."

"Whatever it's worth," Winston said as he looked down at that marble floors, "I have some people checking into your story. My colleagues would never want to send an innocent man to prison."

Cyrus extended his hand to Winston. "Thank you. Well, I'll get out of your way. Good luck and I'll call you once I hear from Arnelle."

"Thanks for..."

"I felt it was the least I could do. Goodnight."

Winston walked Cyrus to the door. When he was alone, he stared at the floor and whispered, "I'm a father" to the empty hotel room.

∞

A couple of hours later, Winston was sitting in the airport waiting for his flight. He'd called every hospital in the Houston area until he found the one where MaLeah was admitted. His mind was racing. He had no idea what he was about to face. Seeing Arnelle again after their fight was going to be stressful enough, let alone seeing the daughter he never knew he had. When his boarding call was announced, Winston walked down the tunnel to the plane.

∞

Arnelle hadn't left MaLeah's side since she arrived at the hospital. Everyone in the room had a worried look.

"Momma, Daddy, Keaton, I'm so sorry for leaving you guys responsible for MaLeah."

Judge Lapahie came to her side. "Arnelle, you are our daughter. There's nothing we wouldn't do for you, Keaton or our grand-child."

Arnelle was trying to be strong, but she felt now was the time to be honest with her family.

She leaned over and whispered, "Keaton, could you sit with MaLeah? I need to talk to Mom and Dad."

"Is everything okay?"

"I just feel like it's time I told them about Winston."

He kissed her forehead. "Everything will be cool, Sis. Go handle your business. I'll look after my little rugrat."

"Thanks, Bro."

Downstairs in the cafeteria, Arnelle shared the truth with her parents. Zenora frowned and asked, "Arnelle, have you've been carrying this burden around in your heart all these years?"

Arnelle fought to keep from crying; she could only nod. She made eye contact with her dad who said, "Why didn't you come to us? You know we would've helped you and Cyrus."

"See, Daddy, that's the point. I needed to learn how to fix things without running to you and Momma all the time. I needed to learn how to be Arnelle Lapahie, not Judge Lapahie's daughter."

"Do you love MaLeah's father?"

Arnelle raised her left hand and said, "Yes, Daddy. He asked me to marry him, but after I told him about the blackmail, he walked out before I could tell him about MaLeah."

Judge Lapahie stood and kissed her on the top of her head.

"What's done is done and there's no turning back. You knew

what you did was wrong and now you're suffering the conse-quences. Did we not teach you anything?"

"Herbert!"

"No, Zenora!! Arnelle needs to understand how many lives this idiotic scheme has affected. What you guys did to that young man is serious!! You're my daughter and I'll always love you, but you're going to have to face the music. I don't blame him one bit for being upset. I just hope this thing doesn't end up ruining your career because you damn near ruined that young man's life."

Arnelle lowered her head and said, "I'm sorry, Daddy and you're right."

Her mom patted her hand. "Arnelle," she said, "while your father and I are understandably shocked and upset, what's impor-tant right now is MaLeah."

"You're right, Momma. I'd better get back upstairs."

"Go on, Baby. Your father and I will be right up."

"Okay. Momma, Daddy, I'm so sorry I made such a mess of my life."

Zenora hugged her daughter tight. "Arnelle, there's no reason to keep beating yourself up about it because it's in the past now. Your job is to concentrate on MaLeah and getting her well."

Arnelle kissed her Momma's cheek. "You're right, Momma. I'll see you guys upstairs, and I love you."

In unison, they replied, "We love you, too, Arnelle."

When she walked off, Herbert said, "Now we know why she never wanted us to know who MaLeah's father was."

∞

The cab driver dropped Winston off at the front entrance to the hospital. He gathered his luggage and walked through the automatic door. When he walked up to the receptionist, she asked, "May I help you?"

Winston paused to calm himself. His adrenaline was rushing, causing him to hesitate.

"Yes, could you tell me which room MaLeah Lapahie is in?"

The elderly operator keyed in the name on the computer slowly.

"She's in room 6212 on the children's wing. Go around the corner and take the first set of elevators. That'll take you right to her."

Winston picked up his luggage. "Thank you."

The ride up to the sixth floor seemed like an eternity. He wondered what he would say to Arnelle when he got there. He also wondered how he would react when he saw his daughter for the first time. The doors swung open and he came face-to-face with Keaton. Surprised, Keaton said, "Winston, where did you come from?"

"I just got in. How's MaLeah?"

Keaton took a step back so Winston could exit the elevator. He looked at him in shock and asked, "Arnelle said she didn't get a chance to tell you about MaLeah. How did you find out about her?"

"Cyrus told me. How is she doing?"

Keaton took the luggage from his hands. "Why don't you come see for yourself."

Winston followed Keaton down the long hallway. Before entering the room, he grabbed Keaton by the arm.

"Keaton, Arnelle and I broke up, and it wasn't pretty."

"She told me and I'm sorry."

Keaton opened the door and allowed Winston to walk in ahead of him. He saw Arnelle leaning over the bed and could hear her whispering. He couldn't see MaLeah, but he knew she was there. His heart started pounding in his chest as he approached. Arnelle's body stiffened.

"I can't believe you actually came, Winston."

He looked at Keaton, awed by Arnelle's ability to know when he was present without looking. Keaton placed Winston's bags in the corner and said, "I'm going to run some errands but I'll be back. Are y'all cool? Winston, can I get you anything before I leave?"

"No, I'm fine. Thanks."

"Arnelle?"

"No thanks, Keaton. Drive safely."

Keaton left the room slowly, noticing that Arnelle had not turned around and Winston still hadn't approached the bed. Arnelle softly said, "She's awake if you want to see her."

Winston's legs felt like lead, but somehow he made his way over to the bed. He raised his eyes to look upon the face of a little angel…his angel.

Cyrus was right, he thought. *She does have my eyes*. He felt like he was going to break down and cry, but he couldn't, not now. MaLeah lay there obviously weak, but she noticed Winston immediately. A small voice whispered, "DaDee?"

That was all it took to cause the tears to fall from his eyes. Arnelle looked over at him, with surprise on her face. "She's much better than she was earlier," she said.

Clearing his throat, Winston asked, "Did she say what I think she said?"

"Yes, Winston."

"But how could she know that I'm…."

Arnelle turned to face him and said, "She knows who you are. I've been showing her your picture ever since she was born."

Winston discreetly wiped away his tears and asked, "What picture?"

Arnelle sighed. "A snapshot we took on the beach in California."

"I see. Why didn't you tell me about her, Arnelle?"

"Not now, Winston. Please…not now. I don't have the strength."

Winston looked around the room, not knowing what to do next. He walked closer to the bed and MaLeah once again said, "DaDee."

He went to her bedside, leaned down and gently kissed her. He felt an overwhelming flood of emotion. She looked like Arnelle, but definitely had his eyes. He knew without a doubt that MaLeah Lapahie was his daughter because those eyes had run in his family for generations. She stretched out her small arms for him, but he panicked, not knowing what to do.

"Winston, sit down on the bed. I'll put her in your lap if you'd like."

He nodded in acknowledgement. Arnelle slowly placed MaLeah in her father's lap for the first time.

"Watch her oxygen tube."

Winston realized how different it felt holding her. It wasn't the same feeling he had when he held his godchildren, Clarissa and C.J. He looked up at an exhausted Arnelle as he stroked MaLeah's pigtails.

"You look exhausted. Why don't you go home and get some rest?"

"I'm not leaving her for one second, but I'm sure you could use some rest. Have you checked into a hotel yet?"

Winston stroked MaLeah's cheek and said, "I'm okay and no, I haven't checked into a hotel yet. I came straight here from the airport."

She sighed and said, "You can stay at our house if you'd like. Momma and Daddy will be here in a minute."

"I don't think that would be a good idea. I'd be more comfortable in a hotel."

"If you say so, Winston."

Winston rocked MaLeah and asked, "Do your parents know about me?"

"They didn't until today."

"Winston, I hope we can put our issues aside until MaLeah's better. How long are you planning on staying?"

"I don't know. I'm not leaving until she's better."

Arnelle lowered her head and asked, "What about the trial?"

"It's in good hands," he answered as he checked his watch.

"Where did Keaton run off to?"

"He probably went to check on his restaurant. I'm sure he didn't go far."

Winston skillfully placed a sleeping MaLeah back in the bed and stood. He came around the bed and gazed down at Arnelle. He had to put his hands in his pockets because after all they had been through the past twenty-four hours, he still felt a strong urge to embrace her. However, his hurt overpowered it. Any other emotions would have to take a back seat for now because of MaLeah.

"I would like to freshen up a little, but I want to come back and help with MaLeah," Winston said. "You could use some rest."

Arnelle folded her arms. "I can manage, Winston."

"I know you can, but I want to help, so let me. Okay?"

She stared at him but couldn't figure out what was going on inside him. Did he still love her? Only time would tell. Arnelle thought for a moment and said, "If that's what you want to do, fine. Momma and Daddy can take you by our house to freshen up before you check into a hotel."

As if summoned, Judge Lapahie and Zenora entered the room.

"Momma, Daddy, this is Winston Carter, III, MaLeah's father."

Winston held out his hand to shake theirs, but Zenora pulled him into a warm embrace, cupping his face. She kissed him on the cheek and said, "I'm so glad you came."

"It's nice to meet you, Mrs. Lapahie. Sir, it's so nice to meet you."

Herbert smiled and said, "Likewise. I guess it's better late than never."

"Yes, Sir."

Judge Lapahie stepped forward and shook Winston's hand.

"Well, son, some years have been lost, and some undesirable things have happened to you; try not to look back. Instead follow your heart and try to move forward."

"Yes, Sir."

Arnelle whispered, "Daddy, Winston wants to freshen up. He hasn't had a chance to check into a hotel yet."

Zenora frowned. "Don't you want to stay at the house?"

He cleared this throat and said, "I appreciate your offer, but I'd feel more comfortable in a hotel under the circumstances."

Patting his shoulder, Herbert said, "I understand, Son. We can take you to the house to freshen up and work out the hotel details later."

"I would like to come back to the hospital as soon as possible."

Zenora said, "Winston, let's get you to the house so we can get some hot food in you. Herbert, let's go. Arnelle, I'll call you from the house to see if there's anything you need Winston to bring back."

Hugging her mom and dad, Arnelle said, "Thank you."

Winston went over and glanced at MaLeah one more time before picking up his luggage.

"I guess I'm ready, Sir."

Judge Lapahie smiled. "At ease, young man. Herbert is good enough."

As Winston walked toward the door, he turned and whispered to Arnelle, "I'll be back shortly."

She gnawed once again on her fingernail and nodded in agreement.

CHAPTER FOURTEEN

At the Lapahies' home, Winston was led to the guest room to freshen up.

"Winston, the towels are in the linen closet in the bathroom," Zenora said as she stood in the doorway. "When you're done, come on downstairs so you can eat before going back to the hospital."

Winston smiled . "Yes Ma'am."

∞

He quickly showered and dressed into some comfortable jeans and a T-shirt. He packed a small bag with a change of clothes to take back to the hospital. When he returned to the kitchen, Keaton was at the table adding food to his plate. He looked up and said, "Winston, you're following me back over to the hospital in Dad's car after we eat. He said he wanted to check into a hotel. Are you sure?"

"Yeah, I'm sure and I was planning on renting a car once I reached the hotel," he explained.

"You're family now, Winston, and Daddy doesn't mind you using his car. Look, you have a right to be pissed off because I know I would be if some shit like that happened to me. Arnelle is my sister and despite her bad decisions, I love her. I tried to get her to tell you the truth a lot sooner but she wanted to handle it her way. Cyrus is like a brother to her and I'm sure they never envisioned things would spiral out of control like they did. Arnelle loves you…that I do know. I just hope you two can work things out for my niece's sake. If not, I won't hold any animosity toward you because I understand."

Winston stared at the floor and said, "I can't promise anything right now. This thing has cut me too deep."

Keaton turned to him slowly and said, "I just want her to be able to let it go and move on with her life now that things are out in the open."

Winston shoved his hands in his pockets. "Keaton, I came to see MaLeah. I don't know if I'm able to deal with what happened between me and Arnelle. I need some time to think, okay?"

"Understood," Keaton responded as they shook hands.

"Where are your parents?"

"They had a campaign fund-raising dinner tonight."

"What type of campaign?" Winston asked as he fixed his plate.

Keaton looked up. "I guess Arnelle didn't tell you Daddy's a judge and he's running for mayor? That's one of the reasons she kept things on the DL. She didn't want to cause a scandal for Daddy's campaign."

Winston didn't comment. Instead he scanned all the food gracing the table.

"When did your Mom cook all of this food?"

Keaton laughed. "Momma always cooks like this. She makes sure plenty of food is around at all times."

Keaton and Winston shared small talk as they finished their dinner. Later, Keaton washed dishes while Winston prepared Arnelle a plate. With everything back in its place, they entered the garage. Winston eyed a champagne-colored Lexus LS 430 and a silver F150 pickup truck. He watched as Keaton went to the Lexus and opened the door. He turned and tossed Winston the keys. "Here you go."

Winston caught the keys and asked, "What are your parents

driving tonight?" Keaton laughed and said, "Mom's Escalade. The truck is Daddy's and the Lexus is Momma's. Daddy got Momma the Escalade for her birthday last year. She's a caterer and needs the room to transport her food. You know?"

Winston smiled. "Nice. Is it okay if we swing by a hotel so I can check in?"

"Sure. I'll take you to one near the hospital."

Keaton let the garage door up and noticed Winston's solemn gaze. He asked, "You got everything?"

"I think so."

"Okay. Now if we get separated, call me on my cell. Here's my card with my number on it. Let's roll."

Winston backed the Lexus out of the garage, activated the garage doors and followed Keaton down the street to check into a hotel.

$$\infty$$

Arnelle paced the floor not knowing how the hours would pass with Winston hanging around MaLeah's room. She knew that eventually they would have to talk about their relationship and what had happened between them.

A nurse came in and asked, "How's my little patient?"

"She's finally sleeping."

"Oh my. I need to get a blood sample."

"Can't you wait until she wakes up?"

"Miss Lapahie, your little girl is a tiger. It's best I get it while she's asleep."

Arnelle was exhausted and started to get angry. She raised her voice slightly. "I'm sorry, nurse, but you're not going to wake her up. I just got her asleep about thirty minutes ago. She needs to rest."

"Ma'am, you don't understand. It's best I do it now."

Arnelle stepped between the nurse and the bed and said, "You're not going to stick my daughter with that needle!"

The nurse tried to step around her saying, "Sorry, doctor's orders."

An unexpected baritone voice broke the exchange between the two women.

"Nurse, if you value your job, you won't take another step toward my daughter's bed."

Both women turned to see Winston standing in the shadows of the doorway. He walked further into the room, coming to a stop next to Arnelle. The nurse put the syringe away and said, "Since it seems like we have a disagreement here. I'll send the doctor in to speak with you."

Winston stared her in the eyes and said, "I think it would best if you did and your rudeness has been noted."

The nurse quickly left the room. Winston turned to Arnelle, who was clearly on the verge of tears. Still upset, he was unable to console her so he kept his distance.

"It's okay, Arnelle. I'll request a different and nicer nurse to tend to MaLeah," he whispered as he sat his bag on the floor.

"Thank you," she nodded in agreement.

"How's she doing?"

Arnelle walked over to MaLeah's bed and kissed her cheek.

"She's still coughing, but not as much."

"I brought you something to eat. Your mom and dad had a dinner to attend."

"Where's Keaton?"

Winston sat the plate down and said, "He was downstairs talking to one of the nurses. He said he'd be up in a minute."

Arnelle rolled her eyes. "Another woman is all Keaton needs."

"Really?"

Relationships were not a subject he wanted to discuss that night.

Arnelle looked at the food on the plate. "He claims running his restaurant doesn't leave him time for a serious relationship, but it doesn't stop him from adding to his harem of women."

"I see. So is there anything you need me to do?"

"Would you stay here with MaLeah so I can go down and warm up my plate?"

"Why don't you let me do that for you?"

"It's okay. I really would like to stretch my legs for a minute."

"Go ahead. I'm sure you could use the break."

"Thank you."

Arnelle exited the room. Winston watched her departure, still feeling mixed emotions. He turned and walked over to MaLeah's bed and sat down. He played with her pigtails and said, "My little angel. You have to get better so my mom can help spoil you."

His mom and dad were the two people he hadn't thought about in a while. He had been too consumed with Arnelle. He picked up the phone and dialed.

"Hello?"

Winston stared at MaLeah and said, "Hello, Momma."

"Hey, Baby! How are you? What's wrong?"

Winston sighed. "Momma, why did you ask that?"

"I know you, child. I changed your nasty diapers; now tell me. What's wrong? Is it the trial?"

Winston bit his lip. "Where's Daddy?"

"He's right here, now quit stalling and tell me."

"Tell Daddy to pick up the extension."

Winston's mom was now getting worried, and he could tell she was about to get upset with him. He didn't know how else to tell them but to just spit it out. He did decide to spare them the full details of the drama with Arnelle.

"Momma, I found out that I have a two-year-old daughter. I

didn't know anything about her until today. I ran into her mom a while back, and we started seeing each other again. We got engaged, then had a fight so now I don't know if we're able to mend the relationship."

"Why?" his mom asked. "What happened?"

"I'd rather not go into it, but Arnelle did some undesirable things and I can't handle it. I'm in Houston right now because the baby's in the hospital with pneumonia."

"Is she okay?" his father asked with concern.

"The doctor said she'll be okay in a few days."

In unison they answered, "Good."

"Momma…Daddy, I'm trying to deal with this situation between her mother and me, but it's not easy. My main focus is to concentrate on helping the baby get well."

Winston's mom and dad listened quietly. They could hear their son's pain in his voice.

"So what you're saying is you finally got your heart broken by a woman?" his mother asked. "I knew something like this would eventually happen to you. You've been fooling around with too many women for too many years."

His dad spoke up and asked, "You're not running away from adversity, are you, son?"

"Daddy, it's not that simple. There's more to it than that."

"Now you know how all those women felt when you used them for your simple little pleasures, then broke their hearts," his mother said, slight anger in her voice. "I hope you remember what I told you."

Winston sighed. "Yes, Momma. How could I ever forget? What goes around, comes around."

"Hold on, Sadie," Winston's father said. "We don't know the full story. At least hear the boy out."

"It's okay, Daddy. I did find out what it's like to love some-one and then have your heart ripped out by them."

"I warned you, Winston," his mother mumbled.

"Momma, I wanted to spare you and Daddy the details, but, Arnelle was involved with a couple of people who planned to blackmail me so I would drop a court case. I was deceived, drugged and lost some of my memory because of it. Now, I've learned that I have a daughter as the result."

Sadie Carter sighed. "Winston, I'm so sorry, Baby.

"It's okay, Momma; you didn't know."

"That's no excuse. I should've given you a chance to explain. You're my son and I'm supposed to stand by you and protect you. It's obvious you're hurt, and I certainly didn't make you feel any better with all my ranting and raving. Will you please forgive me, Winston?"

"Of course, Momma."

"Is this the thing that happened to you in California?"

"Yes, Ma'am."

His dad cleared his throat and asked, "Son, you don't remember this woman at all?"

"No, Sir."

Sadie interrupted saying, "I didn't mean to be so hard on you, Winston, but you have to admit there's been a lot of women. I knew it was only a matter of time before a child came into the picture."

The conversation went back and forth between them for several minutes. Winston needed to talk to someone about his ordeal and he did feel a little better talking to his parents.

He sighed. "I'd better go before I wake her up. I'll call you guys tomorrow and keep you posted on her condition."

"Winston, could you at least tell us the child's name?" she asked like a true grandmother.

"Yes, Son, we would like to know that much," his dad added.

Winston smiled. "MaLeah. Her name is MaLeah."

"Well, we hope MaLeah gets better soon, son. Keep us

posted and we can't wait to meet our granddaughter. Good-night, Winston."

"Goodnight, Momma…Daddy. Thanks for listening. I love you."

In unison they said, "We love you, too. Goodnight."

Winston hung up the phone and looked at MaLeah. She started coughing and within seconds was wide awake and crying.

"Mommy," she cried out.

"I got you, angel," Winston said. "Daddy's got you."

∞

Days passed and finally MaLeah was well enough to go home. Winston and Arnelle took turns staying by MaLeah's side. Back at the Lapahie home, an exhausted Winston collapsed onto Keaton's old bed. He'd checked out of the hotel, so that he could be closer to MaLeah. Before he could drift into a deep sleep, he heard a soft tap on the door.

He moaned, "Come in."

"Winston, I'm sorry to disturb you, but I need to wash my hair. Can MaLeah crash with you for a little while?"

"Sure."

He rolled over and saw MaLeah smiling at him. He smiled back at her and stretched his arms out for her.

"Come to Daddy, MaLeah."

Arnelle walked over and laid MaLeah across his chest. She giggled, then coughed softly. Winston kissed her forehead and said, "Take it easy, angel. You're still on the sick and shut-in list."

He looked up at Arnelle and asked, "Do you want me to wash your hair for you?"

Arnelle looked away. "Thanks, but I think I can manage."

He stared at her, causing chills to run over her body. She didn't know what kind of game Winston was playing, but she wasn't up for any games. She wanted to know if there was any hope for their relationship. So far, the subject hadn't come up. She did miss him terribly, and it had been agony being so close to him the past few days. Not being able to touch him had been sheer torture. Arnelle stood there a few more seconds, and then answered, "Thanks for watching MaLeah."

Before he could respond, she closed the door. He looked at MaLeah and said, "Your Momma just broke my face. You know that?" MaLeah played with the gold necklace hanging around his neck. He leaned back against the pillows and said, "Sweetheart, I'm leaving in a couple days, but I'll be back. Now, Daddy's tired so let's take a nap, okay?"

MaLeah snuggled up to Winston and closed her eyes. Minutes later, they were both asleep.

∞

Days later, Winston couldn't believe how attached he had become to MaLeah and Arnelle's family in such a short time. They had spoiled him to no end and still he hadn't talked to Arnelle about their relationship. He was going back to California the next morning. He figured tonight would be the best time to talk. After helping with the dishes, he volunteered to give MaLeah her bath. Arnelle took that time to go for a walk down by the lake. This was the place where she found her solitude. As a child, it had become her special place and if anyone needed to find her, that's where she would be.

Darkness had fallen, so she took her flashlight, gun and their German shepherd, Prince, and started through the woods.

Winston had enjoyed his playtime with MaLeah and so had she. MaLeah had gotten to the point where she would cry for

Winston to pick her up. This melted his heart each and every time. After putting her to bed, Winston returned downstairs to the family room. He looked at his watch and noticed it was about eight o'clock. He saw Judge Lapahie reading the paper and asked, "Herbert, do you know where Arnelle is?"

Her dad closed the paper and said, "She's down at the lake. Have you two had a chance to talk yet?"

"No, Sir. That's what I plan to do now. Which way did she go?"

Judge Lapahie grabbed a flashlight and walked onto the front porch. Winston followed behind and listened as he pointed in the direction.

"Winston, be careful. Do you have your cell phone with you?"

"Yes, Sir."

"Well, call if you get lost. Now, Arnelle has Prince with her and a gun so when you get about a hundred yards out, call out to her. I would hate for Prince to take a bite out of you or worse, Arnelle might put a bullet in you."

Smiling, Winston said, "Thanks for the information."

"Here, take her a jacket. I don't think she had one on when she left."

"You're not worried that she's out there alone?"

Herbert laughed. "Arnelle has been hiking these woods all her life," he replied. "She's right at home out there, and she has the dog with her, so she's okay."

"If you say so, Sir."

Winston took the jacket from him and started through the woods. He wanted to make sure he followed his instructions to the letter.

"Arnelle!"

She didn't answer, so he yelled again.

"Arnelle, where are you?"

Moments later, he heard her yell back, "Over here. Follow

my flashlight." Winston made his way through the trees until he came upon Prince who growled. Arnelle was sitting on a blanket, hugging her knees.

She said, "Down, boy. It's only Winston."

The German shepherd licked Arnelle's hand and lay back down.

"What are you doing out here?"

"I brought you a jacket. Your dad thought you might need it."

She took the jacket from him and laid it on the blanket beside her. Winston also could see the .38 revolver sitting next to her.

He slid his hands inside his jeans. "You know how to shoot that thing?"

Reaching for the gun, she asked, "Do you want me to show you?"

Winston threw up his hands. "I believe you, never mind."

Arnelle continued to stare out over the water in silence.

"Do you mind if I sit down?"

"Help yourself," Arnelle answered.

Winston sat down next to her and also gazed at the lake.

"Arnelle, I'm leaving tomorrow, and I thought we'd better talk before I go back to California."

She didn't blink or breathe. She only sat there in silence.

He looked at her and noticed she showed no emotion. He played with a blade of grass and said, "I appreciate you giving me the envelope."

"I would've never let Cyrus use it, Winston."

"Thanks for protecting me. That has to account for something."

Wiping her tears, she said, "But, it's not enough, huh?"

"I just don't know, Arnelle. I do have some good news though. My colleagues told me it looks like Cyrus was telling the truth about his accountant. I found out tonight that the accountant's brother was shot to death last night in a drug deal. Before he died, he gave a confession that Cyrus was innocent, so I guess it worked itself out after all."

DARRIEN LEE

"What do you want from me, Winston?" Arnelle asked, her voice thin. "I can't go on not knowing where we stand."

He reached over and turned her chin so she would face him.

"Arnelle, I don't know what I'm feeling right now. I mean I'm still hurt…very hurt. I never in my wildest dream thought something like this could happen to me. It's devastating to find out that you've been set up. Then to find out that you have a child as the result of it. The worst of it is that the person I cared about played me."

Butting in, Arnelle said, "It wasn't like that, Winston."

"Well that's how it seems to me, Arnelle. Look, all I know is I need time to deal with this. I know MaLeah is my daughter without a doubt, and I'm going to love her no matter what… that I'm sure of. Before I leave, I'm going to write you a check to compensate you for MaLeah's care."

"What are you talking about? She's my daughter!"

"She's my daughter, too." Winston sighed. "Arnelle, let me do this. It costs money to raise a child and in spite of what has happened between us, I want to do this."

Angry, Arnelle stood and said, "Well, I don't want your money, Winston, and I've been able to support MaLeah just fine by myself!"

"I know you have, Arnelle. Let me do this…please. It's the *least* you could do."

Arnelle sat back down and sighed.

"I don't want to fight, Winston," she said. "All I'm saying is I don't want you to feel that you have to pay me money for raising her."

"I'm writing you the check, period. If you want to start a college fund for MaLeah, fine. I don't care what you do with the money. I won't feel right unless I do something to make up not being there for her."

"It's not your fault that you weren't able to be there."

Winston didn't say anything because he knew that much was true.

"I wish I could feel differently about us," he whispered, "but I can't. I just can't be with you right now, Arnelle."

Tears fell from Arnelle's eyes as she slipped the engagement ring from her finger and handed it to him.

"I didn't ask you to give the ring back, Arnelle."

She stood and gathered her belongings.

"What's the point, Winston? You've made yourself clear. Wearing it would only be fooling me and everyone else."

He also stood, not wanting to accept the ring back. He put it in his pocket and folded the blanket for her.

"For what it's worth, Winston, I'm sorry about everything that happened and for the pain I caused you. I still love you very much, and I'm heartbroken that things have to end like this. I tried to prepare myself for this, but it doesn't make it any easier. I want you to be a part of MaLeah's life, so if you want to draw up some papers about joint custody, I'll sign them."

Winston walked closer to her and said, "That won't be necessary. I'm sure we can come to an understanding without the courts becoming involved."

Arnelle swallowed hard. "We'd better get back to the house."

"Arnelle, I…"

His words fell on deaf ears. Arnelle was already making her way through the woods, behind Prince.

∞

When they returned to the house, Judge Lapahie was still up reading.

"Goodnight, Daddy," Arnelle said before running up the stairs to her room and slamming the door.

Judge Lapahie met Winston coming in the door and asked, "How did it go, son?"

"As well as to be expected. I didn't ask for the ring back, but she gave it back to me anyway."

Judge Lapahie patted Winston on the shoulder. "Don't beat yourself up about it. What happened to you is not something a man can forget about overnight. I pray that with time, things will work out between the two of you. Son, I just want you to know that you can come here and visit MaLeah anytime you want until she comes to Philly. She's your daughter, and she needs her daddy and her mother. Now, go get some rest. I'll drive you to the airport in the morning, but I'm hoping my daughter will step up to the plate."

Winston handed him the flashlight. "Thank you, Sir. Goodnight."

Arnelle cried herself to sleep. She heard Winston knock on her door several times the next morning before he left. She couldn't bear to tell him goodbye, so she ignored his knocks. She knew once she got back to Philadelphia, she would run into him. She had to get tougher to be able to deal with the emotions she still carried for him. One of the first things she'd do was ask Venice's babysitter, Camille, if she would be MaLeah's sitter as well. As soon as the weather warmed up, she would bring MaLeah to Philly permanently.

CHAPTER FIFTEEN

Winston made it back to the California courtroom in time to see all charges dismissed against Cyrus. As they left, Cyrus said, "Hey, Winston. I just want to thank you for your help."

Winston closed his briefcase. "It's my job, Cyrus. Try to keep yourself out of trouble, okay?"

Cyrus laughed. "You don't have to worry about me. How did it go in Texas?"

"Not good. I mean MaLeah is fine and thanks for telling me about her. It's just that my relationship with Arnelle is basically over."

Cyrus put his hand on Winston's shoulder. "Winston, I'm sorry. This whole thing is my fault. Arnelle was only helping me out. You would expect her to help a friend in need, wouldn't you?"

The words Cyrus spoke hit home. He had said similar words to Victoria when he ran out to help Arnelle the night her home was burglarized. But this was a different situation with other people involved. Winston shook Cyrus' hand and answered, "Cyrus, I have a flight to catch. Good luck."

"Thanks, Winston. Good luck to you also."

Winston left the courthouse and was driven straight to the airport. He couldn't wait to get to the solitude of his own home. He had been on an emotional roller coaster the past few weeks and needed a much deserved rest.

∞

As the plane leveled off thousands of feet in the air, Winston pulled Arnelle's engagement ring from his pocket and stared at it. He remembered picking it out especially for her. He did miss her, but the pain she caused seemed to overshadow his loss. He tucked the ring back into his pocket and pulled out a picture of MaLeah. He smiled looking into the angelic face he had fallen in love with. He knew his life would never be the same having a child to raise and love.

∞

A couple of days later, Arnelle said goodbye to MaLeah and her parents. She knew she had to get back to work and start rebuilding her life. Losing Winston had shaken her emotionally. She had called Venice several nights earlier and told her the rest of the story she'd shared with her weeks earlier. Venice did her best to comfort her and told her to have faith and not let the breakup with Winston consume her. She told Arnelle to stay strong for MaLeah's sake. Venice gave her the good news that Camille agreed to keep MaLeah when she came to Philly. Arnelle felt a weight lift from her heart. She didn't want just anyone looking after MaLeah. She told Venice that she had decided the best thing to do was to go on with her life. Her love for Winston was still strong, but she had to face the fact that he couldn't deal with what had happened between them. They hung up from each other after shedding a few tears together.

∞

Arriving back in Philly later that night was bittersweet. She felt the loss as soon as she entered her home. It seemed like she had been gone forever. She called her parents and Venice to let them know she was home. She then ran a hot bath and eased into the bubbles. She was exhausted and wanted to get a good night's sleep before returning to work in the morning. Her heart was aching terribly, but minutes later, she was able to climb into bed and drift off to sleep.

∞

Winston had played several games of racquetball, and now, just before bed, his body was a little sore since he hadn't had a chance to work out for a couple weeks. He walked into his kitchen and looked at the clock. It was almost ten, and he subconsciously wondered what Arnelle was doing. He knew she was back in town because Craig had told him. Craig also informed him that they were having a dinner party at their house in a couple of weeks. He couldn't help but wonder if Arnelle would be there and how it would feel to see her after all they'd been through. That is, if she showed up at all.

Winston walked into his bedroom and sat down in the chair. He lowered his head and started talking to himself.

"Damn. Winston, my man, all you need to do is dust yourself off and move on. Chalk it up to being a fool."

He walked into the bathroom, showered and climbed into bed. Before going to sleep, he opened up the drawer to his nightstand and pulled out the velvet box. Opening it, he gazed upon the ring once more.

"Damn, Winston," he said out into the darkness of his room, "you're losing it. Forget about her. She played you."

He closed his eyes and tried to sleep.

∞

Arnelle thought her heartache would've eased by now, but it

hadn't. It had been a couple of weeks, and Venice noticed Arnelle had become a workaholic. She was the first to come in and the last to leave every day. She called her into the office for a talk.

"Arnelle, I know you're still going through some serious pain, but you have got to slow down a little bit."

"I know, Venice, but it's so hard. I feel like I need to stay busy."

"If anyone understands what you're going through, I do."

A knock at the door halted the conversation.

Venice opened it. "Damon, come in. I have your invoice all ready for you."

Damon Kilpatrick was one of the assistant coaches for the Philadelphia Eagles. Calling him tall, dark and handsome was an understatement.

"Hello, ladies."

In unison, they responded, "Hello, Damon."

He looked at Arnelle, smiled and asked, "Where have you been hiding lately? It seems that every time I come in here to invite you to dinner, you're MIA."

"I've been around, just busy," she softly answered.

Venice discreetly looked up from her computer screen at the two exchanging conversation.

Damon folded his arms and asked, "Are you ready to go out with me, Arnelle? You've been putting me off a long time now, and it's starting to hurt my feelings."

Arnelle smiled back at him. "Damon, I haven't been putting you off."

"Well, you've been doing something. What? Are you spoken for or something?"

Arnelle thought to herself, not knowing how to answer his question. She had told herself she was going to try and move on with her life, but it hadn't been easy. Damon was offering the perfect opportunity, but was it too soon? She had been back in Philly for almost a week now and she hadn't heard a word from Winston. It sunk into her that very moment that Winston had moved on. Now it was her turn.

"Come on, Arnelle. It's only dinner. You'll have fun, I promise."

Venice could sense Arnelle's reluctance to accept his invitation.

"Damon, Venice is having a dinner party at her house tomorrow night. Would you like to go as my date?"

Venice's eyes widened. She knew Winston would also be at the dinner party. Whether he would be bringing a date was unclear. It would be typical for him to be upset if Arnelle showed up with Damon.

Damon smiled. "You bet. What time should I pick you up?"

Arnelle wrote down her phone number and told him to call her later so they could discuss the specifics.

"I can't wait," he said as he tucked the paper inside his pocket. "Venice, what are you serving?"

"You'll just have to wait and see; now get out of here," she teased.

Backing out the door, he laughed and said, "I know when I'm being thrown out. Arnelle, thanks again for the invite and I'll talk to you later. Thanks again for all your help."

In unison, they said, "You're welcome, Damon."

When he closed the door, Venice asked, "Have you lost your mind?"

Arnelle sat down and opened some bottled water. "What are you talking about?"

"You know what I'm talking about. Winston will be at the dinner party."

Arnelle sat up and said, "Yes, and he'll probably bring a date. I need to move on. I love Winston, but I'm not going to sit at home crying over him anymore. I'm sure he's not crying over me."

Venice turned to her computer and said, "You don't know that for sure."

"Yeah right!"

"I hope you know what you're doing."

"I'm just trying to move on with life, Venice. That's all."

∞

Winston arrived at the dinner party early. He brought a colleague from his office as his escort. He had no intentions of starting a relationship with her, but for tonight, she was welcomed company. As more guests arrived, Winston couldn't help but look over at the door every time it opened. He felt nervous, and knew it was because he had no idea whether Arnelle would be there tonight. He turned for a moment to talk to Craig's assistant, Francine. When he turned back around, he saw Arnelle standing in the foyer with a man he'd never seen before.

He swallowed hard and noticed the dress she wore was elegant, but revealing. The royal blue fabric showed what no other man should see. Craig looked over at him and saw that famous vein appear on his forehead.

He walked over and whispered, "Down, boy."

Winston tried to remain calm, but his words came out angrily: "Who is that brotha with Arnelle?"

"One of the Eagles' coaches. I think his name is Damon. He's a client of theirs."

Winston noticed Damon's arm around Arnelle's waist. "He's not acting like a client."

Craig put his arm around Winston's shoulder and said, "You broke up with her, remember? She's fair game now, and there are a lot of brothas in Philly who would love to get with a woman like Arnelle."

Winston let out a breath and asked, "Where's Venice?"

"In the kitchen. What are you…"

Winston walked away before Craig could finish his sentence.

He stalked toward the foyer and locked gazes with Arnelle. He told himself to remain cool.

"Hello, Arnelle. You look beautiful, as usual."

He kissed her on the cheek, causing her heart to flutter.

"Good evening, Winston."

He looked at Damon and waited for Arnelle to introduce them. Damon noticed Winston's territorial stare and said, "Arnelle, introduce me to your friend."

Arnelle took a deep breath because Winston looked so handsome and he smelled heavenly. The spot he kissed on her cheek still burned from the softness of his lips. She snapped out of her trance and said, "Winston Carter, III, meet Damon Kilpatrick. Damon, Winston."

They shook hands and Damon said, "You look familiar."

"Unfortunately, my face gets plastered on TV more than I would like. I'm a lawyer."

Damon laughed and said, "More power to you. Nice to meet you, Winston."

He then turned to Arnelle and asked, "Arnelle, would you like something to drink?"

"Yes, I think I would. Lead the way. Goodbye, Winston."

They left him standing there with that vein pulsating on his forehead. Winston rubbed his face and felt the beginning of a severe migraine. After becoming involved with her, he hadn't been able to tolerate seeing any man put his hands on her. Tonight would be no different even though they were no longer together. He saw the way this Damon person looked at Arnelle. He was a man and he knew the man wanted Arnelle. But, what man wouldn't? She was beautiful, intelligent, fun, sexy as hell and happened to be the mother of his child. All the qualities he had fallen in love with. It was going to be a long night. He just prayed he could get through it.

∞

Sitting around the dinner table, the guests enjoyed various subjects of conversation. Winston noticed that Damon kept leaning over, whispering into Arnelle's ear. Each time he did, she would smile and lower her head shyly.

Winston couldn't eat his food for staring at the couple sitting across from him. One of Craig's female guests spoke up and said, "Arnelle, I don't see how you and Venice work around all those jocks all day. Isn't it hard?"

Arnelle smiled. "It's my job and I like what I do. I don't pay them any attention. I guess you can compare us to male OB-GYNs. Besides, we work with female athletes as well."

Everyone laughed at Arnelle's answer. The lady then said, "Well, I've heard nothing but great things about Bennett Clinic."

A male guest added, "Damon, I hope Arnelle and Venice are keeping your guys healthy so we can go all the way to the Super Bowl this year."

Damon took a sip of wine, smiled at Arnelle and said, "Mayor, I wouldn't trust them to anyone else. These ladies are amazing and a true asset to our staff."

Winston could see the longing in Damon's eyes when he looked at Arnelle. He wanted to change the subject. The conversation was getting way too personal. Craig watched Winston's facial expressions from afar. With the mayor of Philly in attendance, he prayed Winston didn't make a fool of himself. He knew his friend was in agony, but now was not the time to show it.

The mayor smiled. "Damon, you and Arnelle look good together. Could wedding bells be in the future?"

Arnelle nearly choked on her dinner. She coughed and took a sip of wine. She looked up at Winston, who was staring a hole through her. Her face was burning with embarrassment. It was obvious that Winston wasn't happy with the flow of the conversation. The mayor's wife nudged him and said, "Honey, stop embarrassing them."

Damon smiled. "Slow down, Mayor. You're all up in our Kool-Aid."

All the guests laughed. Damon continued, "Arnelle and I are friends. As far as anything more, well, that's between us. Now, enough about us; I want to know what's for dessert."

The guests laughed again and steered the conversation to another subject. Arnelle stood to excuse herself from the room. All the men rose as Arnelle headed out of the dining room and up the stairs. She had to get out of there.

∞

A few minutes later, Venice entered the nursery and found Arnelle sitting in a rocking chair.

"You okay, Girl? I warned you things might get ugly tonight."

Arnelle rocked the chair. "So you did. I can't believe the mayor was so nosey."

Venice sat in the other rocker. "He didn't mean any harm. I'm sorry about that. Winston looked like he was going to freak out. I'm glad he didn't show his ass. You know he's still in love with you."

"Please!"

Venice stopped rocking and said, "He is, Arnelle. You can look at him and tell. He cornered me in the kitchen earlier, asking about Damon."

"What did you tell him?"

Venice fumbled with her hair. "I told him Damon was a client and that you two have known each other for a while. Then I told him if he wanted to know more he would have to ask you himself."

Laughing, Venice said, "You should've seen his face! He is jealous as hell!"

"I don't know why. He made it clear that he couldn't be with me anymore and I can't say I blame him."

"I know, but I'm sure he'll be back. Damon is a handsome, successful man. Skeeter is just being a typical man. He can't handle seeing you with anyone else regardless of what happened between you guys."

Arnelle sighed. "While we're on the subject, who is that woman with him?"

"She's just a coworker. Don't worry because they really are just friends."

Solemnly, she responded, "I don't know about all that, Venice. Considering what I've done to him, I wouldn't blame him if he did find someone else. It would be hard for any man to get over what happened. He'll never trust me again."

Venice pulled Arnelle out of the rocker, hugged her and said, "Well, we're rooting for you two. Now let's go get some dessert."

When they got back downstairs, the guests were eating dessert. When Arnelle sat down, Damon leaned over and asked, "Are you okay?"

"I'm fine, just a little tired."

"We can leave whenever you're ready."

Arnelle smiled. "Thank you, Damon. I'm ready."

Damon stood and helped Arnelle from her seat.

"Craig, I'm sorry, but we have to leave. Venice, dinner was excellent."

Winston frowned and watched Damon pour on the charm. Before he knew it, he had put his foot in his mouth.

"Leaving so soon? Arnelle, I've never known you to eat and run."

Arnelle's head snapped around, and she gave him a warning look not to start tripping.

Damon smiled at Winston. "Arnelle and I have other plans, so we have to be going. It was nice meeting all of you. Have a nice evening."

The guests all said their goodbyes to the couple as Craig and Venice walked them to the door. Winston's escort whispered, "Is there something going on here that I need to know about?"

"No. I'm sorry. I'm just a little on edge. I guess I'm still exhausted from my West Coast trip. Do you mind if we leave, too? I'm really not up to being sociable tonight."

"Fine with me, Winston."

A few minutes later, Winston and his guest also left. He couldn't wait to get her home so he could call Arnelle. He wanted to know what all that flirting was about at the dinner table.

He had called her house a dozen times since arriving at home. He looked at his watch and noticed it was near midnight. He wouldn't leave a message; he just hung up when her answering machine came on.

He poured himself a drink and yelled, "Damn it, Arnelle! Where are you?"

Winston fell asleep in his recliner. When he awakened, it was one-thirty in the morning. He called Arnelle's house again and still no answer.

"To hell with this," he said. "I'm going over there."

It took Winston all of thirty minutes to get to Arnelle's house. He walked up to the door and rang the bell. Upstairs, Arnelle was startled out of her sleep by the doorbell. She first thought it was her phone ringing, then remembered she had the ringer off so she could get some rest. Her heart was pounding in fear. She noticed the time was two a.m., which made her even more nervous. She put on her robe, grabbed her gun and headed downstairs. When she reached the landing, she took a deep breath and looked through the peephole.

"Winston?"

She deactivated the alarm and opened the door.

"What the hell are you doing here?"

The air was cold and Winston had left his house without a

coat. He stood there in jeans and a sweatshirt. He noticed the gun. "Where have you been? I need to talk to you."

She bit her lip and laid the gun on the table.

"What? Winston, where's your coat?"

"I forgot it."

She grabbed his arm and pulled him inside.

"Get in here before you catch pneumonia. What is wrong with you? What are you doing here?"

Winston lowered his eyes and shoved his hands inside his jeans. Arnelle tied her robe over her scantily clad body and said, "Wait for me in the den while I make you some coffee or something."

Winston did as he was told. He had no idea what he was going to say to her. He just needed to be reassured that Damon wasn't with her.

Arnelle came back within minutes with a pot of hot coffee. She sat it down on the table so he could pour a cup. Arnelle sat next to him and folded her legs under herself. She watched him in silence as he drank the coffee.

"Thank you, Arnelle. This really hit the spot."

She looked at his handsome face. He looked so tired and exhausted. She, too, had been without a decent night's sleep since they'd gone their separate ways.

She softly asked, "Are you ready to tell me why you're at my house at two a.m.?"

He sat the cup down and ran his hands over his face. She looked so beautiful with her tousled hair.

"Arnelle, I'm sorry for coming over so late, but I've been calling you and when I didn't get an answer, I got a little worried."

"Why didn't you just leave a message?"

"I don't know. I wasn't thinking. Are you alone?"

Frowning, she answered, "That is none of your business, Winston."

They looked into each other's eyes in silence. He leaned in closer and asked, "Are you getting serious with that guy?"

"Excuse me?"

Winston couldn't believe his thoughts had slipped from his lips. Since he'd put the question out there, he had no choice but to continue.

"You heard me. Are you getting serious with him?"

She frowned and explained. "What I do with my life doesn't concern you anymore, remember?"

"It does if you're going to bring him around MaLeah."

She stood and said, "You have a lot of nerve, Winston."

"I'm just looking out for MaLeah," he responded. "It's my job to protect her, so I have a right to know."

Walking over to the door, she opened it. "Goodnight, Winston."

Knocking lint off his pants, he announced, "I'm not going anywhere until I get a straight answer from you."

Slamming her door, she yelled, "Why do you care? You don't own me. Instead of getting all up in my business, you need to be keeping up with the chick you were with tonight."

Winston stood up, clearly angry. "What? This ain't about her!"

"You can't tell me who I can or cannot spend time with or who I can have around my daughter. Now get out!"

He laughed out loud in anger as he put his hands over his face. Shaking his head, he pointed at her and said, "We're not through talking about this."

Shaking her head in disgust, she headed for the stairs.

"Lock the door on your way out, Winston. This conversation is over."

He blocked her path, not allowing her to leave the room and said, "We *will* talk about this tomorrow."

"Move out of my way, Winston. I have nothing else to say on the subject."

He slowly stepped aside and said, "I know you're trying to make me jealous, but Babe, Winston Carter, III don't go out like that."

"Whatever."

"I want MaLeah to come to Philly, now."

Arnelle's eyes widened. "Where did that come from? Are you trying to pull rank on me?"

"No! But she's my daughter and I want her here."

"She's my daughter, too, and I don't want her up here until the weather's more predictable."

"Why?"

"Because I said so, now go home!" she screamed.

Walking toward the door, he yelled, "I'm sorry I ever met you!"

His words sliced straight through her heart. A lump formed in her throat. She swallowed hard and whispered, "Winston, please...just go."

He stood there angry and upset. He wanted her to hurt like he was hurting. When he reached the door he turned and once again allowed his thoughts to slip from his lips.

"I need to know something else."

Arnelle felt emotionally drained. "What now?" she asked as tears stung her eyes.

"Have you slept with Kilpatrick?"

Turning away, she answered, "Lock up on your way out, Winston. Goodnight."

He watched her disappear upstairs, leaving his question unanswered. He didn't know what made him challenge her like he did, but she was right. Even though his heart wanted him to, he couldn't reveal that he still had feelings for her. The fact still remained that she had played him. Turning slowly, he locked the door and headed back home.

CHAPTER SIXTEEN

D ays later, Winston found himself working vigorously to try to keep Arnelle off his mind. He tried not to imagine her spending time with Damon Kilpatrick. His caseloads were heavy, and he spent a lot of time at the office. He decided his best bet was to stay away from Arnelle and give things time to cool down before talking to her again about MaLeah. He made sure that before going to bed each night, he called MaLeah to tell her he loved her. It had gotten to the point that she knew his voice, which made his heart swell with love. He also flew to Houston to visit her, unknowingly to Arnelle, every other weekend. This pleased Judge Lapahie very much knowing Winston was making a dedicated effort to be a father to MaLeah, especially since his relationship with Arnelle was still estranged. Judge Lapahie kept telling Winston to follow his heart and stay focused on his job. Even though Arnelle was his daughter, he was also a man and knew that men didn't recover from deception easily, or if ever.

∞

The fellows' standing basketball game had to be changed this weekend from Sunday evening to Saturday morning. It didn't matter one bit because Winston didn't feel like going anyway. Craig knew Winston still hurt from the things Arnelle did, but he also knew Winston still loved and missed her very much whether he admitted it or not. He decided to pay him a little visit. When he arrived at his house, Winston opened the door looking terrible.

"What's up, Bro?" Craig asked, giving Winston the once-over.

Walking away, Winston said, "I told you I didn't feel like playing ball today."

Craig followed him into the family room. "I know what you told me. Skeeter, man, you can't keep doing this to yourself. You look like hell! Why don't you go ahead and tell the Witch Doctor you still love her?"

"Stay out of this, Craig," Winston said before dropping onto the sofa. "All I'm concerned about right now is my daughter."

"The hell you are. Skeeter, if you could've seen your face at dinner the other week when Arnelle showed up with Kilpatrick. It was obvious that it pissed you off, especially when the mayor started talking about them getting married. I thought your ass was going to jump over the table and act ghetto."

Winston put his hands over his face. "I can't deal with it, man. This shit is driving me crazy, but I just can't be with her, Craig."

"Then why aren't you going out with other women? Maybe that will help you get over her."

"It's not about them."

Craig laughed. "That's what I thought. You're not even interested in any of the others anymore. Not even for a casual relationship."

Winston sat in silence. Craig laughed.

"All right," Craig said. "I'll leave it alone, but don't come crying to me when it's too late."

Winston sat and stared at MaLeah's picture on the mantle. Craig glanced at it. "Your daughter is very beautiful. Just like her mother."

"Thanks."

Craig walked toward the foyer. "Come on, Skeeter. If you

don't come play ball, the team will be uneven. It'll do you good to get out of the house so you can do something besides work."

He kept sitting there staring at MaLeah's picture. "Craig, how is Arnelle?" he asked.

He walked toward the door and said, "I don't know and if you want to know, pick up the phone and call her yourself. Better yet, go over to see her. Skeeter, if you're not at the gym in thirty minutes, we're playing without you." Craig closed the door behind him, leaving Skeeter alone with his thoughts.

A few seconds later, the doorbell chimed again. Winston slowly walked over and opened the door.

"Well, well, well. You are still alive."

Winston sighed. "Victoria, what are you doing here?"

She pushed past him. "Aren't you going to invite me in?"

"It looks like you already did." He closed the door. "What do you want, Victoria?"

She slid up to him and purred, "Haven't you missed me, Baby? You know we've had some good times together. What happened to us?"

Winston maneuvered around Victoria and re-entered his family room. She was stunning in her jeans and gold, low-cut silk blouse. He sat down on the sofa. "I'll ask you again," he said. "What do you want?"

She sat next to him and immediately started caressing him intimately. He was startled, but his body responded like clockwork. He closed his eyes and allowed her to continue her sexual massage. He missed the intimacy of touch and had been without sex for several weeks now. What Victoria was doing to him felt wonderful. She had always been aggressive and now was no different. Victoria kissed him on the neck and said, "Come on, Baby. I know you want some. Let's go upstairs so I can really make you feel good."

Winston opened his eyes, looked at Victoria and said, "You really want to make me feel good?"

"Oh yes, Baby."

He looked into her eyes and said, "I know just the thing. Let's go."

Not long afterwards, he grabbed his keys and walked Victoria to her car.

∞

Arnelle woke up feeling tired, as usual. She didn't know the last time she had had a solid night's sleep. She climbed out of bed and slowly walked over to her closet. Damon was taking her to breakfast, and she didn't have much time to get ready. Spending time with him lately had been nice, but nothing other than friendship. She knew he wanted more, but friendship was all she could offer him.

After looking through the closet, she decided upon a pair of black leather pants and a lavender cashmere sweater. Her black boots would complete her ensemble. She glanced at the clock and hurried into the bathroom to shower.

∞

Winston was glad Craig pushed him to go play basketball, though his game was completely off.

"Hey, Skeeter," Craig called out. "Even though you didn't play worth a damn today, I'll still buy you breakfast."

Skeeter put on his sweats. "Whatever. If you're buying, I'm eating."

They jumped into the truck and headed to one of the finest family-owned restaurants in the city. When they walked in about fifteen minutes later, both stopped in their tracks. Across the room, they saw Arnelle and Damon enjoying breakfast together. Craig turned and said, "We can go somewhere else if this is going to be a problem."

"No, I'm cool. As a matter of fact, I'm going over to say hello."

Before Craig could protest, Winston was halfway to the table. He approached without them noticing and said, "Good morning, Arnelle. Good morning…Damon, isn't it?"

Damon stood, extending his hand and said, "Yes, it is. Good morning, Winston. Nice to see you again."

"Likewise."

Arnelle closed her eyes briefly, not believing who had crept up behind her back. She opened her eyes, turned and locked gazes with him.

"Hello, Winston."

"You're looking nice as always, Arnelle."

"Thank you."

Damon pointed to an extra seat and asked, "Would you like to join us?"

"No, thank you. I'm here with a friend."

Arnelle's heart started beating hard against her chest. She would be devastated if she turned around and saw a woman waiting on Winston. She relaxed when she heard a familiar voice. She smiled and turned around. Craig walked over and said, "Good morning, everyone." He leaned down and kissed Arnelle on the cheek. "What you doing out so early, Witch Doctor?"

She punched him on the arm. "Mind your business."

Winston and Damon watched their playful exchange in silence. The waitress finally called out, letting Craig and Winston know their table was ready.

"Well, our table is ready," Craig said, "and I'm starving. You two have a nice breakfast."

"Goodbye, Craig," Arnelle said. "Tell Venice and the kids hello."

"I will."

Craig walked away, leaving Winston standing. He extended his hand to Damon one more time before saying, "Enjoy your breakfast. Arnelle, you have a good day."

As he walked off, his mind started wandering. It was early, and he wondered if Arnelle and Damon had spent the night together. That was a visual which elevated his blood pressure as well as angered him. The vein appeared on his forehead as he arrived at the table gritting his teeth. Craig looked up and said, "Damn, Skeeter. You are so pitiful."

"Go to hell, Craig. I'm not up for your shit right now."

Craig smiled and said, "You don't have to be hostile with me. She's just having breakfast with the man. Look, why don't you come by at noon and help me build Brandon's tree house? I'm sure he would love to know you helped me build it. It'll help get your mind off things for a while."

Winston looked at Craig, seeing through his transparency. Deep down he appreciated his best friend trying to console him.

"A tree house?"

Craig pulled out his chair. "Remember the one I had when we were growing up?"

"Yeah, it was so cool. We had some good times up in that tree." Winston's eyes glazed over.

Craig took a sip of orange juice. "Skeeter, are you going to help me or not?"

"I'll be over. Tell Venice to cook something good."

Laughing, Craig said, "That's a bet."

Winston turned one more time and glanced at Arnelle and Damon before turning his attention to his breakfast.

∞

Arnelle was heartbroken. Winston couldn't show her even the tiniest bit of affection. Arnelle truly believed Winston hated her. She started playing with her food.

"Are you okay?" Damon asked. "What's wrong?"

Arnelle looked at him with sad eyes. "Can we get this to go? I'm not hungry anymore."

"Sure. Let's go."

∞

Back at her house, Damon sat the food on the kitchen counter. Arnelle sat down at the table and motioned for him to sit opposite her. She looked up at him and took his hand in hers.

"Damon, you are a wonderful man and I really enjoy your company," she said. "But, before we go any further, there are some things you should know."

Squeezing her hand, he smiled and said, "It's okay, Arnelle. You don't have to talk about anything that'll make you feel uncomfortable."

"I'm fine, but I need to tell you that I have a two-year-old daughter named MaLeah. Right now she's staying with my parents in Texas. She'll be living here with me in about a month or so."

"That's great, Arnelle. I know she's adorable and I can't wait to meet her."

She continued to hold his hand.

"There's more, Damon."

She took a deep breath and said, "Damon, Winston is my daughter's father."

He leaned back in the chair and said, "I knew something was

up. I could tell you two were more than just friends. He never could take his eyes off of you."

Arnelle lowered her head and said, "We were engaged, but we had a big fight, so we're not together anymore."

"He's a fool."

"It was my fault, not his. He didn't do anything wrong. I ruined everything."

Damon caressed her hand. "Arnelle, he still loves you."

"I don't think so. I hurt him too bad."

"Yes, he does, Arnelle. It shows all over his face. It's also obvious that you're still in love with him."

Arnelle closed her eyes, not wanting Damon to see just how true his statement was.

"Arnelle, I was hoping that you and I could've been more to each other, but now I know that can't happen...at least not right now. Look, for what's it worth, why don't you come down to Miami with me on the fifteenth? It's my brother's thirtieth birthday and we're giving him a big party. It'll be a nice, relaxing getaway for you. How about it? No strings attached."

"No strings?"

"Just two friends hanging out."

Arnelle came around to Damon's chair and hugged him. "Thank you for understanding, Damon. I'd love to go, but I have to be back on Sunday, okay?"

"Cool."

She smiled and said, "Okay, Damon. I'll go."

"Great. We'll leave late Friday night. Now let me get out of your way. Thanks for having breakfast with me."

"Next time it's my treat."

Arnelle walked Damon to the door and gave him a soft kiss on the lips.

"Thanks for everything, Damon."

He kissed her again and said, "Anytime, Sweetheart, and I just want you to know I'm here for you."

"I know. I'll talk to you later."

Arnelle watched him walk away. He was the perfect man, with a wonderful personality. Damon was a great catch for any woman, just not for her.

∞

Craig and Winston worked diligently on Brandon's tree house. It was almost finished. To make sure it was a surprise, Venice had taken the kids out on the town for the day.

"Skeeter, hand me that two-by-four," Craig said.

Winston gave it to him and proceeded with his end of the tree house in silence.

Craig looked over. "You want to talk about her?"

Winston sighed. "She's driving me crazy, man. I've never let a woman get into my head before. I don't even know when or how it happened."

"You do know it's because Arnelle is the real thing."

"What do you mean?"

Laughing, Craig stood to measure a section of the tree house. He turned and stared down at Winston, who was looking like a sick puppy.

"I tried to warn you in the beginning that she was different. Now, look what has happened. She's not one of your little sex buddies. You can't dismiss her so easily, huh? "

"I don't know anything anymore."

Craig picked up the nail gun. "I do because I've known her longer than you have. Especially since you don't remember being with her out in Cali. I kind of got an idea of where her head was."

Winston worked in silence for a while before saying, "Craig, that woman has made me feel things I've never felt before."

"Really?" Craig asked, a smile on his face. "Damn, that's deep."

Winston went back to work, but Craig could hear mumbling coming from Winston's end.

"What are you saying over there, Skeeter?" he asked.

"The woman turned me out," Winston replied simply. "She makes my body react to her in a way that's indescribable."

Craig laughed and asked, "What did she do to you?"

"Let's just say that making love to her makes me feel like my damn heart is going to burst out my chest and some other things I'd rather not mention."

"You *are* turned out. No wonder you're dying a slow death seeing Kilpatrick pawing at her."

Winston gritted his teeth hearing Craig mention Kilpatrick.

"Why don't you just tell the woman you love her and want to be with her?"

"I can't."

"Why not?"

Winston finished his side of the tree house. "I just can't. She hurt me and no woman hurts Winston Carter, III."

"You're acting like a fool. You're going to mess around and let her get away."

Winston was silent. He'd never lost a woman, only dismissed them. So why was Arnelle causing him so much heartache? Why couldn't he dismiss her as easily as the others? He knew the answer; he just couldn't admit it to himself or bring himself to say it.

"There," Craig said, looking at the tree house proudly. "It's finished. Brandon will love it. You do know we're going to sleep out here with him the first night to initiate it? Next weekend, I'm planning to have some of the kids from his Boy Scout troop over. I might need your help since it seems you have extra time on your hands."

"Go to hell, Craig!"

Laughing, Craig said, "I'm just messing with you, man. It's not my fault that you're making yourself miserable. You need to tell the woman you still love her."

"I can't."

Craig leaned against the wall of the small tree house. He took a deep breath and said, "Skeeter, you don't see it, do you?"

"See what?"

"Even with your memory loss, you found a way to fall in love with the same woman twice. That has to tell you that it's meant for you two to be together."

"What it does, Bro, is make me feel like I've been set up."

"Okay! It's your life. Thanks for helping me with the tree house. Brandon is going to be so surprised."

"No problem. I'm hungry. Please tell me Venice cooked before she left."

Gathering the tools, Craig said, "She cooked your favorite meal. Let's eat."

"I'm right behind you."

CHAPTER SEVENTEEN

T he next few weeks passed quickly. Arnelle looked out the window and noticed that it had started snowing. She looked up at the sky and prayed the snow wouldn't prevent her from going on her trip with Damon. She was actually looking forward to some fun in the sun. She turned and picked up the stack of movies she had rented. Going to the oven, she turned on a pot of her mother's fire-engine chili. She tasted it and even though she followed the recipe to the letter, she still couldn't get it exactly like her mom's. She poured a bowl and grabbed a couple of Coronas out of the fridge. She went into the den and settled down to watch her movies. As soon as she got comfortable and pushed play on the DVD, the phone rang. She sat her bowl down and answered.

"Hello?"

"Hey, Girl! What's up?"

"Hey, Venice. You're interrupting my dinner and movie; that's what's up!"

Venice laughed. "Well, it's nice to hear your voice, too."

"Sorry. You know I've been on edge since...well, you know."

"I know, Boo. It'll be okay. Look, I need a favor. Craig and Lamar went out of town today, and he left his truck at the airport. Tressa was going to take me to pick it up, but Clarissa is running a little fever. I called Skeeter and asked him to go pick it up..."

Interrupting, Arnelle asked, "What does that have to do with me?"

"Well, before you cut me off, I was going to tell you."

Venice hesitated, then said, "I need you to pick him up so you guys can go get Craig's truck."

Arnelle sat up straight. "No way! Don't even try it, Venice. You know we're not getting along right now. Please don't put me in this position."

"Come on, Arnelle. I need your help. Skeeter didn't have a problem with it, so why do you?"

Arnelle stood and chewed on her nail. "It's snowing."

"Excuses! You've driven in worse snow than this. Come on, Arnelle, before the snow gets any worse."

Arnelle slid into her boots. "Venice, you owe me big time! I mean it this time!"

"I know, Boo. Thank you, thank you, thank you. I'll call Skeeter and let him know you're on your way. I love you, Girl."

"Whatever."

It took Arnelle thirty minutes to arrive at Winston's house. He must have been waiting for her because when she pulled up, the garage door immediately opened. She watched him get into his truck and drive out. He pulled up beside her and rolled down the window. She also rolled her window down. He looked sexy and raw, but he didn't show any emotions.

"Park your car," he said. "We'll go in my truck since it's snowing."

She didn't answer. She just rolled up her window and turned off the engine. As she got out her car, she took a series of deep breaths and climbed onto the seat next to him. Before she could close her door, he said, "Buckle up."

She snapped the seatbelt. "I hope this won't take long."

He didn't respond. He just gave her a look, a look that was unreadable. This told her he was still angry, so she decided not to try to make any more conversation. Winston maneuvered his truck through the bumper-to-bumper Philly traffic. This was taking longer than Arnelle had expected. He hadn't spoken another word since she initially got in the truck. Only the music from the radio pierced the silence engulfing them.

Winston was dying a slow death. He couldn't stand to look at her. His conversation with Craig weeks earlier still haunted him. Her scent was already driving him mad, and the thought of Damon Kilpatrick touching her made him tighten his grip on the steering wheel. But the fact remained that she had betrayed him. His twice-a-month visits to see MaLeah were slowly helping him cope with his newfound responsibility of being a dad. Making amends with Arnelle was going to be very difficult, if at all possible.

Arriving at the airport, Winston entered the airport garage and quickly found Craig's truck. Pulling up behind it, he put his truck in park.

"Arnelle, you drive my truck back. I'll follow you to my house because I don't think we'll be able to make it all the way over to Craig's. The snow is coming down too fast."

Their eyes met briefly before she climbed out and walked around to the driver's side. He held the door for her and watched her slide into the seat. Her jeans fit exceptionally well. He blew out a breath, closed the door and tried to shake the image of her from his mind. It wasn't working. He'd been without the sex for over a month now, and he felt like a bomb that could detonate any second.

Back out on the expressway, Winston noticed that some of the drivers were making some careless and reckless moves. He was anxious to get their vehicles off the road before the conditions worsened.

An hour and a half later, the snow was still coming down in blankets. Winston followed Arnelle into his neighborhood until they finally came within one block of his house. When

Arnelle pulled up to the four-way stop sign, she stopped, then pulled out. A car came careening through the intersection without stopping. The other driver missed her by inches. Quick thinking on her part avoided the accident, but sent the vehicle into a three-sixty spin. The other car came to a stop in a nearby ditch.

Winston yelled, "Son of a bitch!"

He quickly jumped out of Craig's truck and ran over to his truck. He swung the door open. "Arnelle, are you okay?"

Shaken, she answered, "I'm fine, Winston. Scared...but fine."

The vein popped out on Winston's forehead as he stalked toward the other driver's car.

Worried that Winston was about to do something he would regret, she jumped out of the vehicle and screamed, "Winston...don't!"

He wasn't hearing Arnelle at all. He walked right up to the driver who stumbled out of the car, clearly drunk. Winston grabbed the guy by the collar of his jacket and slammed him over and over against the side of the car.

"You stupid bastard! Don't you know you almost killed her?! What the hell is wrong with you?"

Winston kept slamming the guy against the car, who was too drunk to protest or feel the pain. Arnelle finally made her way over to them after stumbling and falling in the wet snow.

"Winston, stop it! He's too drunk to know what happened!"

Winston threw the man to the ground just as a patrolman pulled up to the scene. The drunken driver slid to the ground, mumbling. Winston was too upset to speak to the officer, so he went back to the truck and climbed in, hoping to calm his temper. It would be up to Arnelle to explain what had happened. The officer could smell the liquor on the man's breath and quickly arrested him. The air was freezing and Arnelle was cold and wet. She walked back over to the truck and knocked on the window. Winston opened the door and looked at her with eyes she never thought she would see...fearful.

"You okay, counselor?"

As if he had experienced a vision, he softly said, "That idiot almost killed you."

She tried to be strong even though she was still shaking, inside and out.

"I'm fine, Winston."

He cleared his throat. "You're freezing. Let's go."

Winston had never been so afraid in his life. Well, when his mother had become ill, it scared him. Then when MaLeah was sick, that worried him also. But those cases were different from witnessing something potentially tragic right before his eyes, especially since it involved Arnelle. He closed his eyes and thanked God for sparing her life.

Arnelle ran back to the truck and drove the block to his house. They pulled up to his house and he motioned for her to pull his truck into the garage. He joined her inside, leaving Craig's truck in the driveway beside Arnelle's car. He started lowering the garage door.

"What are you doing, Winston?" Arnelle asked. "I have to go home."

He gave her a firm look. "Not tonight. The roads are too bad. You can go home in the morning. Anyway, your clothes are wet and you need to get out of them before you get sick."

She opened her mouth to protest, but he had already entered the house. She had no choice but to follow.

Inside the kitchen, Winston called Venice and told her they were leaving Craig's truck at his house for the moment. Arnelle walked into the family room so she was unable to hear whether he told Venice he was holding her hostage. After hanging up the phone, he joined her. "Are you hungry?"

"No, but thanks for asking. I could use a drink though. My nerves are shaken a bit."

He twirled his keys on his finger and stared at her with those eyes. She couldn't help but tremble. Having on wet clothes didn't help the situation either.

"Come on upstairs so you can get a hot bath and some dry clothes. I'll bring you a glass of wine if you think that will help."

"I'm sure it will. Thanks."

She stood and followed him silently up the stairs and into the guest room.

"Do you remember where everything is?"

She sat on the bed. "I think so."

"Holler if you need anything," he said before walking out.

After the door was closed, she slipped out of her boots, wet jeans and other articles of clothing. As she ran the hot bath, there was another knock on her door. She wrapped the towel around her body and opened it. Winston froze as he stood there with the glass of wine in his hand. He wasn't prepared for seeing her nearly nude. It was difficult to stay angry with her when she looked so beautiful. Breaking his trance, she accepted the glass.

"Thank you."

Without saying a word, he backed away, closed the door, and sighed. On the other side of the door, Arnelle exhaled loudly.

After a while in the tub, she hated to get out of the relaxing bubbles, but Arnelle found herself falling asleep. When she walked back into the room, she noticed that Winston had left a T-shirt on the bed and a hot cup of cocoa on the nightstand. She dried her body and slipped into the shirt. She needed to wash her clothes so she opened the door and padded down the hall to the laundry room.

Back in the bedroom, she sat in the room, sipped her cocoa,

realizing just how thick the tension was between her and Winston. The stress of their breakup gnawed at her gut, but she was unsure how he was coping with it. He could barely look her in the eyes, and he looked fatigued. The house was quiet...too quiet. She sat not knowing what to do with herself. The man she loved despised her and she couldn't sit under his roof and take it any longer. She waited patiently until her clothes were done and pulled them from the dryer. On her way from the laundry room, she decided to tell Winston that it would be best if she went home. His door was slightly opened, so she entered.

"Winston?"

As soon as she called out to him, she noticed the sound of the shower. The telephone started ringing and almost immediately, the answering machine clicked on.

Hey, Baby, it's me. I thought I would call you up to see if I could come over and warm you up on this cold evening. I could also give you one of my famous massages. I have something very special to give you. Give me a call a-sap, Winston. I love you.

Arnelle stood there, stunned. She couldn't believe what she had just heard. The reality that Winston had moved on and found someone else shook her foundation. Tears formed in her eyes as she stood there clutching her clothes. She was so shocked, she didn't even notice that he was standing there with a towel wrapped around his waist. He had heard a portion of the message and recognized Victoria's voice. Arnelle finally noticed him.

"Winston, I came in to tell you that I was going home...now!"

She turned to walk out of his room, but he quickly blocked her path.

"You're not going anywhere, Arnelle. I told you the roads are too dangerous."

She pushed him aside and walked out into the hallway. "You can't tell me what to do!"

Frustrated, he grabbed her clothes out of her hands and threw them on the floor.

"I'm not going to tell you again," he yelled. "You're not going anywhere tonight!"

The tears were stinging her eyes now. She stooped to gather her clothes.

"I said I'm leaving!"

Winston saw the keys in her hand, so he grabbed her wrists and tried to take them away from her. He wouldn't be able to live with himself if he allowed her to leave and she was killed or injured. He was still trying to shake the earlier image out of his head when the drunken driver almost killed her. He wasn't about to let her put herself in harm's way again.

"Give me the keys, Arnelle."

"No! What do you care anyway? That woman can come over and keep you company as soon as I get out of here!"

Not responding, he continued to wrestle with her. He could care less about Victoria. Arnelle was the only one he loved, but he just couldn't admit it.

Still wrestling, he yelled, "Give me the keys!"

Seconds later, Arnelle lost her balance and fell to the floor. Winston tried to break her fall, but she still hit hard. Her hair swung wildly over her face. When she tried to remove it from her eyes, Winston pinned her arms over her head and tried to pry the keys out of her hand.

She raised her legs and tried to push him away. Instead, his towel fell to the floor. Neither noticed because they were too busy struggling over the keys. Winston noticed that Arnelle was tiring, but she was still putting up a good fight.

"Let me up! Stop, Winston! I'm going home and you can't stop me!"

The vein had popped out on his forehead again and she knew he was angry, but so was she.

"Forget it, woman!"

The softness of her body wiggling against his nude body sent his mind and body into overdrive. He had almost forgotten how heavenly her skin felt against his. His anger slowly changed to heated desire as he noticed Arnelle's T-shirt had slid up over her waist.

"Stop fighting me, Arnelle, and give me the keys!"

"No! Let me up, Winston!"

Winston felt like he had finally lost it emotionally. What he was feeling now was hot passion. Arnelle's blood was boiling with searing heat as well. Her skin had taken on a strange hue, and she felt defeated from resisting the desire she had for him.

Before either of them realized, Winston lowered his mouth and kissed her hard on her lips. He didn't know why; he just did. She tried pushing him away, but his strong grip wouldn't allow it. Winston's lips ignited her body and started a smoldering flame within her. One free hand roamed under her T-shirt and over her curves. Moisture pooled in her lower body as his tongue put her into a hypnotic trance. She was still trying to get away, but not to run. Winston had opened the flood gates to all the emotions she had pinned up in her over the past month or so. She kissed him and moaned as his mouth suckled her stiffened nipples. She arched and wrapped her arms around his neck, pulling him closer. Winston couldn't control what had come over him and neither could Arnelle. The rawness of their relationship caused a throbbing in his rigid sex.

Arnelle squirmed to get closer as she felt his flesh pushing against her moist canyon. Their bodies were covered in perspiration as they intertwined wildly on the floor in his hallway. He ran his tongue up the column of her neck as he entered her body. She let out a loud scream and pulled him into the abyss, allowing them to become one with explosive passion. He made love to her like a man on a mission. Her body shook with each thrust of his hips. She held onto him and raked his back with her nails. Winston moaned loudly as this took him to a point of sheer pleasure. Winston had never in his life been so out of character with any woman. He always remained in total control, but Arnelle had taken his mind, body and soul to the peak of desire.

He could feel Arnelle's body grip his sex and create a spasm. She screamed into his ear as her release came hard and in multiples. His climax wasn't much different. He felt like his heart would burst as his body continued its release. He let out one final groan as he collapsed onto her body. Their breathing was erratic and loud. He kissed her one last time and slowly rolled off her body, totally spent. He covered his eyes with his arm as he tried to recover. Seconds later, he turned to look at Arnelle who had also covered her eyes. The difference being she seemed to be crying. He sat up, stroked her cheek and picked up the car keys. He sat them on a table in the hallway. Embarrassed by his behavior, he slowly stood up and wrapped his towel around his waist.

Softly, he said, "Arnelle? Come on, Babe. Let me help you up."

She uncovered her eyes and with hesitation, allowed him to help her up, but she couldn't make eye contact with him. Her body was still tingling from the effects of his loving. This was much more than she could handle because they were not together as a couple anymore.

Sobbing, she said, "I love you, Winston, but I can't continue like this."

He cupped her face and kissed her gently on the cheek.

"Arnelle, I'm sorry. I didn't mean to come onto you like this. Are you okay?"

"I will be."

He sighed. "Regardless of the drama that's happening between us, I do have feelings for you and I'm trying to protect you. You are the mother of my child, and I don't want you to get hurt. So, please wait until morning before driving home."

She quietly nodded as he helped her gather her clothes. Without speaking another word, he watched her slowly walk into the guest room. She closed the door without looking back. Winston remained standing in the hallway, upset with himself for his behavior, but happy he convinced her to stay the night. He quietly walked into his bedroom and closed the door. The next morning, when he woke up, she was gone.

CHAPTER EIGHTEEN

A few days later, Winston and Venice met for their weekly lunch. She hugged him upon arriving at the table and said, "How are you, Skeeter? You look like you've lost weight. Are you eating or are you trying to starve yourself to death?"

He took a sip of water. "I'm fine, Venice."

"Skeeter, what are you doing?" Venice looked at Winston as if he had lost his mind. "Why are you being so stubborn?"

"Venice, I didn't come here to talk about my love life. I thought we were here to have lunch."

"We are having lunch, and we're talking about your stubborn ass."

He stared at her, realizing she wasn't going to leave it alone. Venice took a sip of water and said, "You're going to lose her if you keep it up."

He perked up. "Why do you say that?"

"I have my reasons. Let me ask you something. Did something happen between you two the night you guys went to the airport?"

"Why?"

Venice sighed. "Because Arnelle seems different. I can't put my finger on it, but something's changed with her."

Winston leaned forward. "What do you mean you have your reasons?"

"All I'm going to say is you need to go visit her today."

Winston nervously fumbled with his tie. "I have no reason

to show up on Arnelle's doorstep. We're not together anymore, remember?"

Venice hit the table with her fist. "Damn it, Skeeter! Just go see her before it's too late, and I mean today!"

Winston knew that whatever Venice was concealing about Arnelle was serious.

"Okay, Venice, I'll go by and check on Arnelle if that will make you happy."

"That's all I ask, Skeeter. I don't know why I let you get my blood pressure up. Let's eat."

$$\infty$$

Winston arrived home, quickly showered and changed clothes. He laced up his tennis shoes, grabbed his keys and headed out the door. It was dark when he pulled into Arnelle's driveway. Before exiting the truck, he took a deep breath. He had promised Venice he would come over, but he still was clueless about Venice saying he was going to lose her. Even though they were broken up, he wasn't ready to completely let go of her.

After climbing out of the truck, he walked up to the door and rang the bell. He fumbled with his keys as he waited for the door to open. He hadn't laid eyes on her since that night at his house. He had no idea how his life gotten to this point. What he did know was that he needed to get it back under control.

Arnelle finally opened the door and he wasn't prepared for what he saw. She was breathtaking as usual.

"Winston, what are you doing here?"

He forced a smile. "I was in the neighborhood, so I thought I would stop by."

Arnelle looked at her watch. "Well, come in."

She backed away and allowed him to enter. He couldn't take

his eyes off her. She was dressed in white cotton gym shorts and a sports bra. It was obvious she was not wearing any undergarments and seeing her midriff exposed made his lower body stir. Upon entering the house, he noticed a suitcase near the door.

"Are you going home to see MaLeah?"

Arnelle ran up the stairs.

"Not this weekend. I'm bringing her here for good next week."

He followed, slowly confused. In the bedroom upstairs, Arnelle had clothes and shoes scattered about. He slid his hands into his pockets and leaned against the door frame. He watched as she hurried around the room. She glanced over at him and asked, "What's on your mind, Winston? Are you here to talk about MaLeah?"

He walked further into the room and sat on the bed silently.

"No. Where are you headed, Arnelle?"

She came out of the closet. "That's none of your business. Why are you here anyway? I thought you hated me."

"I don't hate you, Arnelle. I just don't like the shit you did to me."

"Then stay away from me then!"

He felt a migraine coming on as he covered his face with his hands. He looked over at her. "I don't want to fight, but I think I have a right to know where you're going."

"I have parents that I give that information to. I don't have any obligations to you anymore."

"We have a child together, so I believe that counts."

She stopped gathering clothes for a minute and just stared at him. He looked into her eyes and as if a light bulb had gone off in his head, he said, "You're going somewhere with Kilpatrick, aren't you?"

She lowered her head and walked back into her closet. In anger, he jumped up from the bed and walked over to the window. His mind was racing and he felt lightheaded. Arnelle stepped out of her closet and put another garment into her bag. She looked over at him standing at the window. She worried about what he was thinking. Then from nowhere, he asked, "Has he touched you?"

He was even surprised that he had asked the question because now he feared the answer.

In shock, she asked, "Excuse me?"

Turning, he said, "You heard me. Has he touched you?"

"I don't see why that would matter to you."

Towering over her, he said, "Well, it does."

"Why?"

"It just does. Don't push it, Arnelle."

She sat down on the bed feeling defeated. She wanted so much for him to hold her.

"Look Winston, I'm not trying to push your buttons. You left me. What do you expect me to do, stop living?"

He walked over to her. "I didn't expect you to fall for the first man that came along."

"Winston, I've always made it clear to you what I wanted, but I will not put my life on hold or wait for you any longer. I've apologized for what I did to you. You're the one who decided that you didn't want to be with me anymore."

He turned away and walked back over to the window in silence.

"You caused the end of us, Arnelle."

Arnelle shook her head, frustration building behind her eyes, making her head thump in pain. "Then why are you here?"

He turned and softly said, "Believe it or not, I still care about you and you have to admit that there's still something between us. What happened between us at my house the other day proves that."

"We were both emotional that night. I'm sure you're not stressing over it."

"What if I am?"

She turned. "You've got a lot of nerve, Winston. I hear some woman on your answering machine talking about she loves you and you show up at my house, trying to tell me not to date anyone? You're crazy!"

He walked over to her and did something he never dreamed he would do...beg a woman.

"Arnelle, I'm asking you not to go wherever you're going."

Arnelle stared at him.

"I have my reasons for asking you not to go," he said.

She touched his cheek. "I'm sorry, Winston. I love you, but it's not worth a damn if it's one-sided. I just want you to know that I would never interfere with your relationship with MaLeah. That is one thing you will never have to worry about. I'm trying my best to move on with my life since you've made it clear that you don't want a relationship with me anymore. Now, if you don't mind, I'm busy."

Walking toward the door dejectedly, he asked, "Could you at least tell me when you're leaving?"

She sighed. "Later tonight."

He took a deep breath. "I won't interfere, but I would appreciate it if you would also tell me where you're staying. It's for emergencies only, I promise."

Arnelle fought back the tears as she wrote down the information. She handed it to him and said, "Emergency only. I'll be back on Sunday."

He tucked the paper in his pocket and said, "Be safe, Arnelle. Goodbye."

∞

Once outside in the cold night air, it hit him and it hit him hard. He had never felt the kind of pain he was feeling at this very moment. Why couldn't he be honest and tell her that Victoria meant nothing to him and was in his past? Why couldn't he tell her he was still in love with her? He finally drove off wondering if he was doing the right thing or was he being too stubborn. His heart was aching and his pride was bruised, so he decided to go see the only person who could help him through this.

∞

Winston followed Craig into the kitchen where he and Venice were feeding the twins. Venice looked up at him and immediately knew his visit with Arnelle didn't go well.

"Hello, Skeeter. Do you want some dinner?"

"I'm not hungry, but thanks anyway."

Brandon ran around the table and hugged his leg.

"Hey, Uncle Skeeter!!"

Rubbing his small head, he solemnly answered, "Hey, Lil' Man."

"Will you play video games with me, Uncle Skeeter?"

"Maybe later, okay?"

"Okay."

Brandon gave Winston a high-five and ran out the door and up to his room.

Winston walked over, picked up Clarissa and her baby food, and left the kitchen. Venice looked at Craig and just shook her head.

"Craig, you need to go in there and talk to your boy," she said. "I told him at lunch that if he wasn't careful, he was going to lose Arnelle for good."

Craig picked up C.J. "Do you really think she's getting serious with Kilpatrick?"

"I don't know. What I do know is that Skeeter's still in love with her, but he's too stubborn and proud to tell her. She didn't go through with the blackmail. What she did was fall in love with him and they had a daughter. They need to try and work things out so they can raise her together. If she hadn't told him the truth about everything, they probably would be married today. I know he feels scammed, but Arnelle really does love him. You know that."

Craig picked up two bottles of milk and said, "I'll see what I can do. In the meantime, give me some sugar."

Venice smiled and gladly planted a kiss on his lips before he left the room.

"Mmmm, that was nice. I'm going upstairs to hang out with Brandon for a while, then I'm headed to bed. I hope you can help him."

"Me, too."

Craig walked into the family room with C.J. and found Winston playing with Clarissa. He handed Winston her bottle and asked, "You okay, man? You don't look so good. What happened?"

"I stopped over to see Arnelle after Venice told me to go see her. When I got there, she was packing to go on a trip. I think she's going to Miami with Kilpatrick."

Surprised, Craig asked, "For real? Did she tell you that?"

"She gave me an address, but she didn't come right out and tell me she's going with him. My gut tells me I'm right."

Craig watched Winston's facial expressions for a moment. "You gonna let her go?"

"What do you mean? I can't control Arnelle."

Craig looked at him seriously. "I'm not saying control her. I'm asking are you going to fight for her or just hand her over to Kilpatrick? You know you're still crazy about her, and I know how upset you get when any man comes within ten feet of her. Now you're going to sit here and just let her jet off to some romantic getaway with another man? Hell, I thought you loved her."

"I do love her!" Winston snapped.

His loud outburst startled the twins, and they began to cry. As the two men tried to comfort the babies, Craig spoke first. "Well, you need to be telling that to the woman who might be jetting off with another man. Look, Skeeter, you're older now. Let that pride shit go. I would understand if Arnelle didn't give a damn about you, but I agree with Venice. You are going to mess around and lose her for good."

"Craig, I'm not used to this."

It was Craig's time to raise his voice. "As messed up as that situation was, out of it you got a woman who loves you and a beautiful daughter. Now stop being stupid! If Arnelle comes back from Miami married to Kilpatrick, you'll have no one to blame but yourself. You need to do whatever it takes to fight for the woman you love. Otherwise, you're going to be miserable for the rest of your life. I know this from experience, Skeeter."

Winston kissed Clarissa on the cheek. "I hear you, man. I'd better be heading home. Thanks for everything, Craig, and I'll consider your comments."

They stood up together and Craig said, "Come on and help me put them to bed before you leave."

"Cool."

∞

Back in the quiet confines of his house, Winston entered his empty kitchen. He used to love his solitude, but since Arnelle had spent time with him there, things had changed. Now the house seemed so cold and lifeless. He went into his office and sat down at his desk, not knowing what to do. He looked at the wall clock and realized the mother of his child and the only woman he'd ever loved was possibly gone out of town with another man. He laid his head down on the desk and tried his best to make the pain go away, but it wouldn't. His eyes wandered over to a picture they'd taken together in one of those photo booths in the mall. He began to remember all the things he loved about her: her beautiful smile, her touch, the sound of her laughter and the way she snored as she slept. He remembered how good it felt to fall asleep lying next to her, the smell of her perfume and the softness of her skin. He didn't have any of those things anymore because he allowed his pride and unforgiving heart to get in the way. He closed his eyes and said a very personal prayer. Once he was done, he picked up the phone and made several important phone calls. Moments later, he hurried upstairs to put into motion events that could change the rest of his life.

Arnelle tried her best to take a nap, but as usual, it was difficult. The visit from Winston earlier had unnerved her. She wasn't sure if this trip was the right thing to do, but at least it would give her a change of scenery and possibly a fresh start. She looked at the clock and decided to get dressed. She put on some jeans and a sweater. Going from one climate to another was going to be a shock to the body, but a welcomed one.

Damon arrived right on time and within minutes, they were on their way to the airport. After checking their bags, they sat down to wait for the boarding call. Arnelle couldn't seem to relax. She occasionally looked around, expecting Winston to come for her, but he didn't. Damon did his best to make her laugh, but it wasn't working. Once in Miami, he hoped her spirits would be lifted.

"All passengers for Flight 418 to Miami can now board at Gate 11," a voice boomed over the PA system.

Damon took her by the hand. "Ready for some fun in the sun?"

"Lead the way."

He tightened his grip. "It'll be fine, Arnelle. Relax, Baby."

She smiled and followed him toward the gate. She took one final look over her shoulder and realized all hope with Winston was gone.

∞

Hours later, Damon pulled up to a spacious beach house on a secluded section of Miami Beach. Even in the dark, Arnelle could see the house was gorgeous.

"This house is beautiful," she said. "Is it yours?"

He came around to open her door, smiled and said, "A little collection of mine."

"Wow. Some collection."

He gathered their bags. "Come on inside. I know you can't wait to get out of those hot clothes and relax."

She smiled. "You got that right."

Arnelle was in awe at the immaculate interior. They headed upstairs where Damon showed her to her room.

"Make yourself at home. You should find everything you need. If not, just let me know. If you're up for it, we can go for a swim at daybreak."

"Sounds great."

Arnelle closed the door, broke out into a cold sweat and hurried to the bathroom. Returning to the bedroom, she pulled her swimsuit and sarong from her bag and laid it out for their swim later. She was exhausted from the events of the day and she hoped a nap would refresh her.

∞

Waking up hours later, she found Damon on the patio. The view was breathtaking. He already had sliced fresh fruit, croissants, and coffee waiting for her when she joined him.

"Good morning," she said. "Where did this all this food come from?"

"I told my housekeeper that we were coming and to make sure the place was stocked for the weekend. We're going out to dinner tonight. Tomorrow, I'll cook for you."

Arnelle sat down across from him and took a bite of fruit while Damon poured her coffee. She smiled. "You cook?"

"Of course. I'm from the South and my momma taught me all her cooking skills."

"That's great, Damon."

He felt proud that Arnelle was impressed. He smiled. "You okay? You look a little flushed."

"I'm fine. I'm just trying to adjust to the change in climate."

He touched her hand gently. "Relax. You're here to forget all your worries."

They ate mostly in silence before heading to the warm ocean water for a swim.

Damon and Arnelle spent most of the day sunning and swimming. She actually had fun. He checked the time and said, "Arnelle, we'd better get ready for dinner. Last one in is a rotten egg!"

"Oh no, you don't," she called out.

They raced up the beach toward the house. Damon won. Laughing, he said, "Maybe I'll let you win next time."

"You cheated."

"Arnelle, you're a sore loser. Go get ready for dinner. We have reservations for five o'clock."

She punched him on the arm and said, "Just for that, you're buying."

"I wouldn't have it any other way, my dear."

Smiling, she entered the bedroom, stripped out of her wet swimsuit and once again broke out into a cold sweat. Her nerves had her on an emotional roller coaster being in Miami with Damon.

∞

The restaurant was filled with many hungry patrons. Arnelle and Damon had been seated and were enjoying appetizers.

"So, Arnelle. How are things between you and Carter?"

Arnelle sighed. "The same. Please, I don't want to talk about him tonight, okay? I came here to try and relax."

"I'm sorry. I didn't mean to upset you."

"I'm not upset, Damon. I appreciate you trying to help me forget my problems. This getaway was a nice idea."

Damon raised his drink. "It was my pleasure. Look, here comes our food."

"Everything looks so yummy."

Damon stared at her. "I could say the same about you in that beautiful dress."

Arnelle blushed. "Thank you, Damon, but remember...friends. Okay?"

"I can't help it, Arnelle," he said, laughing. "You can't blame a guy for trying, but I'll behave."

"Good. Now, give me a taste of that fish."

Arnelle's long, floral halter dress was perfect for the occasion. The colors were vibrant against her bronzed skin tone and long raven hair. An hour or so later, they drove around Miami to catch some of the sights and sounds. They stopped at a salsa club and watched the dancers swirl and twirl erotically to the allure of the music. Arnelle yawned and Damon said, "We'd better head back. Tomorrow we can go shopping and whatever else you would like to do."

Holding onto his hand, Arnelle followed Damon through the crowd.

"Sounds good to me," she said. "I am a little tired."

"I must admit, I am, too. Let's roll, pretty lady."

∞

The next day, Arnelle and Damon continued to enjoy the peacefulness of the sandy beach and blue tide after a long day of shopping. The Miami sunlight beamed down on them as they talked about their childhood memories, careers, and futures. Damon could see the bags under her eyes and realized she'd had another sleepless night. He was concerned whether this trip away from Winston was doing her more harm than good.

"Arnelle, you have a great career ahead of you and a beautiful daughter. You have nothing to be sad about."

Playing in the sand she answered, "I know what you're saying is true, but you know why I'm sad."

Damon smiled and said, "I have an idea. Look, let's go grab some dinner and talk about it when we get back. How does that sound?"

She stood and said, "We'll see. Look, I'm sorry, Damon. I'm not trying to hurt you, but I can't help the way I feel."

He also stood and knocked the sand off his legs.

"Don't worry about me, Arnelle, but I do appreciate your concern for my feelings."

She hugged him lovingly and said, "No, thank you for being concerned about my feelings. You're a wonderful man."

"Yeah, a wonderful man who's starving. Let's eat!"

They walked hand in hand back to the beach house to dress for dinner.

∞

The sun was starting to set as they drove back to the beach house. It didn't take long and when they pulled into the driveway, Damon noticed someone sitting on the steps of the beach house.

"Who the hell is this?"

CHAPTER NINETEEN

Arnelle was drifting off, not paying attention until Damon's small outburst. She lifted her eyes and peered out the windshield. Her mouth dropped and her eyes widened.

"Oh my God," she said in a hushed tone. "It's Winston. Something must be wrong with MaLeah. I gave him the address in case of an emergency."

Damon brought the car to a stop and shut off the engine. Winston stood. His demeanor was stoic, serious. Arnelle quickly opened the door and jumped out.

"Winston," she said, "what's wrong? Is MaLeah okay?"

He met her in the driveway and said, "MaLeah's fine."

"Is it Momma or Daddy?"

He shoved his hands into his pockets and said, "Arnelle, calm down. Everyone's fine."

"Winston, you're scaring the hell out of me. What are you doing here?"

Winston took his eyes off Arnelle for a moment to greet Damon. Extending his hand, he said, "Hello, Damon. Sorry for the intrusion, but do you mind if I have a word with Arnelle?"

He saw the look in Winston's eyes. He knew once again, that he had no chance with Arnelle.

Shaking Winston's hand, he said, "If it's okay with Arnelle, it's okay with me."

Arnelle nodded.

"Arnelle, I'll be inside if you need me," Damon said.

Winston turned again to Arnelle and asked, "Is it okay if we take a walk on the beach?"

"Fine with me."

She led the way around the house and down the stairs to the beach. When she got there, she took off her sandals and they started walking along the sand. The sun was continuing to set and it began to give the ocean water a reddish, orange glow.

"What do you want to talk about, Winston?"

"Us."

She looked over at him. "The last time I checked, there wasn't an *us*."

Winston's heart began to race and his mind began to whirl, but he had come to Miami for a reason. He stopped walking and turned Arnelle to face him.

"Arnelle, I came here to do something that I should've done over a month ago. Since I walked away from you and what we had, my life has been miserable. I don't know what I was thinking. I mean...Arnelle, I felt used and betrayed by you. A man's pride is something he values very much. I finally realized that my pride was going to cause me to lose the one person I've ever loved...you."

Arnelle looked out across the water and asked, "What are you trying to say, Winston?"

He took her hand and linked his fingers with hers.

"Sweetheart, I came here to tell you that I still love you and that I want my family together. That is if you'll still have me. I know I haven't been there for you, but honey, you have to realize the trauma you put me through. I didn't mean to push you away, and I definitely didn't mean to push you right into the arms of Kilpatrick."

Tears stung her eyes as she started playing in the sand with her foot. She looked up at Winston and asked, "Why should I believe you? You didn't seem to care until I started going out with Damon. You don't trust me and for all I know, this is some desperate attempt to keep me away from him."

Raising his voice, Winston asked, "Do you want to be with Kilpatrick? If you do, I'll walk away and never bother you again."

She looked away and fought to hold back her tears. He continued to hold her hand as he finally confessed, "Arnelle, I love you. I've never loved anyone like this before. The woman you heard on my answering machine was my ex, Victoria. She became my ex the night your house was broken into. I haven't slept with another woman since you came into my life. You mean everything to me."

Arnelle couldn't help but search his eyes for sincerity and she was beginning to see it. Winston's voice was cracking now as he spoke.

"Arnelle, Victoria has tried everything she could to seduce me, but, Babe...all I can think about is you. You and MaLeah are all I need in my life to balance it. I'd marry you right here, right now, on this spot if you wanted me to. There is no other woman for me, Arnelle."

Arnelle fought her emotions; she wanted so much to believe him. She wanted to feel that his love was truly sincere and not because of MaLeah. She also wanted so much for him to trust her. She watched him pull what appeared to be his small black book from his pocket and a cigarette lighter from the other. He lit it and they watched it burn to ashes together.

"Winston, you didn't have to do that."

Linking his fingers with hers again, he said, "I wanted to. Those women are in my past. You're my future if you'll have me."

She still wasn't completely convinced and felt like this might be Winston's last attempt to get her away from Damon, so she called his bluff.

"Okay, Winston, if that's the way you want it. Let's get married…right now. Let's go find a justice of the peace."

He smiled and pulled her into his arms and waved his hand in the air. Within seconds, the sound of vehicles approached nearby on the beach. She looked up at him in confusion, then turned to see two SUVs full of people pull up. The first person out of one of the vehicles was her father, Judge Lapahie.

"Daddy," Arnelle asked, totally stunned, "what are you doing here?"

Her father approached, taking her into his arms and giving her a kiss. He hugged Winston, and then motioned toward the vehicles.

"What's going on, Daddy?"

"Winston gave us the signal that you wanted to get married right here on the beach. So, I'm getting ready to marry you two."

Her mouth fell open as she watched her mother, with Keaton carrying MaLeah and two other people who appeared to be Winston's parents exit the truck. In the other truck, Craig, Venice, Lamar, Tressa, Cyrus, and finally Damon filed out and walked toward them. Winston was pleased to see the shock and joy on her face as their family and friends had come to share this special moment.

There were a lot of hugs and kisses exchanged, and then Winston said, "Arnelle Lapahie, for the third and last time… will you marry me? Right here, right now because I'm not going back to Philly without you and MaLeah."

He produced a ruby and diamond engagement ring out of his pocket and slid it on Arnelle's finger. It was different from the one she had returned to him weeks earlier. This one consisted of rubies: MaLeah's birthstone. Arnelle stared at the ring and then all of her family members and friends.

"Are you sure about this?" she asked when her eyes finally met Winston's.

He kissed her and asked, "What more do I have to do to prove to you that I'm sure?"

Tears fell from her eyes as she looked over at MaLeah, who smiled their way. Arnelle threw her arms around Winston's neck and said, "Yes, Winston; I'll marry you. Right here, right now."

Zenora Lapahie kissed her daughter's cheek and handed her a lovely bouquet of flowers.

"Arnelle, every bride should have a bouquet at her wedding," Zenora said. "I'm so happy for you, Baby, and I'm glad things worked out between you two."

Zenora kissed Winston's cheek and said, "I'm glad you finally came to your senses, Darling. We were all getting pretty nervous. It was difficult for us not to interfere."

He looked at Arnelle, smiled and answered, "Thanks for believing in me."

"No, thank you for believing in your love for our daughter."

The setting couldn't have been more perfect. The sun was kissing the ocean on the horizon as Judge Lapahie recited, "Dearly beloved. We are gathered here to join Winston Fredrick Carter, III and Arnelle Elease Lapahie in Holy Matrimony."

Minutes later, Herbert Lapahie said, "Winston, you may kiss your bride."

Winston gladly caressed Arnelle's face and kissed her lovingly on the lips as their family and friends applauded.

After the ceremony, Winston told everyone to meet at the LaBrenna Hotel for a private wedding reception. He escorted Arnelle back to the house she was sharing with Damon to retrieve her belongings. Winston hung around outside talking to Keaton while MaLeah played in the sand. Damon and Arnelle walked inside arm in arm.

She turned to him and said, "I hope you're not angry with me, Damon."

"Well, I am a little jealous, but I'm happy for you and Carter. I knew you really loved him and you two have a daughter to think about."

She kissed him on the cheek and said, "Thank you for understanding and thank you for being there for me."

"You bet, pretty lady."

She sighed. "Well, I guess I'd better get my things. You are coming to the hotel, right?"

"I wouldn't miss it for the world. You'll always be my friend, Arnelle, and I wish you and Carter the best. You two have a precious daughter. She looks like both of you."

Laughing, she said, "She does, doesn't she?"

"Come on. I'll help you with your things. You can't keep your husband waiting, Mrs. Carter."

∞

Winston had outdone himself. He had arranged for the hotel to set up a private room for the reception, wedding cake and all. After the traditional cutting of the cake, the family sat down for a delicious dinner. The photographer Winston had hired continued to take pictures and assured him that he captured some spectacular scenes of the ceremony on the beach. Winston told him he couldn't wait to see them. Arnelle was still in awe of the whole evening.

"So, Mr. Carter," Arnelle said, "now that you have me, what are you going to do with me?"

He leaned over and whispered into her ear. Arnelle screamed out, then turned a shade darker with embarrassment. Everyone looked their way, then realized Winston had said something very personal and intimate to her.

Keaton took a sip of champagne. "You guys really need to save that for your hotel room."

Zenora Lapahie said, "Stop hating, Keaton. I can't believe you never met a nice girl all those years you played in the NBA. You're just too picky. You need to settle down before you get too old."

Keaton rolled his eyes. "Oh, here we go. I told you and everyone else that Keaton Mathew Lapahie enjoys his life just like he has it...single!"

Winston kissed Arnelle lovingly and said, "Keaton, my man, I used to think the same way. That was until I met your sister. You'll see, Bro, when it hits you, there's nothing you can do to fight it."

"I'll drink to that," Judge Lapahie said.

The whole table erupted in laughter, and everyone agreed with Winston and the judge. Keaton still didn't believe any of their nonsense. Married was not for him, period.

MaLeah sat in her grandfather's lap and yelled, "DaDee!"

Winston smiled with pride and held out his arms for her. MaLeah happily crawled over into her daddy's lap and stuck her hand in his cake. She grinned, then placed her sticky fingers into her mouth, smearing icing on her face. Winston kissed her cheek, then said, "I love you, MaLeah."

∞

Hours later, Arnelle lay in Winston's arms. He couldn't believe how he had gone from a confirmed bachelor with more women than any man should have in a lifetime to a happily married man with a beautiful daughter.

Arnelle noticed him smiling and asked, "What are you thinking about?"

He hugged her tighter. "You and how I was prepared to kidnap you if you would've dissed me out on the beach tonight."

She sprinkled his chest with butterfly kisses.

"I would never leave you, Winston. I had to be sure you loved me for me and that you didn't come back to me because of MaLeah."

"I never really left you or stopped loving you. You did take a playa through a serious boot camp though."

Caressing him, she said, "I'm glad you never stopped loving me because I can't raise MaLeah and our son without their father."

Winston's eyes widened and he looked at her suspiciously.

"What did you say?" he asked.

She smiled and placed his hand over her stomach.

"Winston Fredrick Carter, III...meet your son."

Winston sat up in bed and said, "Don't play with me, Arnelle."

"I'm not playing. We're pregnant...again."

He was shocked and happy at the same time.

"When? Wait! That night at my house...Damn! How did I miss that one?"

"According to my doctor, I'm further along than that. Remember our steamy shower in California?"

Winston remembered that night very well.

"But you said..."

"I know. I thought we were safe, but my doctor assures me that I got pregnant around the time when we were in California."

Tears welled in his eyes when he asked, "Were you going to tell me if I hadn't come for you?"

Kissing his ear, she said, "I prayed you would come back to me and you did. Yes, I would've told you. I was wrong for keeping MaLeah from you. I wasn't about to make the same mistake twice. You're too important to me."

Running his hand over her hips, he whispered, "I have a confession to make. I never really left you, Arnelle. I've been through hell these past weeks without you. I tried to deny my feelings because I was hurt. But in my heart, I knew I was going to eventually make you my wife because I'd be damned if I was going to let Kilpatrick have you."

Laughing, she said, "Damon is and *was* only a friend, but I do love you for being concerned."

He caressed her abdomen and asked, "Does anyone else know?"

"I wanted you to be the first to know. We can tell the family in the morning if you like."

He nuzzled her neck. "I'm sure they'll be quite excited but let's enjoy it in private for a while. Between my mother and Zenora, we won't get any peace until the baby's born."

"Sounds good to me."

The reality of having another child with Arnelle overtook him emotionally.

"Thank you," he whispered. "I do love you."

"You're welcome, counselor, and I love you back."

EPILOGUE

Living in Philly made the weather very unpredictable and the snow was a hindrance getting to the hospital. It took both Zenora and Winston's mom, Sadie, to calm Winston's nerves when Arnelle informed them her water had broken. Sadie knew her son very well. He was cool as a cucumber in the courtroom, but when it came to his loved ones, he fell apart. Both mothers had decided to stay with them in Philadelphia when Arnelle's due date became closer. They knew Winston would freak out when this day came. Arnelle's screams of pain on the ride to the hospital didn't help matters either as he frantically drove to the hospital. To help him cope, he blasted the jazz music of Najee on his stereo. By the time they got to the hospital, Arnelle was almost seven centimeters and an epidural was out of the question.

An hour later, Winston proudly held his son in his arms as an exhausted Arnelle recuperated from the natural delivery. Winston Fredrick Carter, IV made his appearance to his parents at approximately seven p.m. on New Year's Eve. Weighing in at nine pounds, one ounce, the baby was a beauty; Winston knew his son would have his eyes and Arnelle's features, just like MaLeah. They had decided to call him by his middle name, Fredrick.

The Lapahies and Carters came into the room and quietly placed Fredrick in MaLeah's lap so she could hold her new brother. They took many pictures and when Arnelle finally woke up, they took more pictures. Keaton walked in carrying gifts as did Craig and Venice, and Lamar and Tressa. Venice hugged Winston, and then kissed Arnelle and said, "Boo, you did good! He's perfect."

Craig followed suit, saying, "Witch Doctor, you held up better than I expected. Now as far as your husband, I knew he would be a total mess. You should've seen him when Venice was in labor."

Everyone laughed and continued fussing over Arnelle and Fredrick. The doors swung open, and Fredrick's pediatrician walked in with a smile that lit up the room.

"Happy New Year, everyone. How's my new patient?"

Keaton was now holding Fredrick and when he turned toward the heavenly voice, he froze. Dr. Meridan St. John held out her arms for the baby. Winston grinned, seeing Keaton's immediate attraction to her. He stepped forward and said, "Keaton, this is Dr. Meridan St. John."

She smiled. "And you are?"

Keaton blinked rapidly as he placed Fredrick in her arms.

"I'm the proud uncle, Keaton."

Winston knew Keaton was going to be taken by Dr. St. John's attractiveness. He was taken the first time he'd met her also. She had a fair complexion, short, wavy, cropped hair and dark piercing eyes. She was about five feet ten inches and healthy in all the right places. She would be what a brotha would call, "an Amazon." She was different from the women he'd seen Keaton attracted to, which were slender and runway-model gorgeous. Dr. St. John had a natural, average, down-to-earth appearance with a very special past. From what Arnelle had told him, she was very conscientious about her size and had shared that with her on more than one occasion. Her figure was fine to him because he had never been particular about a woman's size. But he knew Keaton was particular and yet, there was something that caught Keaton's eyes with Dr. St. John, and Winston was curious to find out what he was thinking.

Dr. St. John smiled. "Nice to meet you, Keaton. It's nice to meet all of you. I see my little patients have a lot of people to love them. Isn't that right, MaLeah?" MaLeah smiled and hugged Dr. St. John's leg. Winston went on and introduced the rest of the family to the doctor.

Smiling, Dr. St. John said, "Well, Mom and Dad, I need to take your little man down for his circumcision. Winston, you're going to accompany me, right?"

"I'm right behind you, Doctor."

She caressed Fredrick's cheek and said, "Don't worry, handsome. I'll take good care of you. You can ask your big sister."

As she placed the baby back into his crib, she turned to Arnelle. "Everything will be fine, Arnelle, so don't worry. Get some rest. I'm going to give Fredrick something for the pain after the procedure, so he'll be rather sleepy the rest of the night."

"Thank you, Dr. St. John," she said.

"Please call me Meridan."

Smiling, Arnelle said, "Okay and thank you."

"You're welcome. Well, goodbye everyone and nice meeting all of you."

Dr. St. John wheeled the cart out the door. As Winston followed, he mischievously grinned at Keaton and whispered, "Hey, Bro, you want to go?"

Keaton nodded discreetly and said, "I'm not wild about seeing my nephew get his johnson sliced, but I'll go for support."

He turned to the family and said, "I'm going with Winston just to make sure he doesn't pass out."

Silence engulfed the room as everyone stared toward the door as Winston and Keaton walked out. Arnelle knew what was up. She'd seen the look on her brother's face when Meridan entered the room. Even though she knew he was a sports-loving womanizer, she didn't want him playing around with Meridan's heart. She laughed out loud when she remembered the one thing Keaton and Meridan had in common. Once Keaton found out about it, it would be hard for him to resist her even though it was obvious he was in awe of her beauty. Meridan St. John was just what the doctor ordered for Keaton Mathew Lapahie.

ABOUT THE AUTHOR

Darrien Lee, a native of Columbia, Tennessee, resides in LaVergne, Tennessee with her husband of twelve years and two young daughters. She is excited about the release of her sequel, *What Goes Around Comes Around*. Darrien picked up her love for writing while attending college at Tennessee State University, and it was that experience which inspired her debut novel, *All That and A Bag of Chips*, and its sequel, *Been There, Done That*.

She is a member of A Place of Our Own Bookclub, Women of Color Bookclub and Authors Supporting Authors Positively. Darrien also writes for the hot e-zine, *The Nubian Chronicles*, an online magazine where she shares her opinion on controversial issues on her page titled, "From The Desk of Darrien Lee." You can view her work monthly at www.nubianchronicles.net

Please visit her website www.darrienlee.com for upcoming appearances and events.

WHAT HAPPENS NEXT? AN EXCERPT FROM

When Hell Freezes Over

BY DARRIEN LEE
AVAILABLE FROM STREBOR BOOKS

Keaton entered the bathroom and leaned against the door. Meridan had confirmed everything, and there was no turning back now. He would make love to her and then hope to return back to his life in Texas in a couple of weeks.

When he opened the door to the bedroom, Meridan was sitting on the bed painting her toenails. She looked up and smiled at him. He stood there with his skin still glistening with water. He walked over with the towel still wrapped around his waist. Looking down at her, he said, "Let me do that."

"Are you sure?"

Grabbing her foot, he sat down on the bed and proceeded to finish painting her toes.

This man is killing me!

Meridan was being seduced just by the way he was blowing on her toes. He painted each toe methodically, making sure he didn't make any mistakes.

"You're good at this. You must have done this before?"

He looked up at her mischievously. "Not as much as you might think. MaLeah keeps me busy painting her little fingers and toes."

"I'm talking about big girls, Keaton."

"You're the first big girl's toes I've ever painted, Scout's honor."

Meridan couldn't help but admire his handsome features.

The silky hair on his chest had now dried. His skin was a beautiful brown and his dark eyes were piercing. He wore his hair closely cropped and a goatee neatly trimmed and surrounded by dimples which surfaced with every smile.

"There! You're all done. You have pretty feet."

"Keaton, are you a foot man?"

Keaton put the top on the nail polish and said, "No, I'm just a man. I like everything about you Meridan St. John and then some."

They stared at each other for a moment. He looked down on the bed and noticed the bottle of lotion. She followed his eyes, then looked back up at him.

"May I?"

Handing the bottle to him, she said, "Help yourself."

In her heart, she knew the moment his hands touched her she would fall apart. Keaton poured some lotion in his hands.

"Ready?"

She swallowed and said, "As ready as I'm going to be."

§

It seemed he had pleased her just by his touch. God knows what the experience would be like when they finally made love.

As Meridan lay there trembling, she prayed he would never find out her secret before he returned to Texas. She wouldn't be able to look him in the eyes. A man like Keaton would never understand.

Her lids closed tighter as she felt strong hands caressing her warm skin. She could also feel how he was aroused as he continued to run his hands over her body. The kiss came to her without speaking another word. Her legs became wobbly and her breathing erratic.

"Come with me, Taylor."

"What are you doing?"

"I can show you better than I can tell you."

He pulled her onto the bed with him, gently stroking her cheek with the back of his hand while drowning himself in her desirable eyes.

"I thought you had a hangover?"

Craig answered softly, "It's gone" as he kissed her gently biting her lip. He reached for her robe and tossed it to the floor.

She was still trying to play hard with him, but she couldn't resist lacing her fingers around his neck.

Good Lawd!

He began to run his hands up and down her body in a slow rhythmic motion. Without breaking his gaze, he whispered, "You feel so good, Venice."

She felt like she was going to scream as he dipped and kissed her tenderly while probing her mouth with his tongue. Within a few seconds, Venice noticed something was a little different. He was a little more aggressive than usual. He was working on her weakest hot spots and he knew it. She was breathing heavily and felt a throbbing sensation in her lower body. Venice was getting very excited and found herself raking her nails up and down his back. Craig continued to pleasure her by kissing downward toward her stomach and nipples, taking his time with each one. Her body was burning as she felt his tongue play with her navel.

She let out a loud whimper when he came up and kissed her on the ears and whispered, "I want you."

He moved to kiss her harder on the mouth as he took his time tasting her. Craig gently worked his way downward once again to her stomach. She took a deep breath when she closed her eyes to enjoy the sensation she was feeling. Then, without any warning, she felt Craig's warm lips there.